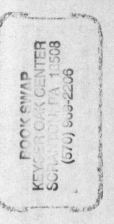

Kendal bolted upright besid g into the dark jungle.

In the same instant they both saw the figure move. It was a young woman, crouching in the undergrowth like a frightened animal.

"It's the same girl who was outside the hotel," Kendal whispered at Jason's shoulder. "The one who had the child with her."

She emerged into the moonlight and beckoned them. Kendal started to get up, but Jason grabbed her arm.

"That little child!" she protested. "What if he needs us?"

The woman led them into the jungle over a dappled moonlit path to a small cave where trickles of water dropped over the opening. "*Aquí,*" she said softly, putting a finger to her lips. *In here.*

Inside, the sleeping form of a tiny boy was visible curled up on a brightly woven blanket. He was pretty, like his mother, except his mouth and jaw didn't look right.

"Oh," Kendal breathed, feeling her heart melt.

Dear Reader,

When I ventured into the Yucatán jungle to visit with a Mayan medicine man a couple of years ago, I had no idea what I would find.

But as I followed my guide deeper into the heart of the jungle, the isolation and the ancient peace of the place closed around me. In such a remote setting, I realized, twenty-first-century trappings could quickly fall away. In such a setting, time would slow, priorities would emerge, sensations and feelings would be amplified.

The medicine man was not what I expected. A humble little man who spoke to my guide in the quiet, clicking cadence of the Mayans, he kindly shared with me his efforts to help his people attain better health, using simple herbs and ancient remedies.

Not long after that, I met a doctor who had performed surgeries for the Doctors Without Borders organization in the same region. I am very grateful to Dr. Michael Bumagin for sharing his technical knowledge of reconstructive surgery and the details of his service in Chiapas. (This is a work of fiction, of course, so any creative embellishments are mine, not Michael's.)

Those experiences came together to form this story, where two people, swept away by both passion and compassion, find something unexpected in the remote jungle. They find a child who opens their hearts. And as they struggle to save that child, they find something else unexpected—a deep and lasting love for each other.

I treasure my reader mail. Contact me at P.O. Box 720224, Norman, OK 73070, or www.darlenegraham.com.

My best to you,

Darlene Graham

To Save This Child
Darlene Graham

HARLEQUIN®

TORONTO • NEW YORK • LONDON
AMSTERDAM • PARIS • SYDNEY • HAMBURG
STOCKHOLM • ATHENS • TOKYO • MILAN • MADRID
PRAGUE • WARSAW • BUDAPEST • AUCKLAND

ISBN 0-373-71202-2

TO SAVE THIS CHILD

Copyright © 2004 by Darlene Gardenhire.

This edition published by arrangement with Harlequin Books S.A.

® and TM are trademarks of the publisher. Trademarks indicated with ® are registered in the United States Patent and Trademark Office, the Canadian Trade Marks Office and in other countries.

www.eHarlequin.com

Printed in U.S.A.

This story, my tenth Superromance novel,
is dedicated with deep appreciation to the gifted and
hardworking editors who have given me so much
encouragement and help over the past five years:

Paula Eykelhof, Zilla Soriano, Laura Shin and
Kathleen Scheibling

Books by Darlene Graham

HARLEQUIN SUPERROMANCE

812—IT HAPPENED IN TEXAS
838—THE PULL OF THE MOON
904—UNDER MONTANA SKIES
958—THIS CHILD OF MINE
994—THE MAN FROM OKLAHOMA
1028—DAUGHTER OF OKLAHOMA
1091—DREAMLESS
1126—NO ORDINARY CHILD
1152—ENCHANTING BABY

PROLOGUE

Somewhere over the remote mountainous regions of Chiapas, Mexico

KENDAL COLLINS breathed a prayer of thanks that at last they were safe. At last. *Safe.*

Though the mountains rolling beneath the belly of their small plane looked rocky and steep, forbidding in their vast isolation, Jason Bridges appeared to be in control, his hands relaxed on the yoke of his Cessna Conquest as he executed flying maneuvers with his usual precision.

Shuddering, Kendal released what felt like the first full breath she'd drawn in days. Even during the dark time of their captivity, Jason had always sworn he would keep her safe, but only now that they were airborne would she let herself believe it. Finally, they were leaving Chiapas far behind.

"Hang in there, sweetheart." Jason released the yoke long enough to squeeze her hand.

She gave him a brave smile, then twisted her torso, extending that smile to the two dear people strapped together into one of the rear-facing seats. Miguel Vajaras, age two, slept like the baby he was with his beautiful dark head lolling against the slender shoulder of Ruth Nichols, Jason's scrub nurse. Ruth adjusted Miguel on her lap and put a shushing finger to her lips. Kendal nodded her understanding. Miguel had been so frightened, confused and crying right up until the plane had lifted into the air.

"Miguel." Jason had distracted the child. "Look! Mountains!"

At the sound of Jason's deep voice, Miguel had quieted abruptly, straining forward in the seat to look out the window. "Moun-nan. 'Moun-nan,'" he had echoed in baby talk. "Moun-nan. Eh-pane." He had repeated the unfamiliar English words over and over, until the drone of the plane's engine had finally put the exhausted toddler to sleep.

Kendal studied her adopted son's innocent brown face, so angelic in repose, not quite able to believe this sweet child was, at last, going to be safe and was soon going to be her very own. This ordeal had been so hard on all of them, but now they were safe. *Safe.*

She longed to be back in Ruth's seat so she could comfort her baby, but Jason wanted, *needed,* Kendal in the copilot's seat. They weren't out of Vajaras's territory yet.

"Get in front in case I need a navigator," Jason had said as he helped her into the plane.

And Ruth would take good care of Miguel. Ruth had always been good with the children, adept at calming their fears. Miguel was in good hands. Kendal tried to relax as she gave her sleeping little boy one last loving smile.

Ruth returned Kendal's smile before she closed her eyes in exhaustion. Their flight from terror had worn the poor woman out.

Kendal glanced at her future husband. His muscular neck was craned as he concentrated on the terrain below.

''Look at that, sweetheart,'' he said.

Kendal glanced out the small plane's window as the Canon del Sumidero came into view. The scenery rolling below them was exotic, breathtaking, but Kendal was sick of Chiapas and its strange seductive beauty. Right now she wanted to feast her eyes on the plains of Oklahoma…and on Jason.

She studied his handsome profile for a second before her gaze was drawn down to his hands gripping the control yoke. She had noticed those hands the very first time they'd met in his office. The rest of his appearance could border on scruffy at times, but his hands were always immaculate, smooth and clean like any good surgeon's.

She would probably admire Jason's hands for the rest of her life. Even the way he wrote was strong. She loved to watch as he jotted orders or slashed his signature across a chart in neat, bold strokes.

But it was seeing him use those hands in surgery that had finally won Kendal's undying admiration. Jason Bridges made real miracles happen every day. She had witnessed those miracles in the worst of conditions down here in Chiapas.

Her eyes trailed from the control yoke down to his legs, also tanned and oh-so-muscular, bulging against wrinkled khaki shorts. It seemed his whole body functioned like one long, taut muscle. A six-foot-tall granite statue—that's what Jason was.

Her gaze flitted up to his cropped hair, dark as midnight, with strands of silver at the temples that created a delicious contrast to his clean profile, his chiseled lips, his square jaw. His skin, deeply tanned from the Mexican sun, glowed in the slanting sunshine that streamed through the plane's compact windshield. She sighed again, utterly content to just admire him.

He glanced over and smiled when he caught her doing so.

''What're you thinking about?''

''How much I love you.''

He smiled. ''I love you, too. Is Miguel okay now?''

She nodded and raised her finger in the same silencing gesture Ruth had used. Jason glanced back at his sleeping passengers. Then he reached across the narrow space and wrapped a possessive palm around Kendal's inner thigh. She wrapped her fingers around his wrist. His pulse felt steady, strong.

''God, I'm glad we're finally out of there,'' he murmured.

''Me, too.'' But Kendal found that she could still summon up the fear. The danger is over, she reminded herself as she suppressed tears, and gripped Jason's wrist harder.

''Ah, now.'' Jason flipped his hand up, capturing her fingers. ''Please don't cry, sweetheart.'' He leaned toward her, glancing back and indicating that he wanted to speak near her ear. Their heads touched halfway over the center console. "Everything's going to be okay."

"I know." Kendal closed her eyes, flooded with relief as she pressed her head into his broad shoulder.

"Just remember how much I love you," he murmured. "And that I can't wait to be alone with you," his voice lowered further still, "so I can show you exactly how much."

She opened her eyes, tilting her head up to flash him another brave smile. The sun bounced off the Cessna's white engine cowling up onto Jason's aviator shades. Behind the sunglasses, Kendal knew, her lover's eyes were as blue as the Pacific Ocean that stretched beyond the endless horizon at their backs. And she knew what those eyes looked like when they were brimming with tenderness, burning with desire.

"I can't wait," she said as she leaned in closer to him and caught a heady whiff of his scent. But in that same instant her vision was snagged by a peripheral glimpse of the fuel gauges.

"Jason!" She jerked her head up, pointing.

"What?" His voice echoed the sudden alarm in hers.

"Shhh!" Ruth shushed them from behind.

But Kendal ignored her. "The fuel!" The dial for pounds of fuel remaining read unbelievably low and the dial for fuel outflow read unbelievably high.

Jason stared at the gauges and Kendal blinked hard, hoping her eyes, her brain, had made some kind of horrible mistake. But when Jason pulled on the red knob to stem the flow and frantically flipped the switch for the backup tank, she knew he was seeing the same thing she was seeing.

"What's wrong?" Ruth, sensing trouble, clutched the still-sleeping child's head to her breast while she twisted to see, stretching her seat harness.

Right then the warning lights flashed, and the low fuel alarm started to blare.

"We're almost out of fuel," Kendal spoke above the insistent warning chimes and the even louder drone of the engine, which to Kendal seemed to be already making an ominous straining noise.

"How can that be? We just left!"

"I will," Jason ground out through clenched teeth, "kill Vajaras with my bare hands."

"How could he do this!" Kendal cried, horrified to realize the man was so evil that he would arrange the death of his own grandchild.

"How could he do *what*?" Ruth demanded, clearly panicking.

"Vajaras must have arranged for one of his goons to puncture our fuel lines before takeoff," Jason explained as he eased the plane to a lower altitude. "He knew we'd be over the continental divide by the time it leaked out." He was executing a careful fuel-conserving turn in a narrow mountain valley. "Stay calm," he said. But his own lips were stretched white with fear. "Our best bet is to circle back to the airport."

Jason gripped the control yoke while the low fuel signal continued to chime like a death knell.

In the back seat Miguel whimpered, awakened by

the loud alarm. Kendal looked back to see his thickly lashed little eyes growing wide with fear.

"It's okay, honey," she said in a Chiapas dialect, *"Mamá está aquí."*

But the toddler started to cry, struggling against Ruth's seat belt and stretching his thin arms toward Kendal. All Kendal could do was reach a hand back, awkwardly trying to reassure the child. She rubbed her palm gently on his little shoulder while Ruth murmured reassurances in his ear.

In only minutes, the mountains gave way to a broad valley, then the patchwork of fields and forest revealed clusters of thatched huts and finally the large metropolis of buildings that was Tuxtla Gutiérrez appeared in the distance. When the airport runway came into sight the three adults held a collective breath.

Maybe they could make it down.

Jason's strong fingers gripped the landing gear control handle as they closed in over the crude airport, but suddenly he lurched forward in his seat.

He cursed and, without further warning, jerked back hard on the yoke. The nose of the plane peeled up in a gravity-defying climb that pitched the three passengers sideways. In the same instant Kendal heard the unmistakable *pop-pop-pop pop-pop-pop* of gunfire from below. A bullet ripped through the fuselage as she twisted her face to the window, looking down to see several men running out of a hangar, strafing the sky with submachine guns.

In seconds Jason had pushed the little plane up to an air speed that made Kendal's hair stand on end.

"What are you doing?" she screamed as he continued to climb.

"Keeping us alive!" he screamed back.

"The fuel!" she argued, knowing his maneuver was gobbling up what little remained. But Jason only pulled the plane up higher, out of range of the gunfire.

The Cessna's engines were tough, but they weren't designed for dogfight maneuvers, and the plane stalled as the fuel was sucked away to mere fumes. They plummeted back to earth in a screeching nosedive.

While the alarms rang and the warning light panel on the Cessna lit up like a Christmas tree, Jason managed to pull the plane out of the dive.

Dizzily, Kendal looked back to see the machine-gunners running across the landing strip toward an aircraft that she hadn't noticed before. In the next few minutes those men would take off, and their plane looked bigger, faster than Jason's.

"We can't outrun them," Jason yelled. He leveled the plane just as the engines coughed once more, sputtered, and died. "Put on the life jackets," he commanded. "And strap Miguel in his own seat. We'll have to go for a controlled landing out on the river."

The Rio Grijalva came into view. It was wide in places where it had been dammed, but it was carved deep into the Canon del Sumidero. From their altitude it looked like a broad navy blue ribbon curving at the bottom of three-thousand-foot-high cliffs. But it was the only place where the jungle canopy and the rugged mountains parted enough to put a plane down.

"Oh, God." Kendal felt her face draining pale,

paler, as with trembling hands she pulled the life vests from behind the rear seats and hurriedly helped Ruth strap the wailing Miguel into his, then quickly slipped on her own. Ruth secured Miguel into the other seat.

Jason grabbed the CB-like microphone off the instrument panel.

"Mayday! Mayday!" he shouted into the mike.

"We are making a forced uncontrolled landing over the Rio Grijalva gorge. Cessna Conquest call numb—"

His words were cut short as the dying plane tilted and careened, and he had to wrestle the yoke with all his might. In a panic Kendal tried to wedge a life jacket behind him, but he shrugged her hands away. She studied his grim face, and then twisted to see the steep rocky walls of the canyon below, hurtling rapidly toward them. *We are going to die*, she thought.

How had it come to this?

She reached back to clutch her howling baby's tiny leg. With her other hand she gripped Jason's muscular shoulder, then pressed her forehead against his hard flesh. She hadn't touched either of them enough, not nearly enough. They couldn't die now. Her mind rolled back to the amazing way it had all begun, and she thought, *Oh, God, please. It can't end like this. Not after all we've been through. Do not abandon us now, God. Not now. Not when at long last we have discovered the meaning of true love.*

CHAPTER ONE

Three months earlier in the tenth-floor Oklahoma City offices of Dr. Jason Bridges. 7:06 a.m.

"I SEE YOU'VE GONE and pulled yourself another all-nighter." Kathy Martinez stated the words calmly, as if all-nighters were a boring fact of life with her boss, which they were.

"Now, now, Mother Martinez. Stop scowling. I feel great."

But Kathy Martinez only frowned harder. "Well, *Doctor*, you don't *look* great." She patted her own kinky dark coif as she studied the young physician who had enticed her with a generous salary three years ago. Jason Bridges was a cutie-pie, all right. *Mmm-hmm*. But this young man could sure use some neatness lessons. Jason Bridges ran around this hospital looking more like a rebel in a Gap ad than a gifted surgeon. Mussed dark hair, an overnight growth of beard, faded jeans, loafers with no socks, a leather jacket opened wide over a wrinkled gray T-shirt that looked like he'd slept in it. "If you ask me, you don't even look like a *doctor*."

"I *didn't* ask you." He reached for the clipboard with the day's schedule.

The faded T-shirt stretched too tightly over a chest sculpted by weight training. But Dr. Bridges didn't spend all that time in the gym so he'd look good. Although he most certainly did look good.

Dr. Bridges built his body up so he could use it like a machine. Or rather, abuse it like a machine. Everything this young doctor did focused on one thing and one thing only—performing surgery. Performing countless surgeries, in fact. Dr. Bridges worked like a man possessed, as if his were the only hands that could undo the damage, the defects, the heartache that fate had dealt his patients.

And in certain respects, it could be argued that his were the only such hands. Because Dr. Bridges frequently, and successfully, attempted risky surgical techniques that other surgeons in his field were too intimidated, too terrified, to even try. Her boss, Kathy always said, was gifted. His hands, especially, were gifted. The most gifted of the gifted.

Others were not so admiring. Kathy had heard the stories. Nurses he'd had affairs with had labeled Dr. Bridges "The Wolf." The image fit. His eyes, deepset and icy blue, often squinted or flicked sideways with a sort of wariness, a watchfulness, that bordered on predatory. He seemed to be consumed by some sort of insatiable hunger, though he hid his drive behind a smoke screen of endless jokes. But when Kathy had seen him angry, which was not often and only in response to some idiot's incompetence, Jason Bridges could be genuinely scary.

Kathy Martinez tugged the lapels of her starched snow-white lab coat over her broad bosom. With a renegade doctor like this one, somebody had to maintain standards. "No, sir. You don't look like a doctor at all," she sniffed. "In fact, I'd say you look like the devil himself."

He looked up from the clipboard, and his bloodshot blue eyes flashed mischievously before they narrowed. He twisted his face into a mock diabolical expression, arched his dark brows and flared his nostrils. "You found me out, Mother Martinez." He rubbed his stubbled jaw and leaned toward her. "I am...the devil himself. *Mwah-ha-ha-ha.*" He punctuated the fiendish laugh with a little pinch at her stout waist.

"Stop that." Kathy slapped his hand. She pursed her chubby carmine lips, refusing to smile.

"You know what I mean." Over her half glasses she skewered him with her black eyes. "You don't get enough sleep and then you come in here looking like something the cat dragged in. It's just plain shameful."

"Ah, now." Jason faked a pout. "Would you forgive me if I told you I had an emergency?"

"What was it this time?"

He sobered, shrugged. "Teenage girl who tried to exit her car via the windshield. Let's just say her face looks considerably better now than it did at two o'clock this morning."

Kathy gave a brisk nod of approval, then returned

to her agenda. Middle-of-the-night surgeries notwithstanding, other doctors managed to shave. "You gonna get cleaned up before you make rounds?"

Dr. Bridges released a long, lionesque yawn. "Already made rounds, sweetie. And I'm sorry to report that the sticky buns on the ninth floor are done gone."

Kathy planted her fists on her double-wide hips. "I didn't say I wanted any dang sticky buns." With a huff she stepped behind the desk and proceeded to rearrange the stack of charts that the staff had pulled the evening before. Only yesterday, she had embarked upon a strict diet. The latest in a long line of strict diets calculated to return her figure—in thirty days or less—to its prepudge state, before she'd added five pounds with each of her five pregnancies. Okay, ten pounds.

"Ah. You've found another foolproof diet?" Dr. Bridges's grin was wicked. He was the devil, all right.

"Absolutely." Kathy squared her shoulders.

"I've told you before, Mother Martinez. If you'd stop messing with your appetite, your body would eventually find its perfect shape." He pulled a PalmPilot out of his hip pocket and started punching at it.

For a surgeon who spent his days repairing faces, Jason Bridges had some pretty laid-back notions about bodies. He always acted like Kathy wasn't really all that fat. But she was F-A-T, fat. And she suspected it was her weight that had gotten her into a teensy bit of trouble. Well, they'd discuss her medical problems in a minute. Patients first.

"I wish it were that simple." Kathy finished putting the charts in the proper order. The staff had to do everything possible to keep their gifted young surgeon on track. "What with the nurses and their sticky buns and the drug reps hauling in trays of food every week. Everybody's always celebrating something around here. Tomorrow's Valentine's Day, and sure enough, a basket of cookies has already arrived." She flipped a dismissing hand at the end of the counter, where a gigantic red basket, lined with pink foil wrap, overflowed with gift pens, notepads, and heart-shaped cookies.

Dr. Bridges turned his head toward the gaudy basket. "Good Lord! Who sent that thing?"

"That drug rep from Merrill Jackson." Kathy watched Dr. Bridges saunter over and pluck out the card protruding from the basket. He read it, sniffed at the paper, raised his eyebrows with interest, then slipped the note in the pocket of his leather jacket.

Kathy rolled her eyes. She would bet her last sticky bun that that young woman, just like every other eligible female around this hospital, was after a whole lot more than the doctor's pharmaceutical business. Heart-shaped cookies. Phooey.

"Those drug reps are after you like ducks on a June bug. Another one was supposed to bring breakfast tomorrow, but she canceled."

"Doubt I could have made it anyway. I've got that periorbital reconstruction at dark-thirty and then a bilateral resection of parotids." Dr. Bridges returned his attention to his PalmPilot. "But you nurses can have a treat now and then without obsessing about your weight."

"Easy for you to say. You aren't a fat black woman."

"And neither are you, Mother Martinez. What you are is the most efficient and kind nurse I've ever had the pleasure of working with. And you are absolutely gorgeous."

Kathy rolled her eyes at him. This is why he was such a lady-killer. "You can just stop that old sweet talk."

"You know you look fine."

She swatted the compliment away. "I wish I could say the same about you, Doctor. You need a shower."

He finished with the PalmPilot, scratched his chin again and checked his watch. "It'll have to be a quickie in the doc's lounge. I've got to be in surgery by seven-thirty."

He probably hadn't caught a wink of sleep since he'd rolled out of bed, jumped in that silly little sports car of his and raced to the hospital in the middle of the night. Kathy frowned at his unshaven face. And he'd probably come back to the office after surgery looking just as scruffy. She had very particular ideas about how surgeons ought to comport themselves, and those ideas didn't include running around looking like a wild man.

He narrowed his gaze at her. "I can either rebuild people's faces or keep myself all purty. Take your pick." He gave her an engaging grin as he thrust out the other hand in a *gimme* gesture. "Are you gonna let me see those charts before I head back down to the O.R.?''

Kathy handed him the charts. ''There's a bunch.''

''Excellent. Now maybe we can pay the light bill.''

She eyed Dr. Bridges's backside as he sauntered down the hallway, already absorbed in the day's cases as he walked. *Pay the light bill.* Because he worked like one possessed, the man was making money hand over fist. But money wasn't his motivation.

Kathy Martinez was one of the few people who knew the truth about The Wolf. Before he'd even arrived at Integris, her sister from Texas had told her all about the new doctor, about his sad history down in Dallas. It had been on TV, her sister said, had made all the papers, back when it happened.

''Oh.'' The doctor stopped and tossed a killer smile over his broad shoulder. ''Could you please get me a cup of coffee?''

When she scowled at him, he said, ''Pretty please, Mother Martinez?'' and blew her a kiss.

The *Mother Martinez* bit didn't bother her. She *was* a mother, the uber-mother, and he gave everybody nicknames. But beneath the teasing, Jason Bridges exhibited more respect for and far more trust in his staff than any other doctor she'd ever worked for. And even if Kathy was old enough to be his mother, that didn't stop her and every other female in Dr. Bridges's orbit from appreciating his astonishing male beauty. It was sad, really, and a major waste that such a handsome specimen of a male remained so stubbornly alone.

What that young man needed was a good wife.

But Kathy suspected that the same thing that made him so driven kept him alone, too. That his past, in fact, was the cause of his loneliness.

She went into the break room and filled a foam cup with the coffee she'd put on to drip when she arrived at seven o'clock. While she stirred in the right amount of sugar, she heard some of the other staff calling out as they came in the back door. She looked at her watch. Seven-fourteen. They were getting a jump start on the day. Well, who could blame them? The week before the doctor left for Mexico was always a crazy one.

"Is Dr. Bridges here?" his scrub nurse Ruth asked as she swept into the break room.

"Back in his lair, getting ready to rev up on coffee." Kathy held the cup aloft. "Pulled an all-nighter. No rest for the wicked today." She headed down the hall. She hated to tell the doctor her bad news right before he went into a difficult surgery, but the sooner, the better.

She opened the door to his office. He was standing behind his desk, threading his long arms into a stiffly pressed lab coat with his name stitched above the pocket. A grudging concession to her standards, she supposed. But the crisp white garment only accentuated his bronzed skin and made his looks seem all the more rugged by contrast.

"*Now* do I look doctorly enough?" he taunted.

"No. Is this car accident case going to interfere with the trip to Mexico?" She handed him the coffee.

He took a sip before answering. "Hope not. I think Mike can cover for me."

He sipped the coffee again with a concerned frown. "My main worry is the kid's maxilla. Both sides were affected, and there was a lot of swelling before I got to her. I couldn't really tell what she was supposed to look like. May end up with a redo. I'll decide once I see her 'before' pictures. The mother's bringing them this morning."

Kathy nodded and stepped to the window where the morning sun was winking up over the matching Doctors' Tower to the east. She closed her eyes against the brilliance. Their work could be so heartbreaking, but they seldom allowed themselves the luxury of dwelling on their patients' grief. Bridges kept his team on an even keel with his own resolve, with his cool decision-making style, with his constant jokes. But it proved a delicate balancing act. Because the more his reputation spread, the more challenging the cases he attracted. His skills just kept growing, and he kept pushing the envelope while the staff scrambled to keep up. He decided what had to be done and then they all did it. They went to the wall for their patients, nothing held back, nothing spared in the fight against their enemies—disfigurement, deformity, pain.

When he had relocated to Oklahoma City three years ago, Jason Bridges had assembled an experienced, top-notch staff. He paid them well and expected them to give their jobs their utmost, just as he did. Every day they threw themselves into the fray, warriors in a never-ending battle.

But no one seemed to mind the long hours and the exhausting work. None of them had ever been involved in a practice this exciting, this dedicated. Dr. Bridges was truly a young miracle-worker, an amazing leader. He had already treated patients from a four-state area. Their work made them all fiercely proud.

And then there was this yearly mission to Mexico. The ultimate payoff—three weeks working down in the remote state of Chiapas. They had started out with the Doctors Without Borders organization, but now Jason had turned renegade, flying his own plane in, circumventing customs.

Oh, yes. Working for Dr. Jason Bridges was exciting, to say the least.

Mexico had become their ultimate proving ground, their yearly high. Every spring Jason Bridges closed his office for three weeks and headed south to continue his humanitarian work. He was welcomed with open arms by the indigenous people in the isolated mountains and jungles.

The back-to-back surgeries in the horrible conditions—dust, heat, mosquitoes, flies—always seemed to go on without end, but when their three weeks were up, nobody ever seemed to want to leave. They'd all become as hooked on the experience as the doctor himself. Every year Bridges took along his scrub nurse, Ruth Nichols. Every year he took Kathy. The rest of his staff rotated, but Kathy and Ruth were indispensable, Kathy because she was the only one in the office who spoke Mexican Spanish fluently. She'd learned it from her husband, a gentle Hispanic from south Texas.

Damn. She was going to hate missing out on the Mexico excursion this year. She so hated to tell Dr. Bridges the bad news.

He had seated himself at his desk, sipping coffee and pouring over the charts with a concentration that seemed totally undimmed by sleep deprivation. He wasn't a wolf. He was a superhero, that's what Kathy thought.

"Doc, I need to tell you something." She turned from the window to face him.

He glanced up, caught her expression. "Hey. You okay?"

She sighed. "Not really."

"Martinez?" His deep voice became quiet with concern. "What's going on?" He stood and rounded the desk, propped his rear on it and folded his arms over his broad chest. His blue eyes fixed on her with the kind of sympathetic attention he usually reserved for his patients.

She crossed to one of the chairs facing the desk and lowered herself into it. "I'm afraid you'll have to find a new interpreter for the Mexico trip."

"Really? Why?" His face was intent, serious. All hints of the teasing Dr. Bridges was gone. She had to hand it too him. The man had infallible instincts.

"I've got to have surgery. Doc Marshall said the sooner the better."

"Marshall? It's a G.I. thing?"

"Gallbladder." Kathy felt her face heat up. Fat,

fifty and flatulent, that's what she was. "He'll do a laparoscopy, of course. No big deal. But I thought I'd better get it over with while the office is going to be shut down for three weeks. I'm sorry. I really hate to leave you without an interpreter. And on such short notice."

"Don't sweat it." His gentle, compassionate tone made Kathy feel all the worse for letting him down. She wished he'd say something smart-alecky now.

But instead he crossed to her chair and squeezed her shoulder with his large, warm palm. "Your health comes first. I'll find another interpreter. No problem."

But it was going to be a big problem, Kathy knew. Jason Bridges understood Spanish, of course, but the Mayan cadences of the dialect spoken in the Chiapas region were tricky. Especially when the patient was a frightened peasant or when Jason started firing off fast and furious instructions to the local help. An interpreter who could put the patients at ease was critical. Finding somebody with the right combination of medical knowledge and compassion was going to be really tough. And finding somebody willing to endure the physical discomfort of the region, the daily rigors of Jason's mission, was going to be an even bigger problem. An enormous problem. But problems didn't stop Jason Bridges. He plowed through them like a machete through jungle growth.

Jason didn't want to make Kathy feel any worse than she already did, but she knew he was thinking, *Where?* Where on earth would they find someone who could drop everything to hop on his private plane to Mexico in only one week?

"I'm sure I can find someone," he repeated.

"I know I shouldn't even ask," Kathy glanced up at him, wincing. "But I don't suppose there's any chance you'd postpone this trip? I'll be good as new in a couple of months."

Jason stepped around his desk to a giant topographical map of Mexico that was anchored to the wall. Just looking at the thing made him wonder what fresh atrocities Benicio Vajaras had inflicted on the people in the Tzeltal villages around San Cristóbal.

"Right here—" he tapped the area at the bottom where Mexico funneled into Central America. "—we have good old Jose and his family. And their baby girl, Chiquita."

Kathy rolled her eyes.

"Chiquita's a sweet-tempered child," he went on, "even if she is named after a banana. Smart, healthy in every respect. Except, of course, for that harelip splitting her face in half."

Kathy frowned. He knew she was seeing the parade of such children they'd treated in the past three years. And others, too. Older children who had been maimed by the faceless monster named Vajaras. Parents who had been wounded in armed combat. Sometimes Jason felt like a surgeon patching up a tide of wounded on a battlefield. Only he fought this war year in, year out. Because his enemies were not only endless disease and poverty, but the cruelty and inhumanity of a ruthless overlord.

"So—" Jason focused his gaze on the map "—at this late date, Jose and Rosita have already loaded up the rental donkey and are making the arduous trip—" he ran his finger over the mountainous region on the map in a slow, twisting path north "—in the hope of getting a miracle for their baby." He flashed a wicked smile at Kathy. "Cancel? Don't think so."

"Then the least I can do is help you find my replacement. I want you to know—" she glanced over at him again, this time with apology in her eyes "—that I only found out about this on Friday."

"Maybe I can locate an interpreter in the region," he offered. The Miami-style hotels facing the turquoise ocean in Cancún were crawling with bright young bilingual Mexicans looking for ways to improve their economic status. But even crossing the border without a Spanish-speaking cohort could be very risky, especially when you were trafficking medical supplies and drugs and sharp instruments past Mexican customs.

"Even if you can hire some bright kid to travel across the peninsula to the Chiapas clinic, if he or she doesn't have a medical background..." Kathy left the rest unsaid—that such a person couldn't adequately explain the strange and frightening procedures to the patients. She stood, facing her boss. "I really am sorry."

"It can't be helped." Jason walked around the desk and gave her shoulder another reassuring pat. "Now get your behind back out to salt mines." He winked at her.

"Watch it. I'll turn you in for harassment." Kathy quipped as she walked to the door. She paused with her hand on the knob. "I hate leaving you with this snafu."

"Go drown your guilt with a cookie, Martinez." He flapped a dismissing palm at her.

"Hold it. I do know someone who speaks fluent Spanish, who might even understand the Chiapas dialects. What was that drug rep's name? The one who brought the cookies?"

"Kendal Collins?" He'd seen the woman around the hospital. Something about Kendal Collins had definitely snagged his interest.

"Yeah." Seeming excited, Kathy hurried back to his desk. "Could I see that card you stuck in your pocket?"

He swiveled the desk chair to his coatrack and dug in the vest pocket of the leather jacket. "Kendal Collins speaks Spanish?"

Kathy took the card. "Yeah. Can I keep this until tomorrow? I might be too swamped to call her until this evening."

"You're going to ask this little drug rep to go to Mexico?"

"No. I'm offering her the open brunch slot. She's on your waiting list. You'll at least need to make an appearance. Maybe if we do her a favor, she'll do us one."

He nodded. The drug reps lined up to get his ear. There was never enough time to listen to everybody, never enough time for anything, which was why he wanted Martinez to cut the blather and split.

"It's worth a shot. Now beat it, Martinez."

Kathy closed the door with a quiet click and a smile.

Jason finished the charts, then sank back in his desk chair with a worried frown. He wondered how long Kathy's gallbladder had been acting up. She never missed a day of work. Sometimes he felt guilty for pushing his staff too hard.

But he didn't push anyone any harder than he pushed himself. It seemed the only thing that gave him any peace was healing the scarred and hurting.

He closed his eyes. He had been too young, too dumb, to save Amy. The pain had dulled with the passage of time, of course, but on some level the tragedy haunted him every day. Every scarred face was Amy's. Every broken nose, every collapsed eye socket, every deformed palette...every burn contracture. He cut and stitched and mended as if he were trying to repair the past. It was like a giant, lifelong *undo*. But what had happened to Amy could never be undone. No matter how hard he worked, it would never be enough.

He placed his open palm on the stack of charts before him. Still, he could save these. And the ones in Mexico. One case at a time. One life at a time.

CHAPTER TWO

ON THE NIGHT of her thirty-first birthday, Kendal Collins sank into her giant Jetta tub until the bubbles grazed her chin. After brooding for one full, uninterrupted minute, she slowly raised a limp hand from the sudsy water and picked up one of the heart-shaped gourmet cookies she'd stashed at the side of tub. She unpeeled the cellophane wrapper, then thoughtfully nibbled the sinful treat. The second cookie went down a little faster. She washed the third down with a tall stemmed glass of very expensive merlot.

The cookies were verboten. So was the wine for that matter. Kendal always struggled with a teeny, tiny weight problem that her best friend Sarah insisted on calling ''voluptuousness.'' But today was her birthday, Kendal told herself. And Valentine's Day. She reached for another cookie. She deserved a little celebration. But as she drained the last of the wine, she knew she wasn't celebrating.

She started to cry.

At first her weeping was gentle, controlled, like a character in a soap opera trying not to wreck a mask of makeup. But before long she broke down, sobbing, hiccuping, letting the tears run down her face as she sank lower into the scented water. Finally, she had scooted so low that her lips skimmed the surface. *Another inch*, she thought, blubbering, *and I could just go ahead and drown myself.*

She rolled her eyes at such a ridiculous thought. But in this past year she had not let herself have one single pity party. And by Jove, she was going to have herself a doozie tonight.

In this past year, she had been brave, trying to show everyone that she was okay. Somehow she'd been strong this whole long, lonely year since Phillip had dumped her. Dumped was such a brutal, ugly word, but nonetheless a true one, and Kendal was all about truth these days. The ugly, unvarnished truth. She was fat. And childless. And Phillip had dumped her.

"It's not working anymore," Phillip had announced on the night of the fifth anniversary of their so-called relationship, which was also the date of her birthday. Which was also Valentine's Day. Which was also this exact hateful date.

"I'm sorry. It's just not." His big brown eyes had looked pained as he'd said it. As if the breakup was something totally beyond his control and he was so sad, so powerless, about the whole thing.

Kendal had asked the usual questions that sputter out of the shocked and bereaved—the dumped.

What do you mean? Are you saying it's over? Just like that? Are you moving out?

But of course he was moving out. Phillip was already packing his bags, right there in front of her eyes. And he was consulting one of his never-ending lists

while he did it. He'd apparently given this considerable thought. But then, Phillip gave considerable
thought to taking a poot. That's why Kendal had never
expected this kind of rash act from him.

Kendal had wanted to scream. *You can't just walk
out like this! It's our anniversary! And it's Valentine's
Day! And it's my thirtieth birthday, for crying out
loud!* Instead she forced herself to remain calm, adult,
as she followed Phillip around the bedroom.

She argued that they'd built a *life* here. That they'd
even bought this town house together.

"I'll need my equity back," he said flatly as he
meticulously stacked underwear into his suitcase.

"You know I can't come up with that kind of
money!" Her false veneer of calm cracked as reality
slammed into her. Phillip was leaving. And on the
heels of that realization came another. This lifestyle
they'd built had become rather expensive. "And you
know I can't come close to affording this place on my
own." The two of them had been on the rise in their
careers, and Kendal had been foolish enough to assume their live-in relationship would eventually lead
to marriage. Though she certainly had no intention of
mentioning the M-word now, not while Phillip was
packing his suitcase like some felon on the run.

Phillip carefully arranged the last of his socks in a
zipper pocket. "This place was your choice, not mine.
Let's face it. We are not a good match in so many
ways."

"How did you suddenly come to that conclusion?"
Kendal demanded. "Did you make another one of

your damned lists or something?'' Phillip was the ultimate anal-retentive pharmaceutical rep. He lived by lists. Elaborate, extensive, three-tiered lists. That was one of the things Kendal had found so comforting about him. With Phillip, nothing was ever left to chance. Once, back when their relationship had drifted into the doldrums and he couldn't quite make up his mind to walk down the aisle, he had actually come to her with a pro and con list, suggesting that she make one of her own.

''As a matter of fact, I did,'' he admitted now, ''right before I made my final choice.''

''Your final choice?'' Kendal echoed.

But he turned away. ''Let's face it,'' he repeated. ''This relationship is just not working.''

Why did he keep saying that? By the time he faced her at the front door with one last parting look of regret and one last ''I'm sorry,'' Kendal was reduced to mumbling, ''I understand.'' Though she really, really did *not* understand. She'd only said that because she couldn't endure the sight of his guilt-stricken eyes for another single second.

But two weeks later, she'd wanted to scratch those big brown eyes out when she learned that dear Phillip was involved in a new relationship—one that *worked*, a woman who fit his *list*, Kendal supposed. The woman, Kendal suspected, who had been at the root of their troubles all along—Stephanie Robinson. The snotty little drug rep who pulled down stellar sales for Merrill Jackson's chief competitor, McMayer. The woman who now had Phillip cozily moved into her condo.

Kendal had seen Phillip only once after he'd moved out, when both of them were in Dallas for a Merrill Jackson sales meeting. He was coming down an escalator at the enormous Galleria mall and there was that hated woman, glued to his side. That hideously tall stick-figure blonde had actually spotted Kendal, grabbed Phillip's arm and steered him in the opposite direction.

Kendal had suffered a very bad moment then. Really suffered.

She'd staggered into a nearby soup shop. Sank into a booth. Blindly ordered French onion, extra cheese. Normally she would have dived into the melted topping with gusto. But that afternoon she had stared at the bowl without so much as lifting the spoon, wondering *why, why, why?*

All their friends, the other pharmaceutical reps at Merrill Jackson, had sided with Kendal after the breakup, labeling Phillip the L.M.B.—List-making Bastard—and labeling Stephanie Robinson an anorectic bimbo. Which seemed like a bit of an oxymoron to Kendal but she enjoyed the sound of it anyway. She tested the words out loud against the bubbles, "Anorectic bimbo."

But her friends' anger on her behalf hadn't really helped. In the long run, she had ended up missing Phillip and their tidy upscale life. Missing him with a strangely hollow pain that surprised her in fresh waves every few weeks.

As the year dragged by, Kendal's long, lonely nights seemed to only get longer, lonelier, while she watched another of her girlfriends get married and another have a baby. And when she'd heard a few months ago that Phillip and Stephanie had also gotten married, the pain had solidified into a heavy, solid thing, squeezing like a vise around her heart. Kendal thought she had succeeded in sealing away the hurt where she wouldn't have to feel it. Except that now, on her thirty-first birthday, here she was, with her tears pouring down into her fancy bathtub.

And fast on heels of the hurt came the fear.

Kendal had to admit that she had some major fears. Her future, without Phillip, looked a little shaky, a little scary. Too scary to contemplate after a hefty glass of merlot. Thoughts of her looming mortgage payment made her wish she hadn't wasted money on a manicure. She raised a hand out of the sudsy water and examined her perfect French nails through the haze of tears. She'd had them done in anticipation of the girls' night out that her friends had cooked up for her birthday. Knowing this was now the worst night of her life, they'd made a big deal out of celebrating "the one-year anniversary of Kendal Collins's emancipation."

She supposed the whole exercise was meant to be therapeutic, and she loved her friends dearly for trying, but she found she simply didn't have the heart for a party.

After a hard day on the road with her boss—he seemed to be insisting on spending field days in the car with Kendal more frequently—the idea of getting all fixed up and oozing false cheer in some trendy bar seemed more like drudgery than fun. She'd called Sarah and begged off. She just could not do it, she told her protesting friend. Not tonight.

The real truth was she wanted to stay home and brood about her life.

She studied her fingers, and suddenly the expensive manicure looked like a metaphor for all that was wrong with her life. It was too perfect. Perfect nails, perfect clothes, perfect car, perfect town house—her whole life looked like a magazine ad. And she hated it. Suddenly it all seemed so sterile, so false. And she hated Phillip for leaving her all alone with it. And all alone to pay for it.

Why did she persist in living a lifestyle that no longer had meaning? Because she didn't know how to do anything else? Because she didn't actually *have* anything else? And if this was all she had, how was she going to continue to pay for it?

Her district sales manager's voice came worming up out of her memory.

"Collins?" They were in her company Taurus, on their way to a tiny hospital in western Oklahoma. What had started out as a quick road trip had been hampered by thunderstorms and road construction. Warren's mood was as testy as the weather. To mollify him, she'd slipped him a Valentine's cookie from her stash in the glove box. But he'd just called her by her last name. Not good.

"I've been going over the western region's sales

figures, yours in particular." Warren bit into the cookie. "Your numbers have certainly fallen off a bit in the past year, haven't they?"

"Yes, but...," *But what?* Kendal didn't have a good answer here. She knew she'd let her sales numbers slide. She regretted that for more than one reason and had vowed more than once to change it—along with everything else about her life. "I'm taking steps to correct that."

"I was wondering...," Warren was talking with his mouth full, a small slight, perhaps another ominous sign. "Have you made any progress in getting Dr. Bridges on board with Paroveen?"

Dr. Bridges. The very name made Kendal's insides seize up. Dr. Jason Bridges, the up-and-coming facial reconstruction surgeon whose thriving practice sat smack in the middle of Kendal's territory, yet remained frustratingly out of her reach. She'd heard all about him. Supposedly, he was some kind of handsome bad boy. The Wolf. That's what the single women at Integris had labeled him. They said any woman who attempted to slip a choke chain onto that man's neck, much less jerk on it, would quickly find herself dumped.

But she also knew Jason Bridges leaped at the chance to use his brilliant mind and his incredible hands to help people. Aggressive was hardly the word for him. Coming straight from an extended residency at Johns Hopkins, he had burst onto the scene at Integris and nothing had been the same in the surgery department since.

People had talked about him from day one. Within months patients had started flocking to him.

Kendal represented Paroveen, the perfect drug for a busy doctor like Bridges. Paroveen was now being aggressively marketed after years of research and development, and promised to dramatically reduce post-op swelling and scarring with almost no adverse side effects. Kendal believed in its efficacy wholeheartedly, but getting Bridges to believe in it was another matter. He stubbornly persisted in using the competitor's equivalent, Norveen.

Warren swallowed his bite of cookie. "When I saw you at the Christmas party, you told me you were going to close in on Bridges right after the first of the year. And now——" he waggled the cookie "——it's already Valentine's Day." Warren smiled a coercive smile that was anything but sweet.

Since Christmas, Kendal had launched a one-woman campaign to get Bridges to switch. To no avail. She'd done everything in her power to forge a positive connection with the man, arriving earlier and earlier at the hospital to catch him on rounds. Didn't the man ever sleep?

But so far she'd barely gotten her foot in the door of his tenth-floor offices. And that was only thanks to getting on a first-name basis with Bridges's nurse, Kathy. And that was only because over a box of doughnuts one morning they'd discovered their mutual loves—chocolate and the Spanish language.

"Uh, actually, I haven't made as much progress with Dr. Bridges as I'd like, but I'm working on it."

She bit her lip before she blabbed about the basket of Valentine's cookies and promos. Recent regulatory codes prohibited such gifts, but Kendal was desperate. She couldn't ever seem to schedule a sanctioned breakfast or dinner in Bridges's office, which, of course, just happened to be Warren's next suggestion.

"Why don't you set up an in-service breakfast in his office?"

Duh.

Kendal wondered if the other reps got micro-managed like this. "I've offered to do that many times, but the nurses keep saying Bridges doesn't have time. He's got an awfully full surgical schedule. The man's apparently some kind of freaky machine—doing surgery from dawn 'til dusk."

"I am well aware of that. That's why he's the number one facial reconstruction surgeon in the region, our highest potential market." Warren had stretched out the words *well aware* with exaggerated patience. Indeed, that was the point. Everybody in the business was *well aware* that if a prolific, fastidious surgeon like Bridges used Paroveen, the rest of the local surgeons would soon follow. "That's why we need to get him to at least try Paroveen. We're never going to get him to prescribe the drug until we get him to at least try it."

Kendal let the wipers beat to the count of two, seeking the right words to defuse her boss. "I know things have slipped in my territory. But I've done everything I can to meet this guy. I try to leave samples. I talk to his office staff a couple of times a week, but I have yet to lay eyes on the man—"

"I don't have to tell you how this stuff works, Collins." Warren pronounced each word as if she'd suffered a lobotomy. "You used to be one of the best reps in the business. I'm telling you, do whatever you can to impress him."

There was her last name again. That and Warren's choice of words—*used to be*—sent a warning buzz ripping straight from Kendal's toes to the top of her head. Kendal *used to be* Merrill Jackson's hotshot sales rep, the one who won all the quota awards at the national meetings. But when Phillip had bugged out on her, it had felt like he'd pulled some kind of plug. All of her confidence had been seeping like air from a tire ever since. While she should have been aggressively garnering new business, Kendal found it was all she could do to get out of bed some mornings. The truth was she had been too busy surviving emotionally to expand her business. And in the cutthroat world of pharmacy sales, stagnation was bad. Real bad. Now she was stuck with a dwindling territory, a lifestyle built around two handsome paychecks instead of a single meager one and a growing pile of debts.

Her manager knew Bridges was a tough sell. Very set in his ways. Very particular about patient care. Very brand loyal. This was a test.

"Look, if you don't want to go after Bridges, I can always call—"

"No!" Kendal wasn't about to let some other rep take part of her territory. She would get Bridges or die trying. "Don't worry. I'll find a way to tap into his schedule, and when I do, I'll wow Bridges and his crew."

"'Atta girl, Kendal." Warren had smiled, and Kendal had actually been grateful when he used her first name.

She sat up and smacked the sudsy water with her beautifully groomed hand, railing at the one who started this mess. "Phillip Dudley, I hate your freaking guts!" She raised her chin higher to the ceiling, shrieking even louder, "And I hope you *die!*" The word "die" echoed back off the Italian tile walls, sounding so ugly that it shocked Kendal to her senses. What kind of bitter woman was she becoming? She slid back down into the water and might have dissolved into tears again if the portable phone on the counter next to the tub hadn't bleated in her ear.

Annoyed, she grabbed the thing. This was Sarah, no doubt, trying one last time to talk Kendal out of staying home alone on her birthday. But the caller ID displayed an unfamiliar number. With a sudsy finger, she punched Talk. "Hullo."

"Is this Kendal Collins?" A vaguely familiar female voice.

"Yes."

"Hi, Kendal. This is Kathy Martinez from Dr. Bridges's office."

Kendal tried not to make watery noises as she sat up straighter in the tub. Dr. Bridges's nurse?

"Did I catch you at a bad time?"

Kendal leaned forward in the water, adjusting the

phone. "No, actually, I was just...relaxing. What can I do for you, Kathy?" She was grateful that she was able to maintain a fairly coherent business voice, despite the wine.

"Stephanie Robinson——" the nurse started, "do you know Stephanie?"

"I know the name." *Stephanie Robinson.* Kendal gripped the phone, thinking that if Stephanie Robinson were anywhere near this bathtub, Kendal would drown the woman. Why was Dr. Bridges's nurse calling her about Stephanie Robinson? To rub in the fact that her boss was still prescribing Stephanie's drug like candy?

"Well, she had to cancel a breakfast she had arranged for Dr. Bridges and the staff. I knew you were on our waiting list in case we had a cancellation. You wouldn't be interested in doing it, would you?"

Kendal almost slid under the water in disbelief. Would she do it? Would she do it? Was the sky blue? Did the Pope wear a beanie?

"Actually, I'd love to." Was she saying *actually* too much? She frowned at the empty wineglass.

"Great! Apparently Stephanie's expecting and has such a dreadful case of morning sickness that she can't even function until noon most days."

Expecting? Stephanie was pregnant? Kendal raised her knees out of the sudsy water and propped her elbows on them. She pressed her forehead with the butt of one hand and squeezed her eyes shut while she fought down tears. *Pregnant.* With Phillip's child.

When Kendal remained quiet too long, Kathy Martinez said, "Kendal? Are you still there?"

By an act of will so fierce it sent a tremor through her, Kendal dragged her mind back to the conversation, focusing on the good fortune that had suddenly dropped in her lap.

"When do you want me to come?"

"Tomorrow. Seven o'clock."

Tomorrow. So much for the pity party. She'd be busy getting her act together for a presentation instead.

"Great. I'll see you then."

They hung up, and Kendal slid back down in the water, feeling far, far worse than she had before the nurse called, if that was possible.

So Stephanie Robinson, no, Stephanie *Dudley* in her nonprofessional life, was pregnant.

She, Kendal, should be the one who was pregnant by now. That had been the plan. At least that had been her plan. To pay down the town house for about a year, then, as soon as they were married, get pregnant. Then combine their home offices, convert the third bedroom into a nursery and live happily ever after. Her longing for a child overcame her suddenly, an ache in her middle, a physical hunger.

Did she really miss Phillip so much, or was it this fantasy she missed? The idea of a family. They weren't getting any younger, she'd told Phillip more than once, hoping to inch him toward the altar. They'd have to start on a family as soon as they were married. She'd never dreamed the malleable Phillip wouldn't go along with her program.

Only in hindsight had she recognized that Phillip had been mostly silent during these one-sided conversations. Ominously silent.

She got out of the tub and pulled the plug. She stared at the draining water for a moment while she thought, *Goodbye tears. Kendal Collins is all done crying.* Kendal Collins was, by Jove, going to have Dr. Bridges eating out of the palm of her hand within the month. She would make so much money that she could pay for this stupid town house outright if she wanted to.

Almost angrily, she started toweling off. She stopped when she caught her reflection in the floor-to-ceiling mirror that covered one wall. She gave herself a determined glare, straightening her shoulders. Yes, indeed, Kendal Collins was going to take her life back, make buckets of money and forget all about marriage and babies…and pain.

But when she started toweling again she thought, *Who am I kidding?* She couldn't forget about marriage and babies. Because that was what she really wanted. Underneath the manicures and cars and clothes, that was *all* she really wanted.

But now, instead of marriage and babies, she found herself on her thirty-first birthday, all alone and struggling to survive in a very competitive business.

She closed her eyes, wondering again why Phillip had left her. Oh, sure, their love life hadn't been the hottest in history. But she had thought that was the way Phillip preferred it. He'd always been reserved…almost to the point of being passive. She had always feared that unleashing her own fierce passions might scare the pusillanimous Phillip off.

So ironic. He had left her anyway, despite her efforts to mold herself to suit him. Was there something wrong with her? She opened her eyes and gave her reflection a critical once-over. She was cute. Everybody said so. She was healthy and…shapely. Was she perhaps a little *too* shapely? Phillip had hinted as much so many times that Kendal had struggled to lose weight, trying to keep him happy. But Phillip had dumped her for the anorectic bimbo anyway.

She turned sideways and lifted her chin. Okay, so she was endowed with some pretty serious curves, but she also had a healthy mane of coal-black hair, riveting green eyes and skin like a China doll. She unhooked the clip that held her hair high and let the heavy waves tumble down. They felt cool against her bath-warmed back. She looked, she decided, like a Madonna, like a woman born to be a lover…a mother.

To hell with Phillip. She liked herself the way she was, and even if she never found a man, never had babies…

She clutched the towel to her front and closed her eyes. *Never?* She had turned thirty-one on this very night. Never was looking like a real possibility.

"Please, God," she whispered to a deity she seldom thought about, much less prayed to. A deity so remote, so powerful and elusive, that she refused to even assign "it" a gender.

"Please," she prayed, "send me a husband." And as long as she was asking she decided to add, "And a child, too. That's all I really want. A family. I don't even care how you do it."

CHAPTER THREE

KENDAL EXITED the elevator at the tenth floor, pulling her rolling travel cart behind her, reflecting that sometimes a pharmaceutical sales rep resembled nothing more than a glorified bag lady. Hauling your business around in the back seat of your car, up and down elevators in a silly rolling cart. So much paraphernalia—the cell phone, the pager, the laptop, the PalmPilot, the boxes of samples, the promo items, the paperwork. Kendal's constant challenge, and one of her chief strengths, was keeping it all organized. From her home office to her company car to the wheelie nipping at her heels, Kendal's life was a study in constant and careful order. Control, unrelenting control, was the key.

She opened the door of Dr. Jason Bridges's office and hoped Daylight Deli hadn't delivered the quiche, pastries and fruit trays yet. The waiting room was empty—a good sign. She wondered what kind of pull Stephanie Robinson had that she could conveniently get a breakfast scheduled on the one morning in a million when Dr. Bridges wasn't in surgery. A youngish receptionist sat in her chair behind a glassed-in cubicle. Kendal didn't see Kathy Martinez.

The lobby window rolled open and the young receptionist said, "May I help you?"

"I'm Kendal Collins, I've brought breakfast for your office, courtesy of Merrill Jackson." Kendal gave her an engaging smile and handed the woman one of her business cards.

"Oh. Of course. Kathy!"

A familiar brown face appeared around the window of the reception area. "Kendal?"

"Hi, Kathy! Thanks for calling me last night."

"No problem. Thanks for coming on short notice."

Kathy Martinez's black eyes fixed on Kendal. "Now, didn't you tell me that you're——" she paused one millisecond before saying the next words as if they had some special significance "—fluent in Spanish?"

"*Sí. Cómo le va?*"

"*Muy bien, gracias.*" Kathy chuckled. "*Ha estado alguna vez en Chiapas?*"

Had she ever been to Chiapas? Kendal's conversational Spanish was excellent, so she hadn't misunderstood, but she didn't get the point of the woman's question. Still, she kept her cordial smile in place. "No, but I've been near there—to the Yucatan Peninsula."

In her business, any connection she forged might help with future sales. It was all about building the relationship. If she was lucky, she and Kathy might move on to the subject of Paroveen sometime before noon.

"Listen. I need to talk to you about that." Kathy Martinez clutched Kendal's arm.

"Okay." Kendal couldn't imagine why this nurse, who barely knew her, was acting so excited. Did they need an interpreter for a patient? "But I'm expecting the food trays any moment, and I'd like to get my brochures and samples set out first."

"Of course. Let me show you to the break room." Kathy's smile seemed unnaturally bright.

Kathy led Kendal through a warren of offices and exam rooms, then opened a door to a sparsely decorated room with green Formica counters on three walls and a large round faux-wood table in the center.

Kendal parked her rolling case against a wall plastered with unappetizing anatomical charts and went to work with her usual efficiency.

First, she pulled all the chairs away from the table and lined them up against the wall. She didn't want people to sit down without looking at her materials. It was better if they moved around.

Then she unzipped the suitcase and whipped out a portable easel. Faster than a magician, she assembled it and set it next to the table. She then pulled out a giant tri-fold poster featuring Paroveen and propped it open on the easel. Lastly, she covered the ugly table with a paper tablecloth—royal purple, Merrill Jackson's signature color. She'd found a stack of the cloths on sale at a paper goods store and bought the lot. Just the kind of subliminal touch that helped people remember the occasion and your product—and you.

She applied this kind of forethought to her personal appearance as well, lacing her business wardrobe with subtle touches of purple.

She felt a teeny bit puffy today after indulging in the wine and cookies last night, so she'd chosen a crisp black suit with a pencil-slim calf-length skirt and a crisp lavender microfiber blouse. Her only jewelry, save her perennial one-carat diamond earrings and a Merrill Jackson name tag, was a sterling silver lapel pin shaped in the Merrill Jackson logo. She'd been awarded that one for high sales.

The skirt felt a tad snug as she squatted to unzip a low pocket where her brochures and business cards were stashed.

The door to the small room opened and a really good-looking guy in a white T-shirt, leather jacket and snug jeans balanced a trio of long rectangular boxes as he entered the room, tilting his broad shoulders sideways.

"Hi," he said.

"Hi." Kendal barely gave him a glance and turned back to her task. "Would you mind taking the food out of the cartons and putting the trays out on that purple tablecloth? I'm running a little late here."

Kendal was very good at making the most of her time by delegating tasks and soliciting help from others.

"Bossy workaholic," her sister Kara had called her one time when Kendal had pressed her into stuffing envelopes while they visited.

"Ah. So you want me to quit working so much?" Kendal, already hard at the task, had asked her sister sweetly.

"It wouldn't hurt you to slow down, you know."

This, Kendal thought, from the woman whose leisurely days included naps with her toddler while her hardworking husband pulled down six figures.

"Then I guess old Matt wouldn't mind paying my bills, too." Kendal knew that was unkind, implying that her sister was some sort of deadbeat, a burden on her poor husband.

But Kara had merely rolled her eyes indulgently at her older sister. "For your information, Matt and I are a team. Matt enjoys taking care of his family. Unlike that weakling you're hooked up with. The way Phillip insists on divvying up every last cent the two of you spend...that's not commitment, Kendal honey. And it's not true love. Don't kid yourself."

Kara's honesty had seemed harsh at the time. But as it turned out, Kendal's younger sister had been absolutely right about dear old Phillip.

Sensing no movement from the direction of the door, Kendal glanced over her shoulder again. The man with the boxes was still standing there, giving her rearview a once-over.

"You are definitely not Stephanie Robinson," he said and smiled.

Kendal frowned at him. What an odd thing to say. And because Stephanie was ultra slim, and Kendal was not, and because he was looking at her backside, his implication pricked her pride a teensy bit. All of a sudden she really didn't care for the way he was looking her up and down. Sort of brash for a delivery boy. She stood and straightened her skirt.

"Stephanie's not coming," she explained in a tone

that was intentionally frosty. "I'm Kendal Collins, from Merrill Jackson. The McMayer presentation has been canceled."

"I know."

"Oh." She had placed a last-minute call this morning to the same caterer that Stephanie used, figuring they'd be glad to switch the order. Daylight Deli was reasonably priced and located right here in the vast Integris medical complex. They were good, even if their delivery boy was a little rough-looking.

"Then would you mind?" She flipped a hand toward the table. "I'd like to hurry and get set up." Kendal walked over and quickly fanned her promotional materials on the countertop next to the coffeepot. "The staff will be coming in here at seven."

"Only if I say so."

An electric rush zapped through Kendal's middle. *Oh, no.* Her eyes fixed on the counter for one split second, then squeezed shut the next as realization turned to horror. People said the elusive Dr. Bridges dressed like a motorcycle punk.

Kendal whirled around, struggling to recover her poise. "Pardon me?" She smiled as if totally confused.

"I'm Doctor Bridges." He sauntered up to the counter where she stood, and slid the cartons onto the remaining space next to the coffeepot. Then he stuck out his hand.

She took it, hoping hers wasn't too sweaty with shock. She'd been trying for months to meet the man, and here he was, big as life. Truly big. Even his hands were large. And very warm. She shook his hand while her mind did an instant replay. Had she said anything rude while she'd been assuming he was just an ogling delivery boy? "I-I'm Kendal Collins," she stammered while he held onto her hand and her heart started to pound. "I don't think we've ever actually met."

"No, I don't think we have. But I've heard of you." He hadn't released her hand. A fact that screamed through Kendal like a fire alarm. Besides being warm, his hand felt smooth. A by-product of being a surgeon, she supposed. And talk about strong. His clasp was electric with purpose, intelligence, life.

The twinkle in his eye acknowledged that the charge passing between them as he pressed her fingers in his strong, warm ones, was very real. She'd never met a man whose very touch sent an electric current all the way to her toes.

"You have?" *He's heard of me?* she wondered. *How?* She hoped it was in connection to Paroveen.

He nodded, smiling, but didn't elaborate, which was unnerving, considering that his eyes were raking over her frame like a tiger sizing up lunch.

He stepped closer. He was much taller than Kendal, and she had to tilt her head back as she looked up into his face. "Well...*huh*—"

His flashing blue eyes, so sparkling and intelligent that they actually made her breath catch in her throat, were scrutinizing her face now with the same avid attention he'd given her figure seconds before. He finally let go of her hand, grinning while he studied her from hairline to chest. He definitely reminded her of a tiger circling a shivering fawn, and he seemed all too aware of his effect on her.

Kendal waved her emancipated hand in the air nervously. "I hope you don't mind, but when I found out that Stephanie had canceled her breakfast, I offered to bring some food in for the staff instead. So they wouldn't be disappointed," she trailed off, "and all."

"How very considerate!" he spoke with the barest hint of sarcasm.

They both knew why she was here. Kendal imagined his thriving practice was overrun with eager drug reps like herself.

"So. What did you bring us?" He raised the lid off one of the boxes. Kendal could see the tray of expensive pastries, covered with cling wrap. "Not too shabby," he said as he reached to lift the wrap. "Got enough here for a hungry doc?"

"Afraid not." Kendal gave his hand a light slap.

He laughed. Then he quirked a smug grin at her, digging around under the cling wrap anyway, and she gave him a wry little smile in return.

"I'd be all too delighted if you'd eat with us," she said, "since *you're* the real reason I'm here."

"You're interested in little old me?" He took a bite of a roll.

She smiled at his flirting. "No. Only in your business. Allow me to introduce my latest miracle drug." She swept an arm toward the easel.

He chewed as he squinted at the giant poster promoting Paroveen. "Always the latest miracle drug," he muttered.

"But mine really *is* miraculous. I'm only asking you to give it a try." She handed him a brochure, then reached around him and slid the box of pastries off the counter. "I'd better get these set out before the staff gets in here." She often found it prudent to give the docs a moment to read her materials uninterrupted.

But to her disappointment, he didn't even look at the brochure. Instead, he folded his arms over his chest and watched her. "I'd rather hear what you have to say about it."

She was aware of his eyes following her as she quickly arranged the food on the table. "Okay. I'd love to."

She spouted a few startling scientific statistics about Paroveen while she pulled out paper plates, forks and napkins stamped with the Merrill Jackson logo from her rolling cart.

When she was finished her spiel, he stuffed the brochure in the pocket of his leather jacket, sauntered over and proceeded to pile food onto a plate. "I'm afraid I've got to get back down to surgery, so—" he popped in a grape, then reached for cubed ham "—maybe we can get together some other time to finish discussing your wonder drug."

Kendal wasn't sure, but her instincts warned that The Wolf was interested in more than the drug. Maybe it was the way his teeth flashed in that cocky smile right before he bit into a cube of ham.

But she couldn't pass up the chance to push her product. "Anytime." She'd worry about his motives after she got his business. For now, she knew she'd only have his ear for as long as it took for him to gobble down that last piece of ham. She had to talk and talk fast.

"You understand that I don't like switching drugs," he said.

"I understand, but our studies indicate that every doctor that upgrades to Paroveen gets an eighty percent reduction in edema in half the time. Plus our physician education and support services are outstanding," she finished in a rush.

"Samples?"

"All you want," Kendal bargained.

"You'll *personally* provide technical support?" He wiped his hands on his napkin and gave her that eager smile again, as if *she* might make a nice little dessert right now.

"Absolutely. I'll be available to you twenty-four, seven." Shoot! Why'd she say it like that?

He smirked. "Day *and* night? *My, my.* You are the dedicated one."

Kendal was about to say something to show that she was totally professional, something that might put this handsome dog in his place, when the door swung open.

"Hello!" As if the smell of food had summoned them, Kathy Martinez and two other nurses, a tall one wearing surgical scrubs and a paper cap and a smaller girl, came waltzing up to the table.

"Hi, doc!" The nurse in scrubs winked at Jason Bridges. "Didn't expect to see you up here, what with no patients out front."

said.

"I'm headed down to surgery in a sec."

"We've got a bilateral resection of inflamed parot-ids," the nurse in scrubs explained to the shorter one.

"Oh, I forgot about that," the smaller office nurse said.

Kendal had heard about the complex microsurgery that could take up to three hours. It was exactly the kind of procedure where Paroveen would be a benefit.

"We're doing the deed right after I have another one of these little muffins. Man. These are good, Miss...tell me your name again?" He popped in a muffin, chewed and frowned at Kendal.

Was he being intentionally obtuse? After all, Ken-dal was wearing a big purple name tag. She pressed her fingers to it and smiled. "Collins. Kendal Col-lins."

"Kendal," he said, and swallowed.

"Help yourselves," Kendal told the nurses as she swept an arm over the food trays.

"Kendal—" Kathy started the introductions as the women filled their plates "—this is Mary Smith and Ruth Nichols. Mary's one of the office nurses. And Ruth is Dr. Bridges's scrub nurse."

Mary, nibbling a strawberry, reminded Kendal of an anxious little mouse. She was short, wearing a faded scrub jacket stamped in a teddy bear pattern, had cropped nondescript brown hair and rimless glasses crammed tightly against the bridge of her but-ton nose.

The one named Ruth was exactly the opposite. Even in the baggy surgical scrubs, her tall body exhibited the svelte lines of a supermodel. Even the ugly paper surgical cap did not detract from her beauty. The dusty blue color seemed to merely emphasize the flawlessness of her ivory skin.

"My extra set of hands." Bridges winked at the attractive young woman. "And my eyes. And my ears. And some days even my sense of smell."

"Just call me the doctor's scrub nose." Ruth giggled and actually tapped a fingertip to Jason Bridges's handsome nose.

Everyone but Kendal laughed. Apparently this was some sort of inside joke.

"I hope I brought enough food." Kendal turned to the table, feeling strangely uncomfortable with the couple's flirting. "How many more people are we expecting?"

"Four more from the office." Kathy smiled. "This food looks fabulous, by the way."

"Too bad you just started that nasty old diet." Dr. Bridges teased his chubby head nurse.

Kathy whapped him on the shoulder and popped a glazed doughnut hole into her mouth.

When Kathy swallowed the treat, Kendal noticed the older lady leaning over toward Dr. Bridges, mumbling something.

From across the table the last of it sounded like, "...about the Spanish."

Bridges shot Kendal a look bright with interest. In that split second when their gazes locked, Kendal began to understand how The Wolf might have gotten his nickname.

He stepped around the table to her. "Kathy tells me you speak Spanish?"

"Yes."

"Fluently?"

"Yes." Kendal frowned.

"Mexican dialects?"

"Yes." Kendal was not at all sure she liked the way he was looking at her.

"Ever been there?"

"Where?"

"Mexico. Chiapas, specifically. You ever been down there?"

There was that weird question again. "I've been to the Yucatan Peninsula a couple of times. To Cancún."

"Did you go out into the jungle or just lie on the beach?"

"I went to some Mayan ruins...in the jungle. Some remote ones." Why was Kendal explaining herself to him? But his eyes were boring into hers with such intensity that she could hardly make herself look away, and her answers just seemed to fall out of her mouth.

"I assume you have some medical background?"

"Of course. Anatomy. Physiology. I specialize in surgical physiology and pharmacology."

"Great! Wanna run away to Mexico with me?"

Behind him, she thought she heard the mousy nurse twitter.

"Not particularly." Kendal didn't get it. *Run away to Mexico?*

"You don't care for Mexico?"

"Love it. Can't wait to go back. But..." she trailed off, leaving him to fill in that the idea of going with *him* was the impediment.

"But not with a guy like me." His blue eyes flashed with amusement.

Another twitter from the nurse entourage.

"Not even if it was for a good cause?"

"What is this about?" Kendal leaned around his broad form to get a look at the nurses, who obviously knew what the doctor was getting at.

But he leaned imperceptibly also, blocking her view. "I have a proposition for you, Kendal."

Kendal wanted to say something sarcastic like *Be still my beating heart* because when a man like The Wolf used a word like "proposition," her urge to resort to sarcasm was strong. "I hope this has something to do with Paroveen."

"It does."

That surprised her. His attitude had been so flippant that she wasn't prepared for this conversation to lead anywhere serious.

"I'm listening."

"For three weeks out of the year, every year, I go to Chiapas, Mexico, to work with the local peasants. I do as much surgery as I can on as many patients as I can for those three weeks. You've heard of Doctors Without Borders?"

Kendal had. The international relief effort manned by idealistic young doctors had originated in France. They brought medical care to the poor in Third World countries around the globe. Their efforts on behalf of children had always appealed to Kendal's altruistic side. "I have. The work they do sounds wonderful."

"My mission is similar. How would you like to be part of that mission?"

"*Me? How?*"

"Because you speak the Mexican dialects. Because I'll promise to give Paroveen a thorough clinical trial down there. You can bring a case of the stuff with you. You can keep your own records. Merrill Jackson will love it. They should even get some great PR out of the deal."

Behind him, Kendal now noticed, Kathy Martinez was smiling broadly, encouraging her. The nurse named Ruth was smiling, too, but with a kind of uncertainty.

"You're saying you need an interpreter?"

"Absolutely. I speak a little Spanish, of course, and so does Ruth—" he motioned to the beautiful nurse "—but not fluently. The patients are hurting, frightened. They talk fast and the dialect is tricky. A good interpreter is crucial. What do you say? Will you consider it?"

"When?"

"Next week."

"Next *week*?"

"Sorry. My regular interpreter got sick. I just found out yesterday." He shot Kathy Martinez a meaningful glance.

"Isn't that pretty short notice for getting me on board for a trip to Mexico?"

"You said you'd been there. I assume your passport is still current."

"Well...yeah, but—"

"The other arrangements won't be a big deal. Every year, I choose my own team, fly my own plane. We take our own security guard, Ben Schulman from the hospital. All of these nurses have gone down there at one time or another."

The trio behind him nodded in affirmation.

"Ask them how fulfilling it is to help the poor, to change lives for the better. It will be a perfect opportunity to demonstrate the effectiveness of your new drug in a setting where it is desperately needed. Maybe Merrill Jackson would donate some immunizations, too."

Kendal didn't know how the conversation had taken this radical turn from slightly flirtatious to genuinely idealistic, but it had.

"I see. I...I'll have to check my schedule. And I'll have to get approval from my company." But that wouldn't be a problem, she was sure. Her boss had been very clear—*do whatever you have to do.*

"Of course."

"We'd better get downstairs," the willowy Ruth interjected. She stepped up beside Bridges.

But Jason Bridges stepped toward Kendal, facing her squarely, moving in close with his palm outstretched. "Give me one of your cards," he said. "I'll call you and we'll set up a time to get together and discuss this. I'll also have to teach you a bit about the types of surgery we do. You'll end up answering a lot of questions for the patients and families. We'll have a lot of preparation to do in a week's time.''

''Okay. I'll think about it.'' But while she was handing him one of her cards Kendal was thinking, *He can't be serious. Me? On a medical mission to Mexico? In only a week?*

He took the card. He glanced at it, then smiled into her eyes again. And again Kendal thought of The Wolf and how thoroughly dangerous it felt to be the object of this man's attention. Like he could talk you into almost anything. She felt her cheeks heating up and was glad when he turned back to Ruth.

He stuffed Kendal's card in the pocket of his leather jacket with the brochure, then said to his scrub nurse, ''The patient is elderly. Very fragile. No room for screwups. I'd like you to be the one to set up downstairs, not one of those O.R. nurses.''

''Already done.'' Ruth favored her boss with a cover model smile and a look of supreme confidence.

''Great. Remind me to give you a big old Christmas bonus.'' Jason put a guiding hand to the small of his nurse's back, and as the two of them hurried out the door his flashing eyes fixed on Kendal one last time. ''I'll talk to you soon, Kendal.''

CHAPTER FOUR

"PARDON ME?" Kendal tapped the security guard's huge shoulder, which felt like it was carved out of marble. "You're Ben Schulman, right?"

He turned, and Kendal looked up into the kindly handsome face that went with the killer body. The name tag on his massive chest read SCHULMAN, so of course this had to be the Gentle Ben that the nurses all talked about. Usually their talk bemoaned the fact that this fabulous hunk of male was not interested in women.

"Yes, ma'am."

Kendal always greeted the younger man when she came into the hospital early in the mornings, when she was trying to catch up with the surgeons before they got too busy. He was always polite, always calling her "ma'am."

Covering the night shift, Ben Schulman made for an imposing presence at the front entrance of the hospital. He was a six-foot-four blond wunderkind with a body builder's physique and a choirboy's face. The endless, swirling hospital rumors had painted Ben with a pretty broad brush. Religious fanatic. But a not-so-latent homosexual. But Kendal's impression of him was that he was totally professional. Stoic; polite, nice. Approachable, should one need help. Aggressive, should one be up to no good. Definitely idealistic. A real "serve and protect" kind of guy.

"I'm Kendal Collins." She extended her hand and he gently shook it. "I understand you accompany Dr. Bridges on his Doctors Without Borders missions to Mexico."

His face broke into a boyish smile. "We're not associated with Doctors Without Borders, per se. But yes, this will be my third trip to Chiapas."

"Could I ask you a few questions about that? When you have a minute?"

He frowned. "Why? Are you a reporter or connected to the hospital PR department or something? I was under the impression you did sales of some kind."

"I do." She handed him the card she had at the ready. "I'm in sales for Merrill Jackson. But Dr. Bridges has asked me to accompany him on the Chiapas trip as an interpreter. I thought we should meet, and I'd like to find out a little more about what I'd be getting myself into."

Ben studied the card, then her. His expression was carefully neutral, not surprising considering his job, but even so, Kendal could see that he was uncomfortable about something. "Working with Dr. Bridges is quite an experience. But I'll be happy to tell you everything I know." He checked his watch. "I get off in twenty minutes."

"Meet me at the Daylight Deli then. I'll buy breakfast."

DAYLIGHT DELI was situated in the middle of the hospital concourse that connected four enormous buildings. It faced an open courtyard and had the kind of atmosphere desperately needed in a place where people were suffering and worrying and working too hard. An atmosphere that said, "*Peace*. Relax. We'll feed you."

The food was excellent, and the place was often packed with hospital personnel in lab coats and scrubs, business-suited executives, casually dressed visitors, exhausted relatives and even the occasional patient. It was especially busy at eight o'clock in the morning. Everybody was hustling for a mug of the deli's gourmet coffee, a cup of fragrant herbal tea, a fresh-baked muffin or one of its infamous sticky buns.

Kendal felt fortunate when two lab techs vacated a small table that was out of the way by the windows. She rolled her cart into the nearby corner, sat down and waited, thinking about what she should ask the security guard.

Before long Ben came in. From behind the counter the owner looked up. The man wore an earring and a kerchief on his head and called most of his customers "sweetie." He hollered, "Ben!" and Ben answered, "Hey, Nolan!"

When Ben spotted Kendal in the corner, she waved at him.

"What can I get for you?" Kendal offered as Ben approached the table.

"A strawberry banana smoothie would be great, thanks."

The owner winked at her when Kendal and Ben walked up to the counter. He was already making the smoothie. "He always has the same thing. What can I get for you, sweetie?"

Kendal craved a sticky bun in the worst way, but she ordered a small serving of fruit salad instead. This kind of discipline was second nature to her by now, but it was never easy.

Once he got the smoothie whirring in the blender, the owner said, "You guys know each other?" while looking back and forth from Ben to Kendal.

"Kendal Collins. Nolan Nelson. Kendal's a pharmaceutical sales rep around here."

"Didn't I fill a big order for you a few days ago?"

"Yes. For Dr. Bridges's office. The quiche was excellent."

"Kendal wants to ask me some questions about the Chiapas trip," Ben said. "Dr. Bridges has asked her to go along."

The owner's eyebrows shot right up to the edge of his kerchief. "Bridges asked you to go to Mexico? Don't do it, sweetie! That man'll break your heart."

The man's tone left no doubt about what he was implying. Kendal felt her cheeks flush to a neon red. "I—"

"Nolan," Ben intoned with undisguised impatience as he looked around the crowded space, "The doc asked her to go along as an interpreter."

Nolan looked abashed, but even so, he said, "Oh, right. That's what he claims." He turned to dish up Kendal's fruit salad.

While she dug in her purse for the money, the caterer studied her with open skepticism. "He sure picked himself a pretty little interpreter. What happened to Kathy?"

"She's sick and can't go," Ben supplied. Apparently Ben had an inside track on events in Bridges's office.

"Nothing serious, I hope." The smoothie was done and Nolan poured it into a glass.

"Gallbladder." Ben took the glass.

"You take care, sweetie," Nolan said as Kendal picked up the fruit salad.

As they walked away Kendal was still feeling her cheeks burn at the caterer's implication that she might be accompanying Jason Bridges to Mexico as some sort of paramour. She wasn't like that. Not at all. In fact, she'd suffered in stubborn celibacy this whole year since Phillip had left. A few men had asked her out, but she wasn't attracted to them. She was beginning to wonder if she'd ever feel real passion again, or if Phillip's betrayal had killed that part of her for good.

"Don't mind Nolan," Ben said quietly when they got back to their table. "He doesn't like Dr. Bridges. Thinks he's a player."

"Is he?"

"How should I know? Nolan's just bitter. His sister's a nurse down in surgery. She dated Dr. Bridges for a while, went all gaga over him, baking him banana nut bread and stuff. Just because it didn't work out, that doesn't make Jason a bad guy.'' Ben didn't elaborate further, but Kendal could fill in the blanks. The relationship between the doctor and Nolan's sister had probably ended with a broken heart—hers—and The Wolf had moved on to his next conquest. But Ben wasn't about to criticize this doctor, who he obviously admired.

''You like Dr. Bridges?''

''Jason's a stand-up guy.''

A small cross shone dully from the open collar of Ben's shirt, and Kendal wondered what ''stand-up guy'' meant to someone with Ben's convictions. Someone who serves mankind under the worst of conditions? Someone who plays around but apparently thinks he's exempt from breaking hearts because everybody understands that he's The Wolf? ''What do you mean?''

''You'll find out what Jason's like soon enough if you go down to Chiapas with him.''

''You mean that he's a good surgeon?''

''He is that, but it goes deeper. He's put himself in some tight spots helping those people.''

''Like what?''

''Like there are factions down there that want to force the government to get involved and bring those people into the twenty-first century, and there are other factions that want the area to stay isolated. Jason has been caught between them a time or two, right along with the poor people he's trying to help.''

''That's why Dr. Bridges handpicked you? For security?''

Ben's handsome face looked abashed. "I can use a gun—and my fists—if I have to, but the truth is, I'm really more like Jason's pack animal," Ben smiled. "Actually, I like to go because Dr. Bridges pays all my expenses and he gives me time off to visit the missions around San Cristóbal de las Casas. That's what I really want to do someday—missionary work."

"That's wonderful! Tell me what it's like in Chiapas."

Ben's descriptions of Chiapas were romanticized, but graphic. He told her about the fascinating culture, of the superstitions that persisted among the descendants of the Maya. About the beautiful waterfalls, lakes and rain forests. He didn't pull any punches as he described the intense heat, the altitude sickness, the man-eating mosquitoes and the inevitable onset of Montezuma's revenge.

"*Turista*, the locals call it. Thought I'd die the first time it hit me. The cramps! Never had such a bad case of diarrh—" He noticed the revolted look on Kendal's face and stopped. "Sorry."

He sipped his smoothie while he eyed her impeccable manicure and silk power suit. "Are you sure you're up to this trip?" he asked. "No offense, but you seem like more of an indoor type gal."

"I've had my share of adventures," Kendal asserted. Which was at the least misleading and at the worst an all-out lie. Her "adventures" consisted of skiing down a double diamond slope at a fancy resort or finding her way on the Metro line in Washington

D.C. "I've been to Mexico before," she added for good measure, leaving out the fact that her trips had mostly been confined to the Miami-style resort areas of Cancún.

"We go down there strictly for work, you know. You'll have to prepare."

"I already bought some lightweight travel clothes, some sturdy walking boots."

"Sunscreen, insect repellent. Start taking your drugs. Cut those nails off." Ben pointed at them. "And get current on plastic surgery.

"Right. Dr. Bridges has been helping me. He's already got me boning up on cleft palates, cleft lips, burn scar deformities, post-op wound care—"

"Syndactyly—"

"Webbed fingers and toes, yes."

"Dr. Bridges will even fix stuff like protruding ears and deviated septums if he has time."

"He told me that."

"You've been with him a lot?"

"Every day. Every night."

"Really?" Ben cut a glance at Nolan behind the counter, as if he was wondering if Nolan's assessment of Jason was accurate after all. "How's that been?"

"It's been...stimulating. Challenging."

But the look on her face, she was afraid, betrayed her true feelings. Now that she'd agreed to go to Mexico, her whole life had shifted into high gear. Jason Bridges had made Kendal dog around after him on his hospital rounds while he dumped information on her faster than a flashing computer. She wasn't sure how she was supposed to remember it all. Chasing him around, trying to remember the staggering amount of material he threw at her, made her feel breathless and headachy. But she wondered if that wasn't because she was also resisting an overwhelming physical awakening. Every night, the doctor had taken her to an elegant dinner while he'd crammed her head full of yet more facts. The whole time she'd been fighting a powerful attraction to the man.

"But some of it was pleasant," Kendal continued. "We've shared some nice dinners."

Ben frowned. "There won't be any fancy dinners in Mexico. Dr. Bridges can be a tough taskmaster. His first priority is caring for the people in the region. The team—that'll be you, me and Ruth this time—is expected to keep up with him, make sacrifices and never, ever complain."

"It's only for three weeks," Kendal stated with conviction. "I can do anything for three weeks."

BUT A FEW DAYS LATER, when Kendal found herself airborne in Jason Bridges's small Cessna, she found herself wondering if she was even going to be able to stand the first leg of this "adventure." They'd hit a bank of storm clouds out over the Gulf of Mexico, about two hours into the flight.

As the small plane bucked and bumped against the turbulence, Jason Bridges seemed unfazed. He maintained control and steadily pushed and pulled at the yoke until he had the plane safely below the level of the clouds. Now they were skimming the tops of the Sierra Madre mountains. Looking at the nearness of the peaks gave Kendal a sick, dizzy sensation.

She and the nurse Ruth were crammed into the tiny rear seats, pressed from all sides by supplies and equipment that were stuffed into every available niche. Jason's instruments, IV bags and IV pumps, suture, meds, syringes, dressings, alcohol, gloves. The boxes of vaccines that Kendal's company had donated. They'd even brought their own Kleenex, paper towels and toilet paper. Even a huge box of individually wrapped hard candy, stuffed between the two women like an ottoman.

All of it left very little room for personal effects. "Clean underwear. A waterproof jacket and two changes of clothes," Ruth had explained during Kendal's last briefing, "spare shoes. The bare necessities as far as toiletries. That's it."

When they'd loaded the plane at dawn, Ruth had smiled and explained that, with the exception of Jason's specialized instruments and the pumps, all the stuff would be consumed by the end of their mission, so there would be much more room on the return trip. "Sorry about the limited luggage, but the supplies take priority on the trip down. If our clothes start to stink—" she grinned "—we can always buy us some *huipiles* to wear."

But right now Kendal could have cared less about shopping for colorful native blouses. She didn't know if it was the claustrophobia or the stuffy air in the tiny cabin or Jason Bridges's hotshot flying maneuvers, but she realized she was definitely going to barf.

Like a good nurse, Ruth read Kendal's face as accurately as a road map. "Gimme a bag, Ben. She's gonna hurl."

Jason Bridges tossed an evil grin over his shoulder. "Go ahead and get it over with, sweetheart. Never flown in a small plane in rough weather before?"

Kendal shook her head "no" as she snatched the plastic bag that Ben had flipped over the seat back.

Ruth patiently held Kendal's hair back out of the way while Kendal puked into the little sack. When Kendal was finished and had tossed her head back, gasping for air, the nurse released Kendal's long, dark hair over her shoulder. "Remember to wear it braided from here on out," she advised without a smile.

Kendal tried to nod, but the last of her breakfast insisted on making an encore. When the next wave of heaves had subsided, Ruth gave Kendal's shoulder a condescending little pat. "You'll live. Jason—" she leaned forward, grinning "—ixnay on the scenic nosedives, okay?"

Ruth had begun calling Dr. Bridges "Jason" the minute they took off. Again, Kendal wondered about their relationship. How close was it? Both of them had been in high spirits the moment the plane had become airborne, and the familiarity and excitement between them was palpable.

From the front seat, Jason Bridges hollered at Kendal over the drone of the plane's engines. "Look out the window, sweetheart. That scenery will cure whatever ails you." He gave the plane a gentle tilt to afford Kendal a better view.

Kendal's eyes grew wide as the enormous Canon del Sumidero split the landscape. Despite her nausea, she felt a shot of exhilaration at the sight. She had never seen anything so beautiful. The steep red rock walls fell in layered shelves covered with lush, brilliant green vegetation that tumbled like waterfalls into the canyon below. At the bottom, a blue-green river filled the gorge. Kendal could see the tiny white wake of a powerboat. The thing looked like no more than a toy in the vast setting. Exotic didn't come close to describing this place.

She glanced at the pilot, surprised to find Jason watching her. His aviator shades masked his eyes, but his full mouth broke into a rakish grin, complete with dimples. "Had that thing dug just for you, sweetheart. Hope you're impressed."

Ruth rolled her eyes at Kendal. And Kendal wondered what kind of situation she'd gotten herself into. Obviously this nurse had a crush on her boss and their relationship seemed slightly more than friendly. Yet he had no qualms about flirting with Kendal right in front of Ruth. She'd heard how Jason Bridges broke all the rules…and all the hearts, too. And, indeed, the rules seemed to have flown out the window the minute the plane took off. What with Jason calling Kendal "sweetheart," Ruth calling her boss Jason, and the normally reserved Ben laughing like an idiot at every dumb joke Jason cracked as if the two were old fishing buddies. Fun times in the little Cessna.

Kendal closed her eyes, pressed her head against the seatback and tried not to barf again. She must have dozed off, because when she awoke, they were making their landing approach to the city of Tuxtla Gutiérrez.

The capital of Chiapas lay spread out on a central plain surrounded by high plateaus. Forest-covered mountains shouldered up around the plateaus, sending rivers meandering down from all directions. The Pacific coast with its estuaries and humble fishing villages lay in the distance, to the south and west.

Jason handled their small aircraft as easily as if it were a giant kite being bent to his will, sending the plane earthbound in a sharp tilt to the left.

Kendal felt her stomach clench up. Ruth patted her arm. "We'll be on the ground soon, and you'll feel better."

But on the ground, Kendal only felt worse. As she hobbled down the steep little steps of the Cessna, the heat and humidity of Chiapas assaulted her like a sauna. A very smelly sauna. What *was* that revolting odor? It had a fishy, sea-salt high note—though the ocean was far away—mixed with a cloying spicy undertone that was akin to, but not nearly as appetizing as, the pungent odor of frying onions.

The blacktop under her feet felt spongy, sticky, in the heat. At ten o'clock in the morning, the sun was already beating down like a merciless spotlight and Kendal's clothes stuck to her skin like cling wrap. She swiped her forehead on her sleeve and longed to be back in Oklahoma, up to her neck in bubbles in her familiar Jetta tub.

"Ben, help Kendal unload her suitcase and those boxes of meds," Jason ordered. The two men were already pulling cargo from the rear of the plane.

"I can do it," Kendal protested and grabbed the handle of her duffel bag.

Jason clasped his hand gently over hers. "Save your strength, sweetheart." A corner of his grin quirked up, his expression amused. "You don't look like you could lift a flea right now. Speaking of fleas...." He released her hand and reached into a pocket of his vest, then startled Kendal by pitching a can of insect repellent at her. "This stuff stinks to high heaven, but you'd better slather up. The mosquitoes'll gobble up a little morsel like you."

Ben took the can from her fingers and gently counseled her. "It's not that bad. Close your eyes and turn your face away." He sprayed her legs and arms with several efficient sweeps of the can.

Not that bad? The stuff smelled positively toxic, like high-powered ant spray. Straight DDT, probably. The chemical stench made Kendal's stomach protest in an upward wave again, and the oily residue left her skin feeling twice as clammy. She touched her fingers to the stickiness and thought she could not possibly get any more uncomfortable.

She was wrong.

They were led across the tarmac to a dented white van, spewing black exhaust from its tailpipe.

Jason greeted the young Mexican driver with a hearty hug.

"*El Médico!*" the skinny youth cried, thumping Jason on the back before turning black flashing eyes on Kendal. "*Dos chicas?*" His toothy smile was too big in his thin face and Kendal could see faint traces of a scar where a cleft lip had been repaired. "*Dos lindas.* Eh?"

Jason smiled, answering the man in Spanish, "Yes, both very beautiful," he said. "But careful, Alejandro. That particular *chica* speaks the language."

Alejandro immediately altered his leering expression into a polite, respectful one. "*Buenos días, señorita.*"

"*Buenos días,*" Kendal replied just as politely. Her voice was cool, but her cheeks were burning at the man's implication that she was another one of Jason's "*chicas*"—girls.

"Get in," Jason said, taking Kendal's arm and guiding her up into the van. This time Kendal didn't argue about helping with the bags, but she felt like a weakling as she wilted back against the seat.

Inside, the vehicle's wheezing air conditioner fought the good fight but was defeated while Alejandro and Ben stowed the boxes and luggage in the back, letting heat and exhaust fumes roll in through the gaping door.

Soon enough, the supplies were loaded, the doors were slammed, and the others had crowded onto the grimy seats.

Beside Kendal, Jason Bridges pressed close and

flung one arm behind her on the bench seat. "Ready for another bumpy ride, sweetheart?" He leaned his head close, his mouth so near that she could feel puffs of his warm, moist breath against her temple. "You'll live." She heard the smile in his voice. "Feel free to put your head on my shoulder if you need to."

She didn't back away from the intimate pose. The Wolf would have to do better than this if he was trying to intimidate her. She smiled, imagining that her breath was not the sweetest thing in the vicinity right now. "Sure, I will." She gave him a thin little smile and kept her expression cool, neutral, while she looked up at her own reflection in the aviator shades.

"Got another barf bag on you?"

He didn't flinch or back away, either. Instead he flashed that wicked smile again. "You'll do, kiddo," he commented, as if talking more to himself than to her. "You'll do." He turned his head and hollered at Alejandro, *"Vámonos!"*

Off they flew with the driver careening and honking his way through the traffic-clogged, potholed streets of Tuxtla Gutiérrez, then over a narrow two-lane highway with a surface like a cheese grater. That road wound ever-higher into the Chiapas highlands and finally dropped down the other side of the mountains, narrowing to a rutted trail. Kendal eventually lost her bearings. All she knew was they had ended up on a dusty path that was leading them into the dark heart of the jungle.

CHAPTER FIVE

JASON EYED the beautiful brunette attempting to slump away from him. The way she was trying to avoid touching him was kind of cute. It betrayed the fact that the attraction he was feeling wasn't all one-sided. During their week of preparation together he'd hardly been able to keep his hands off of her.

Her lush, dark looks were captivating, absolutely fascinating. She had the palest skin he'd ever seen. Milky. He glanced down the open collar of her linen shirt. *Ooo.* Just gorgeous. Her jet-black eyebrows and dark feathered eyelashes made a startling contrast against that pearly skin. She'd chewed all her lipstick off long ago and the contours of her pale nude lips begged to be tasted—that is, once she brushed her teeth. In the meantime, he sure enjoyed looking at her. If he wasn't careful, he was going to stare a hole right through the woman.

He turned away and smiled at the jungle growth scrolling by outside the windows. He hadn't had this much fun in years. He couldn't believe he'd talked a hot chick like this into coming along on the Chiapas trip. 'Course she had her agenda—selling drugs—but then he had his. Seducing her.

No matter. They could both win if he played his cards right. If the drug proved its efficacy, she'd have her new scripts and then some. He had a lot of stroke in his circle of surgeons. And if he seduced her properly, it would be an experience neither of them would ever forget.

She was picking at a fingernail now. That fancy manicure would be history soon. This woman certainly appeared to pamper herself. Every time he'd seen her at the hospital her clothes had looked expensive and her appearance had been immaculate, maybe even a little fussy. He wondered if she'd get all whiney, having to live out of one small duffel bag for three weeks. Well, even if she was shallow, materialistic, spoiled, she was still the prettiest little thing he'd ever seen. Or at least she was the most fascinating and unique thing he'd ever seen. He'd seen a whole lot of pretty little things, after all.

Yep. This particular trip was so going to be a whole lot more fun than any of its predecessors. All because of Ms. Kendal Collins.

THE FIRST HOURS in the jungle passed in a miserable blur for Kendal. It had started to rain as they drove through the trees, and the humidity grew stifling. She was still battling the nausea and had begun to work up a fierce little headache to accompany it. But she had insisted on getting down to business alongside everyone else. The team quickly began transferring their supplies from the van, struggling with their burdens toward a large picnic-style pavilion that actually had a thatched roof. Inside, a tall, handsome Mexican woman greeted Jason with another back-thumping hug.

"*Amigo!* You made it again!"

"That's our anesthetist," Ruth explained to Kendal.

"She's volunteering her time just like the rest of us. Her name's Angelica and she's from San Cristóbal de las Casas. That's south of here. You'll see it in a day or two after we get set up."

"Isn't that where Ben's missionary friends are?" Ben had told Kendal about the historic city.

"Yes. They work with the displaced people in the slums. You'll see."

Kendal thought that Angelica, though large for a Mayan woman, was very striking in a bold, androgynous sort of way. She had massive breasts and a massive black braid that swung across her back as she heaved cartons right alongside the men. Her clothing was plain, functional. A dingy white T-shirt and khaki cargo shorts. But woven into the braid were the jeweltoned ribbons the indigenous women favored, a small homage to her femininity and her culture.

"Why are we setting up way out here in the jungle?" Kendal asked while Ruth loaded her arms with packs of paper towels.

"Secrecy. The local authorities don't like us." Ruth tugged on a box that looked way too heavy for her. "In fact, Angelica's taking a risk by helping us. Even the medical missionaries run into trouble sometimes."

"Why?" Kendal stepped up to help.

"We aid the rebels."

"The rebels?"

"The Zapatistas. Locals who fight for better conditions for the indigenous population. Sometimes—ugh!—" Ruth's words were crushed by the weight of the box.

After they'd lowered the box to the ground, Kendal said, "Sometimes?"

"On occasion, Jason has done surgery on people who've been hurt by a bad hombre named Vajaras, a man who tries to terrorize the Zapatistas. He's not above harming women and children—burning their homes and the like."

Kendal was appalled. "Why would he do such things?"

"He doesn't want anybody running up to Mexico City and bringing law and order down here. Jason thinks he's got some kind of drug operation out in the mountains."

"Why doesn't somebody turn him in to the authorities?"

"Nobody's ever actually seen the man. Nobody knows where his compound is. Anybody who's tried to find it has turned up dead."

"But how will the people who need surgery find us? And when they come out here, won't somebody blab about this place to Vajaras?"

"We'll set up an intake station in the square in San Cristóbal. Word has spread into the outlying villages. The missionaries tell the people—most come from the poor villages and the slums outside San Cristóbal. We'll give the free vaccinations as a cover in case anyone comes by to give us grief. But while we're we're there, Jason can discreetly screen the surgeries. Only the patients and their families will be given directions out to this place. We'll have help from the women in the villages, they call themselves *curanderas*—healers. But they're more like nurses.''

Kendal looked around, astonished at the primitive conditions. The large square room, open on three sides covered with mosquito netting, was dark, dank, dirty. This would be their O.R.? Apparently. There were two identical surgical tables in the center, recovery cots along the railed walls. The anesthetist, Angelica, already had her machine set up. Kendal noted the sparse surroundings with dismay—crude tables and shelves; inferior, bare-bulbed operating lights; a few lanterns for backup; basins for alcohol scrubs; a huge, uncovered box of disposable gloves. Everything seemed to be displayed at waist level. She didn't see one chair—apparently nobody would be doing any sitting around in this place.

Angelica talked a mile a minute. Giving no-nonsense orders to Ben and the driver, appraising Jason of the formidable task ahead, joking with Ruth. She switched from somewhat broken English when addressing Jason and Ruth back to Spanish with everyone else, including Kendal, once she realized the new girl was fluent in the native language.

As long as the fast-talking anesthetist was around, Kendal's role as interpreter seemed superfluous. So she pitched in like a hired hand.

First they all held the mosquito netting in place between the half wall and the thatched roof while Jason secured it with a staple gun.

Then Kendal and Angelica organized Kendal's generous samples of antibiotics, painkillers and anesthetic agents next to the anesthetist's meager supplies. It was apparent that the anesthetist knew her stuff. She struck Kendal as focused, dedicated to her job.

"Man, I can't thank you enough for all these drugs," she gushed in English, examining the boxes of medications with appreciation.

"It's our pleasure," Kendal replied in Spanish. "All I ask is that my company's name gets added to any special recognition by the Mexican government."

"Special recognition?" Angelica replied in Spanish, emitting a mocking huff. "Believe it or not, there are people in Mexico who resent doctors like Jason. When the team came down here with Doctors Without Borders two years ago, the Minister of Health impounded Jason's surgical equipment and supplies at the airport in Mexico City. He had a helluva time getting them back. Ever since that little incident, Jason hasn't taken any chances. That's why he sneaks back down here in his private plane. He's a bit of a renegade, does his missions without going through official channels."

It had occurred to Kendal, when they had been eased through customs by a couple of kind-faced Rotarians in Nuevo Laredo, that Jason was truly acting covertly. The need for secrecy perhaps explained Jason's low-flying maneuvers in the mountains.

"He's doing this completely on his own?"

"Not on his own." Angelica's smile was mischievous. "He has us." When Kendal didn't return her smile, Angelica shrugged. "Who's going to know what he does way out here in the jungle? Unless one of Vajaras's spies finds us."

There was that name again. "You know this Vajaras?"

Angelica hooted. "Sweetie, no one knows him. No one wants to know him. These are very fearful, superstitious people down here. They keep their heads down, see nothing, say nothing."

The secrecy gave Kendal the creeps, and she wondered, what if something went wrong? What if a patient died? She wondered exactly what kind of deal she had gotten herself into. At her worried expression, Angelica gave Jason's back a sly glance and added, "Don't worry. Jason can handle himself. Exactly how long have you known *El Lobo?*" Angelica's tone was teasing as she spoke in the local dialect, looking Kendal up and down, gauging her reaction to the term.

Kendal didn't hide her astonishment. *"The Wolf?* Does the man's reputation stretch all the way down to the equator?"

"Some women like a wolf, you know. How well do you know him?"

Kendal took a closer look at their hostess. Surely she, this Amazon of a woman, hadn't slept with the American doctor. But despite her large size, Angelica was a very handsome woman. Dark skin. Darker eyes. Which were glittering now, waiting for the answer to her teasing question.

"We really don't know each other at all," Kendal answered in the local dialect as well. Jason was only ten feet away, putting his sterile packs in order. "I'm volunteering to represent my company, introducing a new drug and keeping records of the results. We're also providing vaccine as a humanitarian aid."

"Yes, I know." Angelica's jaded expression grew sincere. "The people can't thank you enough. I didn't mean to insult you. I just thought...the way he's been looking at you..." Angelica let the insinuation trail off, then added an afterthought. "I thought he told me you were his interpreter."

"I will be doing that, as well as helping in any other way I can." In the back of her mind, Kendal was still wondering *how* Jason had been looking at her, exactly. Apparently Angelica had observed some things that Kendal herself had missed.

"Well, if you're interpreting, you'll be plastered to that man's side, *chica*." Angelica switched to English, her grammar and syntax making it obvious this was her second language. "He works very long hours. Martinez, she used to get sick of it. You ain't gonna have a moment to breathe in." She raised her voice louder. "If you don't know him now, I'm betting you will know him *too* well before all is over." She switched back to Spanish. "You watch him, *chica*. He can be an *asqueroso*."

Jason had been pointedly ignoring Angelica's speech, but he shot her an evil look when he heard the word *asqueroso*—Mexican for asshole.

The anesthetist ignored his glare, smiling innocently

at the neat rows of drugs and IV bags before her. "Almost done," she said with satisfaction. "Wanna go for having a smoke?"

Kendal shook her head. "No. *Gracias.*" She had always considered smoking the vilest of habits. She didn't even want to be around it secondhand. And she was still feeling ill. "I don't smoke."

"Good for you, *chica.*" Angelica went out on the veranda and lit up.

Jason and Ruth followed her. Kendal finished organizing the drugs. At one point she saw Angelica take the cigarette from her mouth and put it to Jason's lips. He took a long drag, mumbled something as he blew out the smoke and they all laughed. Kendal realized she most certainly did not know this man, not at all.

When the smokers ambled back inside, Jason shot Kendal a disgusted look. "You look like you're about to hurl again, babe. Climb up there and stretch out on one of those tables if you want." He jerked his head toward the worn black leather surgical tables at the center of the room.

"I'm okay." Kendal bent to a carton on the floor to unpack more supplies.

"We'd better get some food into her soon," Ruth commented as if Kendal were their patient.

"Viljo is fixing the *comida* right now," Angelica said.

La comida, the heavy midday meal in Mexico. Kendal could hardly bear the thought. "Who is Viljo?"

she asked Ruth, mostly wanting to get the attention off herself.

"Viljo runs that filthy flophouse out on the road," Angelica answered for her.

"He rips me off to the tune of about ten grand every year," Jason offered from across the room.

"Jason rents the entire old hotel while we're here," Ruth explained. "We take care of the patients over there until they can travel. Viljo provides the food, the linens, all that stuff. Jason foots the bill."

"Wow." Kendal couldn't hide the fact that she was impressed at the lengths Jason would go to in order to help these people.

But he deflected her admiration with a wicked grin.

"Try as I might, I can't spend *all* my money on women and booze."

The team worked for another hour before they trudged down a soggy path to the decaying white stone three-story hotel that looked like it had been plunked down in the middle of the jungle eons ago for reasons long since forgotten.

Kendal felt like she had traveled through some kind of weird time warp and ended up in the movie *Casablanca*. The tall, narrow windows had shutters only, no glass, no screens. The thick red tile on the floor was slick from the recent downpour and the arched doors of the lobby were open to the humid air, flanked by jungle growth.

Inside they were seated at warped picnic tables with sticky plastic tablecloths where they were fed a huge meal of spicy local food that did nothing to settle Kendal's stomach.

Everything—the food, the smells, the accommodations—seemed foreign, dirty, oppressive to Kendal. She was definitely not on vacation, as she had been on her other trips to Mexico. The air in the hotel felt thick, almost too muggy to breathe. As she picked at her meal and tried to finish off a bottled Coke, Kendal could feel Jason eyeing her again.

"Headache?" he said.

She nodded, pressing the cold bottle against her temple. "It's the heat and humidity."

"After lunch, take her over to the physician's on-site quarters." He sounded a little tongue-in-cheek as he addressed this order to Angelica on his left. "Seriously, it'll be cooler out there in the jungle."

Jason's "on-site quarters" proved to be a dirty, sagging tent nestled deep in the shade of some tropical mahogany trees not far from the thatched-roof pavilion that would serve as the O.R. Angelica took care of getting Kendal settled on a narrow cot in the cool, darkened interior.

As Kendal lay down, a distant part of her mind noted the buzz of a fly and that the pillow smelled musty while the sleeping bag was lumpy and scratchy. But her head hurt so badly that she didn't give a fig about these small discomforts.

Angelica pulled off Kendal's sandals while, in English, she asked if Kendal could keep some pills down.

"Why?" Kendal groaned.

"You got a killer headache, right?"

Kendal nodded weakly while the anesthetist dug around in the pocket of her khaki shorts and produced two Percocet tablets.

"Isn't two just a tad too much?" Kendal stared at the familiar yellow narcotic. No prescription needed down here, she supposed. Angelica was an anesthetist, and a rogue one at that.

"You ain't gonna sleep without something to kick the pain, sister. And these here is all I got right now. Unless you want me to take you in there and hit you with some nitrous."

Kendal thought that, considering how she felt, it might in fact be lovely to be gassed into oblivion. But instead she took the pills from Angelica's palm and gratefully downed them with the last of the Coke in the bottle.

Despite her discomfort, Kendal immediately fell into a comatose sleep and was blissfully unaware of her surroundings until she heard the rustle of the tent flap being thrust back. The sun had come out and a shaft of strong orangish light pierced the dusty gloom of the tent interior.

She blinked awake, staring at Jason's massive silhouette hunched in the opening. The slant of light looked low behind him. Hours must have passed while she had slept, knocked out from the Percocet.

"How's our intrepid little drug rep?" Jason teased her as he stepped in under the flap.

He knew very well how she was. She was lousy. She was unwashed, uncoiffed, wrinkled. And still vaguely nauseated. Too sweaty and too tired and too thick-tongued from painkillers to utter a comeback.

He squatted beside her cot, knees spread wide, smiling down at her. This was not the wolfish smile that said, *I've got you backed into a corner.* This smile was kindly, sweet. The kind of indulgent smile a daddy might give a beloved child just waking up from a nap.

"Not so intrepid, I'm afraid." She was suddenly feeling defensive about taking medication and a nap while the others had undoubtedly continued to work like Trojans.

"You're doing fine. The first day is always the hardest. Here. Look what I found." He thrust a small plastic medicine cup toward her. Kendal propped herself up on one elbow and frowned at the familiar viscous pink fluid. She despised Pepto-Bismol.

"Drink it," he ordered.

"Will this stuff really help or will it only make it worse?"

"It'll help. You haven't been here long enough for a real case of *turista*—you did start your Cipro like I told you, didn't you?"

She nodded and took the cup.

"And you started your malaria tablets as soon as you got them?"

She nodded again. She was still taking them.

"Could that be causing my nausea?"

He smiled. "It could be anything. Altitude sickness. Too much sun." His gaze slid lightly over her form again. "I don't suppose there's any chance you're pregnant?"

"Unfortunately, none."

"Unfortunately? You *want* to be pregnant?"

"No! I mean, sure. I mean, eventually I want children. But not by accident. What I meant was, unfortunately there's no...there's no way...not right now." She felt she'd just revealed a bit too much.

"That *is* unfortunate." But his ever-widening smile suggested he thought otherwise. "Drink up." He touched his fingers to hers around the little cup.

While Kendal gagged down the Pepto-Bismol, he perched himself on the edge of her narrow cot. They were both wearing hiking shorts and the feel of his hot muscular leg pressing firmly against hers somehow made it that much harder to swallow the sickeningly sweet pink fluid.

"Bet you're already starting to regret that you came to this place where it's all dirty and buggy." He slapped a mosquito away from her biceps. He was wearing a sweat-stained T-shirt with the sleeves rolled up to the shoulders, Marlon Brando-style. With his five o'clock shadow and damp hair slicked back, he looked as handsome as ever, but he seemed tired. Dark circles were forming under his blue eyes. Kendal wondered what he and the others had been doing all afternoon while she slept. Obviously they had worked straight though her siesta.

"On the contrary. After what Angelica told me, I'm anxious to go to work." She sat up on the cot, trying to subtly inch her bare leg away from his. She felt a little woozy yet from the Percocet.

"Oh? And what did Angelica tell you?" His eyes traveled over Kendal's face, then flickered to her chest, most subtly to be sure, but even so the gesture made Kendal acutely aware of the sweat trickling down her cleavage. Before she thought better of it, she had swiped at the moisture with two fingers. His gaze flicked pointedly toward the gesture before he looked away.

Kendal swallowed. "She said you have come down here without government sanction. She said word always spreads through the population and the poor people have to travel all the way out to this jungle location so you can do surgery on them or their loved ones."

"Oh, that." He looked down at his hands. "True. But I never know what else Angelica's going to say. She has a nasty habit of switching to the local dialect like that when she doesn't want me in on the fun."

"She didn't say anything derogatory."

"Really?" He grinned. "Now I am disappointed. You sure she didn't call me an asshole, or perhaps... *The Wolf*?"

Kendal struggled to keep her face from breaking into an embarrassed smirk.

"It's not nice to look like you agree with her assessment."

Kendal emitted an astonished little laugh.

"Angelica's a real case," he said lightly. "She's the one who came up with that wolf business a couple of years ago, during my first trip to Chiapas. She's very...Mayan about some things. Likes to compare people to animals. Ruth thought the comparison was hilarious. She's the one who circulated the nickname around Integris.''

Kendal wanted to ask him if he hadn't considered the fact that the handle was justly earned. Instead she shrugged and said, ''If the paw fits.'' She found she couldn't look in his eyes for long if she wanted to breathe normally. His eyes were, indeed, strangely wolfish. Penetrating.

''Well, I've got bigger worries on my list than The Wolf's sterling reputation.''

The way he said it made Kendal think that his reputation wasn't even on the list. ''I see.''

''You're going to see a lot of things, I expect, before this is all over. Come on,'' he stood and offered her one of his amazing, graceful hands. ''I'm sorry to interrupt your nap, Sleeping Beauty, but I'm afraid I need your help now. The drawing is about to start.''

Kendal put her hand in his and let him pull her up. An involuntary shiver rippled through her as she came to her feet in the low tent, facing him. He held on to her hand for a beat too long, while his fingers, strong and hot, tightened ever so slightly around hers.

''You're trembling. And you seem a little unsteady. Are you okay?''

She looked up at him. ''Just tired.'' What a ridiculous lie. She'd just had a nap, out cold, for—what?—two or three hours?

Still clutching her fingers, he studied her eyes.

"What did Angelica give you?"

"Percocet."

"Look at me. I need to see your pupils."

As their gazes met and held, the dim atmosphere inside the tent felt close, intimate. Kendal had the strangest idea that the two of them might easily entwine and completely melt into each other. A sudden image of their bodies locked together beckoned at her imagination, promising passion, secrets, magic. This jungle was so strange, so *hot*. Without even trying she could imagine wild things happening in this tent, with this man. Very wild things.

She swayed, pulling her fingers away, shocked at her own debauched thoughts. She told herself it was the drugs, of course. Not him. "I'm okay."

"No you're not," he said and his voice sounded hoarse. He was still studying her face with the strangest look, as if something unexpected had shifted inside of him, too. He flipped his fingers under hers and grasped them again, hooking them tightly as he imperceptibly pulled her hand toward his middle. He leaned his face in, bringing the current of his breath across the current of hers, bringing his mouth in line over her mouth.

Kendal blinked once and came to her senses. "I'm fine. Really." She turned her head and pulled her fingers free of his again.

He had stopped with his lips just short of full contact with hers. He gave her a wicked grin as he straightened to his full height. "I guess as long as you can translate Spanish into English and vice versa, it doesn't matter how gorked you are. Okay then.'' He sighed as he squinted out into the late-afternoon sunshine. "Let's get this show on the road. Where are your shoes, little girl?''

"There.'' She pointed at her sandals. He astonished her by dropping to one knee, then gently and efficiently strapping on a sandal first to one foot, then the other. She turned her face away while he performed the task. The press of his fingers around her ankles felt excruciatingly intimate.

"What drawing?'' she said, wanting to distract herself from the decidedly sensual reaction that his touch had stirred in her. "What did you mean a while ago? You said something about a drawing?''

She felt, more than saw, his sly smile as he finished fastening her sandal. "Like I told you, sweetheart,'' he said as he stood and moved the tent flap aside. "Down here, you'd better get prepared to see a lot of things.''

CHAPTER SIX

OUTSIDE, THE DENTED WHITE VAN sat idling and belching smoke. Alejandro's horsey white teeth flashed into a leering grin in his dark face when he saw Kendal again. "The pretty little *chica*, she gonna live, Doc?" He asked Jason the question in Spanish.

"The *chica* is fine," Kendal shot her reply back at the little man in terse Spanish to remind him that she could indeed speak the language.

"*Sí*. That she is," Alejandro said it politely enough, but his sly glance at Jason made his double meaning clear.

Jason guided her into the van, his hand pressing protectively at the small of her back. "Don't mind Alejandro," he whispered in her ear. "It's the macho way. Just be glad you're not a blonde." He jumped in beside her, slid the side door closed, and yelled, "*Vamos!*"

The young driver goosed the van and it took off like a shot. Kendal looked back. In the rear hold she saw the small boxes of vaccines her company had donated bouncing around like Mexican jumping beans.

"The vaccines!" she cried at Jason.

"Cool it, Alejandro!" Jason yelled at the driver.

"The kid gets excited. Doesn't get to drive much," he murmured in Kendal's ear.

She didn't find that reassuring as they went bumping back down the same narrow jungle road that had brought them there.

Jason flung an arm lazily across the back of the bench seat and asked Alejandro, "So. The people have started arriving already?"

Kendal felt small, dwarfed on the seat next to Jason's bulk. She hunched forward slightly to avoid contact with the muscular arm resting behind her, but she felt the heat radiating from him anyway, from his shoulder and from the side of his massive chest.

Alejandro glanced in the rearview mirror, looking at her but speaking to Jason. "They say some of the people been in the town two days already. You know how it is, Doc. Superstitious devils. They think getting a number early increases their chances in the lottery."

Ruth had told her that they'd scheduled a couple of days to get set up and acclimatized, but it looked like they would have to get started right away.

"What lottery? What is he talking about?" Kendal said.

"The *chica* gonna see it sooner or later, *El Médico*." In the rearview mirror Alejandro's eyes looked solemn now.

With his face close to hers, Jason smiled sadly. "I hope you understand. It's the only way."

"What are you talking about?"

"The people have to draw lots. Only the ones with a lucky number get to have surgery."

Kendal blinked, trying to process the enormous difference between the life she was accustomed to and the lives these peasants had to endure.

"Want some advice?" Jason was watching her face closely.

Kendal studied his face in return. This man, how could he come and do this year after year, and then go back to his playboy life in the U.S.?

"Don't get emotionally involved," he whispered.

"That's your solution, isn't it?"

He nodded, his expression hardening, his eyes narrowing against feeling.

Kendal turned away, staring out the grimy window of the van. "Well, it's not mine. Nothing can make me harden my heart like that."

They left the jungle and took the cutoff to Highway 190, which seemed to climb endlessly into the mountains before dropping like a plumb line into a beautiful pine-studded valley, radiant with highland light. Off the road, Kendal caught glimpses of the mysterious Mayan villages Ruth had spoken about.

"San Cristóbal de las Casas," Alejandro announced. "Beautiful, beautiful San Cristóbal de las Casas."

In the distance, finally, they could see the old colonial town.

"It's gorgeous!" Kendal breathed.

The hilly city was crowded with high stone walls, churches and old Spanish-style buildings.

"Very romantic," Jason added.

On the outskirts of town they passed through clusters of poor one-room shacks, some with concrete or adobe walls. Jason explained that these squalid make-shift colonies were where tens of thousands of refugees lived.

"Refugees from what?"

"They were kicked out of the outlying indigenous villages for converting to Protestantism." Jason's expression grew sour.

"That's crazy."

"This isn't the land of the free, sweetheart."

Kendal looked at the grinding poverty scrolling past the van windows and felt sick. Many of the shacks had no glass in the windows. Kendal stared into the open doorways and saw sparse, crude furniture. In places the people had constructed crooked fences and gates out of spindly sticks of underbrush.

San Cristóbal de las Casas was the farthest thing from what Kendal expected. She had anticipated more of the sweltering urban sprawl she'd seen in Tuxtla Gutiérrez. But San Cristóbal's narrow cobblestone streets rambled tranquilly over cool, beautiful pine-studded hills.

At the center of town a parklike square overflowed with the poor peasants, hundreds of them, patiently waiting in the waning sun. Gum-smacking youth, hawking quick services and cheap wares, mined the edges of the crowd. Mixed in among these locals were Anglo tourists, snapping photos of the Santo Domingo church, buying crafts from more established merchants in tiny open-air stores tucked into the nooks around the square.

"Where did all these people come from?" Kendal marveled at the scene as the van edged through the crowd.

"All around these mountains and hills."

"How did they know to come here? Now?"

"Like Alejandro said, some have been here a couple of days already. Word spreads, mostly through the missionaries. Most of them want the free shots," Jason explained. "But the local medicos don't like my style. We'll vaccinate everybody we can, pick our surgery candidates and get out of here tonight."

"What do you mean, they don't like your style?"

"I fix the stuff they won't."

"You mean, like Vajaras's handiwork?"

"Who told you about Vajaras?"

"Ruth and Angelica."

"Figures. *Chicks.*"

The van ground to a halt in the middle of the pot-holed road on one side of the square. The cathedral towered on the north end. At the center of the square, standing on a small raised platform, was Angelica, who had obviously been waiting for Jason to make his arrival with Kendal.

"Surely you aren't planning to do surgery on all of these people?" Kendal asked as Jason threw open the door and leaped from the vehicle.

"I told you. Only the lucky few." Jason offered her his hand. "Stick close by me. And do what I say. When I tell you to, translate for me. *Comprende?*"

Kendal nodded.

The people had started rising to their feet the moment they saw the Anglo doctor. They surged forward even as Kendal saw Angelica throw up her arms, attempting to motion them back.

"*Esperen!*" the big woman cried. "We will draw the lots in a moment," she yelled in Spanish.

But the crowd ignored her. They were intent on reaching out to Jason. They swarmed around him, calling him *El Médico Jase!* All were smiling, holding children out for him to see, crying out, "*Gracias!*" An old woman elbowed her way to him and held aloft a battered Polaroid of a child. These were the children who had obviously had surgeries a year earlier. Cleft palates, burn scars, hemangiomas and Kendal shuddered to think what else.

"*Esperen!*" Angelica ordered the crowd again. *Wait!* But Jason was already touching people, clasping their hands, mussing a toddler's hair, caressing a chubby child's scarred cheek, talking to the people, while they babbled to him in a mixture of Spanish and Mayan. Everything Jason said in English, Kendal immediately echoed in Spanish and Angelica in Mayan.

But as the crowd grew more excited, calling out, vying for Jason's attention like needy children, Kendal understood that one of them would be needed to keep the mass of people under control while the other one served at Jason's side, interpreting while he saw patients one on one.

"Line up to get shots here!" Angelica shouted, waving her arms in the direction of a rickety card table set up under an open awning beside the platform. "We will draw the lots soon."

Kendal trotted along behind Jason. He was marching toward two chairs set apart from the table but still under the shade of the awning. "Having fun yet?" He tossed the words over his shoulder, and she caught a flash of that wolfish smile she was growing accustomed to.

He directed her to sit in one of the chairs while he stood behind the other one.

"Aren't you going to sit?" She looked at the empty chair beside her.

"Nope."

The people clotted into a mass before the awning, but no one ventured under it. Ruth and Angelica were already set up to give vaccines.

A young Mayan-looking woman emerged from nowhere. She sat at the card table and picked up a pen and a spiral notebook there, her face set solemnly for some predetermined task.

Angelica reached into a large clay pot and withdrew a slip of paper. *"Catorce!"* she called out. Fourteen.

A young man stepped forward, holding a too-thin baby with a gaping cleft in its tiny face, a defect so severe that it looked like a wound from a hatchet. He handed the serious young woman with the notebook a slip of paper and softly said a name. As the father with the baby stepped over, Jason offered him the chair next to Kendal. When the peasant was seated with the baby on his lap, Jason squatted on his haunches and proceeded to examine the baby. Angelica gave the baby her shots while Jason, through Kendal, asked questions—patient's name, age, weight—

while the young woman with the serious expression wrote the information in the spiral notebook.

"You don't use a triage method?" Kendal asked. She couldn't imagine that he didn't attend to the most urgent cases first.

Jason was taking the baby's picture now, using first his digital camera, then the Polaroid.

"No. Some of these people have been living with their problems all of their lives. But each year, also, new babies are born that require surgery. I don't want my judgment to be the factor that determines whose baby must live with a cleft palate for another year. We have to have a system that is rigidly fair. I only have time to complete a hundred or so."

"Surgeries? A hundred or so *surgeries*?" They were going to do a hundred surgeries during their brief stay? That seemed impossible. Kendal did a quick mental calculation. If he was planning on even as little as two days of follow-up for the last of the patients, that meant seven or eight surgeries a day. An inhuman schedule, even for a man like Jason Bridges.

But he seemed unfazed by the number. "I can do up to a hundred if nothing goes wrong. *And* we have to take into account an adequate post-op follow-up. The patients all stay at the hotel a couple of days. Their families and the *curanderas*, the women from the villages, take care of them."

Kendal knew from his reputation back at Integris that Jason was a stickler about post-op follow-up.

"Can't the local doctors help you?" Jason emitted a cynical snort. "*What* local doctors?

Most of these people have never been to a doctor. The Mayan medicine man out in the jungle is good at what he does, but he's only one man and he has no surgical skills at all. He's strictly a herbalist.''

"A medicine man!" Kendal blurted, and the eyes of a few of the people in the line cut to her face, their expressions wary, watchful.

Jason leaned down with his mouth close to her ear, and said, "Careful. Some of them speak a little English. And these people are very suspicious, very wary of strange *gringas*."

Kendal struggled to compose her expression into a neutral one. But her thoughts whirled. They were actually going to do a hundred surgeries in a little over two weeks, then fly away in the doctor's plane, leaving the fresh post-op patients in the care of some Mayan medicine man? Now she understood the rows of cots in the ramshackle hotel out in the jungle. This was a style of practicing medicine that Jason had called risky. But it seemed too risky to even contemplate. Jungle medicine, indeed.

With his face still close to hers, Jason seemed to be reading her thoughts accurately. "I have no choice, unless I want to relocate to this place. And even then, I'd run out of resources. Try to remember that what we're doing here is strictly voluntary, okay?''

"Can you help my son?'' the next man asked anxiously in Spanish. He was supporting his fragile child against his chest with one arm and had whipped off a filthy baseball cap with the other.

"He wants to know if you can help his son," Kendal relayed to Jason.

"Just repeat the exact words the people say," Jason instructed her as he focused on gently listening to the child's chest with a stethoscope. "It will go faster that way. Even if we're very efficient, this is going to be a long evening."

He put a finger in the baby's mouth, gently probing with an examination that seemed like more of a gentle tickling. "Open up, little bird," he said, looking into the baby's huge brown eyes. The infant gummed Jason's finger, cooed and smiled. The euphoric father smiled as well.

Kendal watched Jason as he afforded each patient similar compassionate attention. She also scrambled to keep up with his rapid-fire questions and pithy instructions. She relayed it all, simplifying his words for the unsophisticated people they were seeking to help. Those people came in an endless stream for the next two hours, touching Kendal's heart with their solemn, hope-filled eyes, their shy smiles, their polite deference, and always, always, their humble petition *"El Médico! Puede ayudarme?"* Doctor, can you help me?

But he was forced, with nimble hands and sharp eyes, to cull a few of the candidates. Because of infection, infestation, anemia.

"Next year, next year," Jason soothed regretfully. While Kendal echoed the refrain she began to understand the man's frustration over not being able to heal them all.

The hours dragged on. Nightfall came, and many of the people who had been waiting moved to sit against the buildings. They sat with their legs stretched forth on the grimy sidewalk, dozing. Waiting.

At last the final number was drawn. *"Treinta!"* Angelica called above the heads of the crowd.

An old man removed a battered straw hat as a look of astonishment transformed his mangled features. *"Treinta,"* he croaked out in awe.

"Bring me your ticket, Mr. Alvarez," Angelica beckoned him to the platform, seeming pleased that he was the lucky one. He hobbled forward on arthritic limbs. But halfway to the platform, amid the smiles of his neighbors, he stopped and turned toward the edge of the crowd where a young woman had started sobbing loudly, making a scene. Her young husband tried to quiet her as he looped a protective arm around her thin shoulders. She clutched a wailing baby to her chest.

Everyone in the square, many who had yet been hoping for their number to be drawn and were equally disappointed, stared at the young couple.

The woman repeatedly rocked the baby, crying something in Spanish.

"What is she saying?" Jason asked Kendal, having trouble with the local dialect.

"She's telling her husband she fears that without a doctor, their baby will surely die. Apparently, the baby can't swallow enough milk to gain weight and thrive. The father is trying to calm her and get her to be quiet.

He's telling her they will come back next year," Kendal looked at Jason with horror. "Could that baby actually die?"

"It happens down here, all too often."

"We have to do something!"

"Bring the child to me," Jason called out over the crowd in Anglo-sounding Spanish. But the people gave him uncomprehending looks, as if he were speaking nonsense. "My Spanish sucks," he muttered. "Would you please tell them to bring the baby here," he turned to Kendal.

She repeated his request in Spanish.

"You can't add one on!" Angelica rushed forward.

"Word will spread. We'll be overrun!"

But in the meantime, the old man had changed course. He removed his battered hat as he reached the couple. The crowd quieted as Kendal and everyone else watched him hand the father of the baby his ticket, the one bearing the coveted last number.

The father took the paper with tears in his eyes and quietly said, "*Muchas, muchas gracias, amigo.*"

The mother, who had quieted during the exchange, broke down in tears again as she kissed the old man gently on the cheek.

While everyone else was watching the drama in the square, Jason had been watching Kendal. Between patients, he had snatched every opportunity to study Kendal Collins. She'd been like a little hothouse flower back at Integris, but out here this woman was no sissy. She had stayed at his side throughout the endless evening though she looked hot, exhausted.

Right now she had a sheen of sweat on her brow, her cheeks were burning pink and the damp hair around her face frizzed from the heat and humidity—yet to him she was incredibly beautiful.

"Did you see that?" Kendal turned her shimmering gaze on him. Her eyes were brimming with compassionate tears.

"Tell them to bring the kid here," he said gruffly. He'd fix Mr. Alvarez somehow. Any old guy who'd give away his big chance for surgery deserved the best of care. All it would cost Jason was a little sleep…and listening to Angelica grumble, but what else was new?

His eyes fixed on Kendal's mouth again as she stood on tiptoe and excitedly conveyed his instructions, beckoning to the young couple. For some weird reason her mouth looked even softer when she was speaking in Spanish.

He glanced at her one last time as she sat down and held the wailing baby still for his examination. She was speaking soothingly to the child in Spanish, and every time she murmured, Jason wanted nothing so much as to kiss her. At the moment her honey-pale lips were looking a little cracked with thirst, but that did nothing to detract from their attractiveness. A couple of times he'd seen her smear on some Chap Stick from a red tube. He wondered what her mouth tasted like. Strawberry? Cherry?

He concentrated on his examination of the child—yet another cleft palate, albeit the most severe one he'd seen yet.

"That will be the last patient," Angelica informed the crowd.

"Tell the people we'll finish giving vaccinations after dinner. Tell everyone who has been selected for surgery to return here in one hour for their pre-op instructions," Jason told her.

Angelica started yelling in Spanish, waving her arms as she ordered the crowd to disperse.

"Need a break?" Jason said, watching Kendal as she returned the bawling child to its mother.

"I am a bit thirsty." Kendal wiped a hand across her damp brow. When her fingers started to chase a trickle of sweat down her cleavage, she stopped herself. Ah. There it was again. She was as physically aware of him as he was of her. The sexually charged presence of Kendal Collins was certainly upping the excitement factor on this trip.

He smiled. "We can go in the hotel. They have bottled Coke." He jerked a thumb over his shoulder at the crumbling adobe structure behind them.

"But the people still—"

"If you don't take your breaks, Kendal, you won't last three days. Tell the people that the doctor will be back after dinner."

Rapidly becoming accustomed to speaking before the crowd, Kendal relayed Jason's message but the people in the line didn't budge, though they remained quiet and orderly. Some of them squatted on the ground, right where they were.

She turned to Jason. "They'll just wait like that?"

"Fraid so." Jason took her elbow and led her into

the dark, cool interior of the hotel. "This is Mexico, sweetheart. Time means nothing down here." He made a hand signal at a Mexican youth who was lounging nearby and the boy came running. "*Dos cervezas, por favor*," he said and pressed a handful of pesos into the boy's outstretched palm. The lad smiled broadly at the large sum of money. "*Gracias.*" He trotted off.

"You told him to get two beers instead of Cokes," Kendal informed Jason as he took her hand and led her to a wrought-iron table in the inner courtyard. He liked the way her hand felt in his. Just right.

"The beer's safe to drink, too." He shrugged. "We'll sit here." He pulled out a chair, then realized he was forgetting about her creature comforts. "The bathrooms are this way." He took her hand again, but this time she pulled it back.

"I see it."

Ah. A bit of spirit. He walked ahead indicating that she should follow.

CHAPTER SEVEN

''THE QUALITY of the beer is not my point.'' Kendal pressed as she traipsed along after the man, for some reason feeling the tiniest bit annoyed at having to follow the arrogant doctor. ''We still have to get the patients' informed consents signed this evening. We can't do that under the influence.''

She envisioned the tasks they had yet to do that night—the process, Jason explaining, then herself interpreting. Each fearful, confused patient and family needing to understand what their surgery would entail, the risks, the possible negative outcomes. Undoubtedly some, if not most, of these people were illiterate, so the spoken instructions would be critical. They couldn't forget something. ''This could take all night.''

''Yeah. I guess we're stuck with each other until bedtime.'' Jason smiled at her as if liking that idea. He frowned when she didn't lighten up. ''Look. I can give me one Mexican beer is gonna impair your ability to talk to these people?''

''Of course not. I just don't think it's right to drink while on duty.''

"Sweetheart, I keep telling you. This is Mexico. Down here we are going to be on duty twenty-four/seven. The beer is about the only amenity this hellhole has to offer. I suggest you take advantage of it."

"Stop calling me that."

He glanced back again. "Stop calling you what?" He spoke with a challenge.

That was often the way he started with women, calling them "sweetheart" or "pretty girl" or "sweet thing." Which in his mind they almost all undoubtedly were. *So, so sweet.* He loved women. Perhaps a bit too much for his own good. He loved the way they smelled, the way they'd sniff at their own wrist, then offer it up under your nose so you could sample it. He loved their voices, their thoughts, the way they could talk on the phone for an hour about absolutely nothing. He loved their hair, the look of it, the smell of it, the feel of it. And this one had a ton of the slickest, lushest, blackest hair he'd ever seen. Amazing. He was dying to jam his hands through it. To hold her thrashing head still while he—

"Sweetheart." Her voice, dripping acid, interrupted his fantasy. "Don't call me *sweetheart.*" Kendal had noted that wretched little sparkle in Jason Bridges's eyes. It telegraphed unmistakably his desire to toy with her, to show her that he could cross a boundary. A year ago she would have responded to the doctor's flirting. But not now. Her experience with Phillip had left her a little scarred in those places where she had been burned, a little resistant to the honeyed words of any man. She eyed the backside of Dr. Jason Bridges and told herself she was already on to his little game.

"I'm not one, you know."

"I'll be the judge of that." He winked at her.

Kendal didn't respond. They'd come to the rest rooms, such as they were. The two tiny rooms were side by side and the door to the one marked *Damas* was wide open. An attempt to vent the wretched smell of stale urine that wafted out, Kendal supposed.

She was so horrified by the condition of the facilities that she completely forgot their sparring. *This was a rest room?* She peered into the ladies' side, wondering if there was any paper in there and wishing she'd thought to look for a paper napkin on her way past the bar. A cockroach skated by on the damp tile floor and she averted her eyes.

"They're edible, you know," Jason smirked. He swept a gentlemanly palm toward the seatless toilet. "Your throne awaits, *sweetheart*."

Kendal lifted her chin and marched in, slamming the door shut in his smirking face.

Being careful not to touch any surface except the one beneath the soles of her shoes, she squatted and had no sooner started her stream than from behind the thin wall, she heard his. To her ears, it sounded louder than a high pressure hose at a car wash! She tried to blot out all though, especially the embarrassing one that right on the other side of that wall she could hear a vivid reminder that Jason Bridges was, first and foremost, a *male*. **She couldn't remember when she'd been so aware of a *man's maleness*.**

She felt her cheeks flame as she had to concentrate to finish her own business.

She turned on the tap, rinsed her hands, discovered there was no soap, no paper towels, and cringed as she turned off the tap with the tips only of one finger and thumb.

When she stepped out, still flushed and wiping her damp hands on the back of her shorts, Jason was waiting. His body was a straight lean line, canted with one shoulder propped against the stucco wall. "Here," he said, straightening and holding out a small bottle. It was antiseptic hand wash.

Of course. He was a doctor, a surgeon. He, of all people, would be concerned about sanitation.

"Thank you." Kendal held forth her palms, he uncapped the bottle and splashed on the goo, and she rubbed it in as they walked back to the table, where Jason pulled out her chair as if they were on a date or something.

As soon as they were seated, the boy arrived with two cold Tecates.

"*Solo agua,*" Kendal said, indicating that she just wanted a glass of water. But her thirst seemed too great to be slaked by water. A cold beer sounded like heaven.

"Don't be ridiculous." Jason grabbed the bottles, plunking one down in front of her and taking a long draw from the other. "First of all," he said as he wiped his lips, "that kid will bring it in a dirty glass and the local water will make you sicker than a dog, and secondly, we're not gonna be cutting on anybody tonight. Enjoy the beer while you can. Bright and early tomorrow morning, hell week begins.''

The boy smiled meaningfully at Jason as he returned with the predicted smudged glass of not-so-clear water. He also placed sliced limes and a salt-shaker beside the bottles of beer. Jason smiled grudgingly and dug into his pocket for more pesos.

Kendal looked at the frosty beer and her mouth actually watered. She'd downed several of the luke-warm, tasteless bottles of purified water they'd brought along throughout the hot afternoon, and the brew looked like a delicious, pungent alternative.

The boy returned with a basket of tortilla chips and a small cracked dish of salsa, wearing another expectant smile on his face. Jason obliged him with another wad of pesos.

''So,'' he said when the boy was gone. ''You're happy being single?''

''Absolutely.'' She took a chip, dipped it in salsa, munched. Very good.

''You sound awfully sure.''

''I'm sure.'' She put out the fire of the salsa with a long drag on her beer. ''I had a boyfriend. It didn't work out.''

''What happened?''

''It just didn't work out.'' In the past year, Kendal had grown used to giving that explanation.

''I'm sorry.''

''Don't be. I'm not, except that I wasted five years of my life with dear old Phillip.''

''Phillip, huh? At least you didn't marry him.''

"You think that matters?"

"Absolutely. It's called *vows*. Commitment. It matters."

Kendal wondered how it was that this incredibly handsome man had escaped from *vows*, from *commitment*, for all of his thirty-odd years.

"You ever been married?"

"Nope." He sipped his beer.

They heard Angelica's voice off in the distance, hollering instructions to the crowd.

"Drink up. We'll have to get back out there soon."

"Did you know that old man out there?" Kendal asked, then took a delicate sip of her beer. The stuff really wasn't half-bad.

"Yes. I've spotted the old gentleman on each of my other trips."

"Oh, my. You mean he's participated in the drawing before?" Kendal swallowed and set her bottle down, staring at Jason.

Jason kept his expression carefully impassive. He knew he looked almost, but not quite, cynical. He hated to divest this woman of her illusions about helping these people. Her emotions would not survive the first day if she didn't toughen up a bit.

"You're telling me he's come here before?" she pressed.

"Every year since he got hurt. One of Vajaras's goons sliced up his face for helping a Zapatista get to safety." Jason picked at the bottle, trying to think of a way to change the subject. He couldn't save them all. No matter how bad he wanted to do that, he couldn't. And Kendal Collins, staring at him like that with her big, exhausted eyes, was making him feel like dog doo because he couldn't.

"Drink your beer."

"They come back like that, don't they?" she said with quiet comprehension. "They come back year after year, the ones who get turned away?"

"Yes."

"And this is the first time Mr. Alvarez's number was drawn."

He nodded, wishing she'd stop this.

Kendal's eyes grew wide with comprehension. She covered her mouth. "And then he gave his lot to that little baby?" she said through her fingers. Her voice was tight with emotion. She was tired, he knew, but she was also way too softhearted for this place.

"Mr. Alvarez knows the drill." He took a big pull on his beer to fortify himself so that he could make her understand. He needed to make her see that he was not some coldhearted bastard who turned away a poor old man who longed for a normal face. But he was not a superhero, either.

"Look. José also knows that along with the surgery, the baby will get her shots and a lot of other care she needs, as much as Angelica can squeeze in. They have a big problem with polio myelitis down here, you know."

"Oh, my." Kendal held her beer to her lips but she hesitated and didn't sip. She looked like she might be about to cry.

Jason had to look away from those shimmering

green eyes. Her emotional reaction to the old man's plight sent a pull from his heart straight down to his loins. He wanted to take her in his arms right then.

He didn't trust this connection to her he was suddenly feeling, talking about the old man. It was a pull on his heart that he hadn't felt in a very long time. It was a damned stupid thing he'd done, bringing this woman down here. In this place, he let his heart open up. Here his emotions weren't protected, no matter how hard he tried to stay closed off.

Because in this place, miracles happened. The kind of miracles Jason Bridges had yearned for his whole life, ever since Amy died. In search of those miracles, he came to Mexico, year after year. It was as if he were looking for some magic, a secret treasure, something hidden in these mountains, among these humble people. He couldn't give up until he had found that treasure.

The magic had something to do with the old man stepping aside for that child. That was the kind of stuff that blindsided you almost every day down here.

He shouldn't have brought this Kendal Collins down here where the miracles happened. Ruth, he could bring along, with no consequences. Though Ruth was an undeniably attractive woman, it had always been safe to hang with her in Chiapas. Ruth was good people, but there was no heart connection between them. Only friendship. Back in the real world, she'd rubbed her boobs against him so often in surgery that he'd grown practically numb to any electricity they might have ever generated. He simply did not react to her that way anymore.

Ruth, he could bring to Mexico with impunity. She was sophisticated, battle-seasoned. He could witness the raw suffering side-by-side with her and both of them could keep on going, the same way they did in surgery at home. No problem.

Same with Angelica. Angelica barked orders. She cussed. And she cared about these people with the heart of a lioness.

And Mother Martinez. She was like a big, brown down comforter. Always hugging and praying and mumbling to everybody in Spanish. Maintaining her famous "standards" even in the hundred-degree heat. He smiled, remembering the time she'd actually passed out sample deodorants to the locals.

And Ben. Ben had that God thing going. No questioning that. The boy was destined to be a saint and he was as loyal to Jason as a golden retriever.

The five of them had always plowed through each day in Mexico like it was their last. Working like they were possessed, drinking and smoking and cursing so Martinez and Ben could chew on them about it. Having a great old time, rescuing the needy ones. Ruth and Angelica and Martinez and Ben had become like fellow soldiers in the great war against poverty and disease.

But this Kendal Collins was different. She wasn't battle-hardened. Seeing these people and their problems through her softhearted eyes was dangerous. *She* was dangerous. She reminded him why he had chosen this mission in the first place. *She* touched his heart in a whole new way.

And to top it all off, he wanted her body in the worst way.

The whole combination was dangerous.

What he needed to do was seduce her and get it over with. He told himself, as he always did, that he couldn't afford to get emotionally involved with a woman. He never bothered to dig down deep and ask himself *why* he couldn't, he just heeded the warnings that came from his gut. But suddenly, looking into Kendal Collins's compassionate green eyes, it occurred to him that with her he could lose a part of himself that he'd never get back.

"Drink your beer," he told her.

Kendal took a big sip, looking slightly tougher as she swallowed. With a rebellious expression, she opened her mouth to speak. But he cut her off.

"Look, it's the way things are down here. And listen, sweetheart—"

Her lips immediately pursed, and then that cute mouth popped open. "Don't—," she started.

"—don't tell me not to call you that," he interrupted. "You *are* a sweetheart and you know it."

THEY WENT BACK into the trenches somewhat refreshed. Which was a good thing. Hundreds of people had stayed on in the square to receive the free polio and DPT vaccinations for their children. The line seemed to stretch forever. Ruth and Angelica had eaten and were back under the awning. A large basin was already half full of the spent TB syringes.

Because Jason was no longer doing exams and an interpreter wasn't needed, Jason and Kendal threw themselves into the vaccination effort so that the tired children could go home. Ruth quickly taught Kendal how to draw up an injection, allowing the others to conserve their thumb pads for giving them. After Kendal's thumb grew bruised from repeatedly pulling back on the plastic plungers, Ruth showed her how to give injections and traded places with her.

"This is okay?" Kendal asked nervously as she hesitated before sticking her first needle into a brave little boy. "I mean, I don't have a nursing license or anything."

"This is Chiapas, sweetheart," Jason explained as he popped a needle into a chubby baby's thigh. "We gotta do what we gotta do. Get crackin'. We still have all the pre-op instructions to do."

During the long hours of vaccinating and vaccinating and vaccinating, and then explaining and explaining and explaining to the patients, Jason and Kendal established a kind of sentient rhythm between them. He spoke softly in English. She repeated his words softly in Spanish. Male voice. Female voice. It was as if Jason's instructions flowed right through Kendal to the people in endless undulations.

Jason teased the Chiapans, the same way he did everyone at home, only a bit more gently. He called the little girls, *"las estrellas"*—his stars, and he referred to each boy as his *"mano"*—buddy. Occasionally he would attempt to talk to a child directly in Spanish but sometimes it was so garbled it made the kids snicker.

"What?" He feigned innocence, staring wide-eyed at the giggling little boy on his lap.

"You told him you had a surprise in your purse," Kendal explained with a benevolent smile. "*Bolso* means purse, *bolsillo* means pocket."

"Whatever. Tell this silly little boy——" Jason tickled the child "——to get the candy out of my pocket——" he held the pocket of his vest open "——and that he is going to look like a prince when I'm done with him."

Kendal echoed his words. The child reached in Jason's pocket for the candy and then Jason put him off his lap with a little pat.

Jason, she noticed, was not afraid to touch these people. He hugged the babies. He patted the worried mothers' shoulders. He gave the fathers macho handshakes.

He seemed to have endless energy. She ended up feeling somewhat in awe of him.

In the wee hours the van brought them back to the makeshift medical compound in the jungle. Bearing flashlights, too exhausted for conversation, the three women trudged from the road up the jungle path toward the crumbling hotel where they would share a suite.

"Where did Jason go?" Kendal broke the silence.

"He sleeps in that tent over at the edge of the jungle," Ruth explained.

"The one where I took a nap?"

"Yes. He prefers it—says the jungle sounds lull him to sleep, and that the hotel is too moldy and musty."

"I see." Kendal felt vaguely disappointed that Jason would not be staying nearby. She supposed it was because she had grown used to his constant presence, working shoulder-to-shoulder beside him all afternoon and evening.

Ruth misread her subdued tone. "We'll be perfectly safe. Saint Ben will be staying at the hotel with us." Ruth jerked her head toward something approaching from behind them in the gloom.

Kendal looked back. Sure enough, the hulking form of Ben Schulman was coming up the jungle path, powerful and quiet as a jaguar.

THE NEXT MORNING, just as Jason had predicted, hell week started in earnest. Ben awoke them before dawn with a soft rap on their door.

"Go away!" Angelica whined.

"What time is it?" Kendal yawned from her cot. It looked pitch-dark outside.

"Five." Ruth's voice floated out of the darkness from her bed.

"Five a.m.?"

"Yes. Surgery starts as soon as the sun's up."

"Will we be getting up this early every day?" Kendal stretched, and all of her muscles ached.

"Every damned day." Angelica flipped on the bare overhead lights.

Kendal sat up, blinking at Ruth who swung her legs over the edge of the opposite cot. "I know what motivated me to come down here, but why in the world are you doing this to yourself?" Kendal had to ask.

"She has a thing for Jason." Angelica was already pulling on her shorts.

"Oh, puh-lease." Ruth made a face at her Mexican friend. "I gave up on Jason Bridges a long time ago. Nobody's ever gonna put a choke chain around The Wolf's neck. God help the poor woman who tries."

Angelica hooted her agreement.

Ruth looked at Kendal pragmatically. "Jason and I are just friends, and I love this work as much as he does. You'll adjust," she reassured her.

"Come on. Get dressed," Angelica urged.

"And don't bother with a shower," Ruth advised while they rummaged for their clothes. "Save that for this evening after you've sweated all day. And don't forget to put your hair back in a braid."

Kendal pulled on her baggy camp shorts, then a lightweight T-shirt and finally running shoes. She did her ablutions as best she could in the bathroom's tiny, grimy sink. She divided her hair into two fat braids, then made her sleepy-headed way down the broad stone stairs to the main lobby to face breakfast.

Which wasn't bad. The coffee, plain instant Nescafé, which Viljo stirred into hot water from a battered teakettle, tasted surprisingly good. Kendal had expected world-class coffee here in the middle of a coffee-bean-producing region, but she didn't comment. She downed two cups while their proprietor brought out glasses of lukewarm carrot juice, a steaming platter of huevos rancheros and a stack of fresh, hot, corn tortillas.

Ben bowed his head and prayed out loud, then the volunteers ate in silence as if they were conserving their energy to battle the heat and the daunting tasks that lay ahead.

The path leading off into the jungle was lit by a gray morning light by the time they headed outside. Angelica stopped them outside on the hotel steps and sprayed their arms and legs with that local insect repellent that smelled like ant spray. Could being bit by mosquitoes be any worse?

"Most of it will roll off with the sweat in an hour anyway," Ruth said when she saw Kendal's disgusted look.

Jason was waiting in the surgery pavilion. He looked rested. Unshaven, but scrubbed and handsome. He was disinfecting his hands with alcohol over one of the basins. They would strip off gloves and dip their hands in those basins all day long, Ruth had warned Kendal, until their skin felt like it was on fire.

"Good morning, ladies," he sang out as he shook his hands off and grabbed for a roll of the paper towels they'd crammed onto the plane.

"Good morning," they all said. And that was to be the last good thing for a while.

CHAPTER EIGHT

THE FIRST DAY of surgeries stretched long, full of inconveniences and setbacks. As if the heat and dust and bugs weren't bad enough, there were technical difficulties.

For one thing, the portable surgery lights, which were necessary even in the daytime inside the dim jungle pavilion, flickered repeatedly. When they went completely dead, Jason sang out, "Good thing I can do this in the dark," and Kendal scrambled for flashlights while Ben dashed out to bang on the generator.

Jason worked like a machine, whistled a lot, winked a lot, never lost his cool, even though Angelica and Kendal had to take turns constantly mopping the sweat off his brow.

Jason had filled Kendal in on the routine. Angelica started the IVs and put the patients to sleep. Jason and Ruth stood at either side of the table, working on case after case. They stripped off their gloves and turned to the other table as soon as they were done at the first. Ben carried each unconscious child to a cot at the edge of the room where the local women tended them with verbal supervision from Kendal. Kendal would dash over and get the empty table ready for the next patient. She'd wipe up any blood, lay out clean instruments and wash the dirty ones with alcohol. Then she'd go back to her instructions and teaching until the whole routine was repeated again. At last, the sixth surgery of the day was done.

The men from the villages were carrying the post-op patients to the hotel on crude stretchers, Jason and Ruth were washing their hands, and Angelica was re-covering the last patient when Jason ordered Kendal to get off her feet.

"You look pale," he said.

Maybe so, but she felt great. Her hands were raw, her back and feet were killing her and she'd talked until her voice was hoarse, but she had never felt so powerful and alive, so useful. Pushing Paroveen was the last thing on her mind by the end of that day. Helping these children was the first.

"I'll help." Kendal ignored Jason as she rushed over to help Angelica lift a groggy girl into a sitting position so she could sip water. "You're the one who needs a break."

"Okay. Thanks. Hey, chief," Angelica called to Jason, "want a smoke?"

Jason and Ruth were drying their hands on paper towels.

"No thanks, Ruth," he said. "Take over for Kendal."

"Sure, chief." Ruth appeared at Kendal's side and took the water cup from her hand. "Here you go," she said to the patient in Spanish.

Jason took Kendal's elbow and walked her over to

the area where she kept the drugs. He guided her to a perch up on a stool. "We used a lot of Paroveen today."

His observation reminded her of her purpose here. No, it was her *obligation*. Her *purpose* had shifted in one day, had grown larger and more meaningful.

"I noted it all. We'll know how well it works tomorrow. My company will be very interested in some of the off-label uses you have for the drug."

"I know. Maybe we can collaborate on an article about that."

Kendal smiled. That was exactly the kind of PR she had hoped for when she agreed to this trip. But now the patients seemed more important. "I should help Ruth."

"No. I want you to rest." Jason touched her arm gently. "Please. I'll be right back." After he helped the men get the last patient onto a stretcher he returned to her side.

"We're done for now. Can you come with me for a second?" Jason lightly took Kendal's hand. "I want to show you something special." He led her from the pavilion down the path to the hotel. When they entered the cool lobby, he said to Viljo, *"Dos cervezas, por favor."*

"That's what you want to show me? Two beers?"

But he only smiled. When Viljo came back, Jason took the beers in one hand and Kendal's elbow in the other and led her back out of the hotel.

Out in the overgrown courtyard he guided her to a rusty wrought-iron table.

"Have a seat and look up," he pointed.

Above their heads, enormous palm trees were backlit by golden shafts of setting sun. The stone walls of the hotel appeared lit from within by the reflected light. The huge trees, redolent flowers and lush vines echoed with exotic birdsong.

"Oh," Kendal breathed. "It's beautiful out here." Jason nodded and lifted his beer. "One of my favorite spots."

They sat at the listing table in the sun-dappled courtyard, sipping their beers and enjoying the beauty, too tired to talk much at first.

"An amazing day," Kendal said at last.

"Yep."

"Is it like this every year?"

"Yep."

"Why do you do this?"

"You have to ask?"

"No, I guess not." She had found the work exhilarating, but still she wondered why a handsome, successful surgeon would endure this arduous expedition year after year. "I can't figure you out."

"What do you mean?"

"Back home you have quite a reputation as a bad boy."

He snorted. "Why is it that any man who isn't married and living out in the burbs with two-point-five kids and a minivan is either gay or a bad boy?"

"So you're neither?"

He gave her a smirk. "I imagine I'm just like you, sweetheart. Haven't found Ms. Right."

"I think there's more to it than that. The rumor is you've had an awful lot of women in your life."

He gave her a derisive frown. "You're not one of those pop-psyche types, are you? I happen to like women. I treat every woman I date very well. I've never had any complaints." He sipped his beer, then pointed at her with the neck of the bottle. "And don't even think about giving me a health lecture, okay? I'm a doctor, remember? I'm perfectly capable of keeping myself, and any women I date, totally healthy and happy."

Kendal doubted that. Not the healthy part, necessarily. He seemed to have pretty good self-preservation instincts. But happy? Happy to get tangled up with The Wolf only to be dumped? She doubted that.

"What got you started coming down here?"

"A chick."

"Ah. I rest my case."

"Well, that time I actually thought I was in love, sort of. Beth was a doctor. Talked me into coming along on the Doctors Without Borders trip with her my first year out of medical school."

"You met her in medical school?"

He nodded and sipped his beer, watching her closely. He looked as if anything he revealed about himself didn't matter, but she suspected her reaction to it might.

"What happened?"

"On that trip?"

She nodded.

"I discovered that something about this place ...is magic. It centers me. I can't explain it. It helps the whole rest of the year make sense somehow."

Why wouldn't the rest of his year make sense? Kendal wondered about that. He was brilliant, successful, handsome, with a thriving practice that many surgeons would envy. Yet she sensed there truly was something about Jason Bridges's life that was off-kilter, not centered. Why was that?

"What happened to the relationship?" Kendal wondered if this failed relationship explained his womanizing, his detachment. True love gone bad? It happened sometimes. Well, actually it seemed to happen all the time. "Did you two break up while you were down here?"

"No. We just grew apart gradually. It was just another white-hot romance that burned itself out. We were never committed. We didn't *adore* each other or anything like that."

Kendal thought the way he'd said that word *adore* was revealing. As if he knew exactly what it meant to *adore*, but he had rejected the notion as far too idealistic somewhere along the way.

"Tell you the truth, I didn't even miss Beth that much when it didn't work out."

An uncomfortable silence fell. As if he'd just admitted something he shouldn't have. Kendal decided to change the subject to something more neutral.

"Where are you from, originally?"

"Dallas."

"Your parents still live there?"

"Oh, yes." His voice had a bitter edge suddenly. "Mom in her fancy house in Turtle Creek, and Dad in his fancy house in Highland Park."

"They're divorced?"

"Back when I was a teenager."

"I'm sorry."

"Happens all the time. Doesn't matter." But something in his voice told Kendal it did matter. Why would his parents' divorce still bother a grown man?

"How old are you?"

"Thirty-one."

He'd accomplished a lot for a person so young. Kendal, on the other hand, felt like she was barely getting started with her life. "Me, too. I'm thirty-one." And she hated to think about that. Thirty-one. Unmarried. Childless. Not even left on the shelf. Actually, she had been put *back* on the shelf. She decided she'd rather talk about *him.* "Do you have any brothers and sisters?"

"No." And with that one syllable it *was* as if an iron mask clamped down over Jason's face. He raised the beer bottle and, in one long, deliberate draw, drained it.

He swallowed, tight-lipped, and said, "Why don't you tell me about yourself?" Abruptly, he'd turned the tables. This was interesting. A reversal of the old "talking too much about oneself on the first date" faux pas. Neither one of them, apparently, wanted to talk about themselves.

"My life is rather predictable actually."

"Except that you're healing from a relationship that apparently sucked.''

A little alarm bell sounded inside of her. ''How would you know that?''

"He did marry someone else.''

She stared at him, bug-eyed. ''Phillip married someone else? Are you sure? I hadn't realized that.''

He gave her a reproachful look for her sarcasm.

''All right. I did some checking about you before we left the States. I wanted to be sure you were actually available.''

His admission made her pulse kick up, but she forced herself to let the fact that he was obviously interested in her slide. After all, this love-'em-and-leave-'em guy was not a good bet, especially after the way Phillip had hurt her. ''Phillip and I were committed. We did adore each other. We lived happily together for five years.''

''Then why'd he marry somebody else?''

She didn't respond.

''Sorry. I guess it's none of my business. But I'd just like to go on record here. The guy's an idiot.''

''Yeah?''

''Yeah. Look at you!'' The unmistakable admiration in his eyes gave Kendal a strange thrill low in her belly.

''How do you know so much about me and Phillip?''

''Stephanie Robinson comes into my office all the time.''

"And she told you about *me*?" Kendal could hardly believe that woman would be so low.

"No. She was waggling her engagement ring around one day, talking about *her* Phillip and mentioned the fact that her man had worked for Merrill Jackson. After she left, the nurses said her fiancé had left the woman he'd been living with for five years. I put two and two together when you mentioned a guy named Phillip the other night."

"Oh." At the sound of Stephanie Robinson's name, Kendal's mind had frozen up. A shiver literally coursed through her, despite the steaminess of the jungle night.

When she didn't say anything, Jason offered quietly, "She can't hold a candle to you, you know."

He let his eyes stroke up and down her form again in that way he had that made a woman feel…wanted, if not adored.

And again his unabashed examination gave her the strangest little kick low in her belly.

Kendal gave a derisive little laugh. "Keep talking like that, Doctor, and I might agree to have another beer with you."

He tilted his chair back and yelled into the hotel interior, "Viljo! *Dos Tecates!*"

Kendal studied her nearly empty beer bottle. "I've decided that the whole love thing is a big mystery."

"You mean the *chemistry* between men and women is a mystery?"

"No. I mean the *love*." She eyed him curiously, wondering if he could possibly be as cynical as he sounded. "Look. Just because Phillip dumped me, that doesn't mean I don't believe in true love. Which is far more than chemistry, and you know it."

"No, I don't know that. Two people can have great chemistry, but true love...I'm not sure I believe in that anymore."

"Meaning you used to?"

"Yeah. I used to. But I was very, very young. And I haven't felt it since."

"Was it that woman from medical school?"

"Oh, no, not her. By the time she came along, I was thoroughly jaded. Ruined."

His tone was joking, self-mocking, but Kendal suspected that there was some truth behind his words.

"What ruined you?" she asked quietly.

"You're not even going to argue the point?" he feigned dismay.

"No."

He smiled at her sincerity, as if it were charming. But then his expression grew sad, remote. "It's a long story."

"I've got time." She raised her beer for a sip.

"Okay. Believe it or not, The Wolf, the *asqueroso*, was in love once." He studied her face. "Way back in high school."

"Wasn't everybody in love back in high school?"

"Not like this." His voice grew subdued all of a sudden, and Kendal could see that he was remembering something painful.

"It didn't matter how old we were, or rather, how young. I knew she was the one for me. I never even considered another woman, never even wanted to so much as look at anyone else.''

Kendal was amazed. The man saying these things had ended up as The Wolf? She stared at him in astonishment while he went on talking.

''We were in our senior year. I was a pretty good candidate to play Division One football in college. And she was…perfect. The little blond cheerleader.''

Kendal could not help reflexively comparing her own lush, brunette body to a little blond cheerleader's…and coming up short. She gave herself a mental slap for being so vain and concentrated on the story he was telling her.

''We had our whole future planned. I can't believe I'm sitting in Chiapas telling you these things after all these years. It's the beer and the exhaustion talking, I expect.''

''What happened?'' Kendal waited to hear that the little blond cheerleader had dumped him and married someone else, the way her Phillip had. She was all prepared to commiserate in their mutual victimhood when he said, ''She died.''

Kendal was silent, struggling to absorb what she'd heard. But it was perfectly clear what he said. *She died.* When Kendal found her voice it was too solemn, too quiet. Bordering, strangely, on the reverent. ''That's awful. How did it happen?''

Right then, Viljo arrived with two more beers. When he left, Jason raised his beer and said, ''Mexican champagne.''

Kendal took a sip and waited, wondering if he was going to finish the story.

Instead he watched the retreating Viljo and said, "I'm hungry. How about you?"

"Starving."

"Viljo!" Jason yelled toward the interior of the hotel where Viljo had gone. "Rustle up some grub! The lady's hungry!"

Kendal took a hesitant sip of her beer, and thought that she might be starting to understand this man somewhat. He had learned to be so tough that he could talk about his greatest loss in one breath and order up "grub" in the next.

"You know what I bet happened with that guy?" he said. Apropos to nothing, Kendal thought.

"Viljo?" She had been so focused on the story about his girlfriend that she had lost any thread of their conversation before that.

"Oi! what's his name. Philbert?"

That made her smile, as she supposed it was meant to. She toyed with her beer bottle, trying to decide if she had a right to drag him back to the story of the blond cheerleader. But obviously, he'd rather dwell on her past. "Phillip."

"Ah. Phillip. Want my theory about old Phillip?"

"No."

He went on as if she hadn't even answered. "You made the relationship too easy for him. Most guys, whoever they are, like a challenge."

"A challenge? We were living together for crying out loud."

"Exactly. You started playing house and making life all cozy for the guy, and you made him forget why he started up with you in the first place. You wanted him to be Mr. Right more than you wanted to be *his* one and only. That's the goal, sweetheart. To be his one and only." He took a smug swig of his beer.

Kendal sipped her beer wondering what made this know-it-all such an expert on women. But immediately she realized that here was a man who really believed he had loved a one and only…and that girl had died. Again Kendal wanted to ask how. *How?* But he obviously didn't want her to tell her. Trying to be sensitive to that, she said, "I thought the goal was to live happily ever after. You know, get married, buy a house, have kids, retire and die."

"No, babe, the goal is to be someone's one and only. You chicks get all wrapped up in creating a fantasy world instead of a relationship. Instead of asking if he's treating you like the one and only, you project your fantasy on to some poor guy who's only half-assed into the relationship. That's how you get your hearts broken. Happens all the time."

It was exactly what had happened with Phillip, Kendal realized. She was about to admit that he had a point when she was distracted by an eerie noise. It drifted from somewhere out in the jungle, sounding vaguely like the call of an animal. But it wasn't an animal. It sounded more like…a child.

"Men are different," Jason, still talking, obviously hadn't heard the sound. "They stay detached until something forces them to commit. Even if they're shacking up with you, they might be only halfway into the deal. That's what cohabitation will get you every time. A half-assed relationship. That's why I refuse to do it.''

''Good for you,'' Kendal said it dryly, to convey that she didn't appreciate his judging her past and that somewhere in the back of her mind—or was it somewhere deep in her heart?—she suspected he was the one who was kidding himself. She suspected that his ability to stay detached had more to do with the death of his one and only than it did with being smart.

The sound came again, closer.

''Did you hear something?''

He listened. ''Birds, probably.

''You're probably thinking I just can't commit, but at least I'm honest. What I do is a hell of a lot better than lying to women and playing house with them and breaking their hearts.''

''Oh, surely you haven't broken some hearts?'' Kendal challenged.

This time he smiled at her sarcasm. ''I've tried not to. And when I have, I've tried to make up for it. I've tried to save the friendship.''

His openness surprised her. Her defiance evaporated. He was very good-looking. He'd experienced a lot of women. Maybe she really could learn something here. ''Educate me about men some more.''

''Too many women don't put themselves on an equal footing with men by keeping their boundaries up. They don't protect their hearts. You've got to keep a little piece of your heart in reserve, held back.'' He circled two fingers lightly in the vicinity of his heart.

Kendal frowned. "Is that what works for you? Keeping your heart in reserve?''

"It beats letting it get ground up into hamburger.''

Something about Jason Bridges didn't add up. On the one hand he seemed so open, so real, so compassionate...and so passionate. But on the other hand something about him was definitely sealed off.

"My heart was broken for a while, but it was never *hamburger*.'' As soon as Kendal said the words, she realized it was true. She had gotten over Phillip, in time. "I've still got some stuff to work out, but basically, I've got my life on track again. I'm doing pretty well, thank you. As well as you are, with your constant string of women.''

He turned the focus right back on her. "But I take it you're still not back in the game, still not seeing anyone.''

"Only because I haven't met anyone worth seeing.''

"Not one single man in the past year?''

"I...'' Kendal realized that admitting the truth—not *one*—would sound really bad, like she was living in some kind of sick little shell. It might also be bad to let Jason see how deprived she'd been lately, even if it was by choice. "I have been very happy lately,'' she defended.

"I didn't ask you if you were happy. I asked you

if you'd had a date, if you've been with a man at all this past year."

She wasn't about to admit as much to him. "That is none of your busin—"

Again she heard that sound from out in the trees. When she turned to listen she felt the strangest sensation, like they were being watched. "Did you hear something?"

"Yeah." He frowned in the same direction. "I did this time."

As they listened, the faint mewling sound traveled through the moist night air. With a jolt, Kendal realized it definitely sounded like a baby crying, but she couldn't imagine what a baby would be doing out here in the darkness of the jungle.

"Do you think it's a little animal?"

He put his finger to his lips and they both listened intently for a couple of seconds. "Let's go back inside." He stood and took her hand, pulling her to her feet. "There are worse things than animals out in this jungle."

"But what if it's a baby or—" When she turned her head to the sound, Kendal saw a female figure in a white peasant blouse and a dark skirt. She appeared from amid the fronds of jungle growth looking like a Madonna, clutching a toddler to her side. The little boy whimpered and buried his face in his mother's neck.

"Look!" Kendal stood and started to go to them, but Jason grabbed her arm. "Careful."

At Kendal's questioning look, he elaborated. "Ask her if she's alone."

Kendal did.

In a soft, frightened voice, the woman said, "*Sí*, I am alone. And my child needs *El Médico*'s help."

"She needs our help," Kendal turned to Jason, her face imploring.

"*La comida!*" The shout came from Viljo, who stood balancing two plates of the usual fare in the high arched doorway.

At that, the woman darted into the jungle, disappearing faster than a scared rabbit.

"Oh, no!" Kendal lurched forward, but Jason grabbed her. "She's gone! Oh, Jason, I wonder what the problem was! What could be wrong with her baby?"

"If she really needs us, she'll be back." Jason kept a firm grip on Kendal's shoulders. "We'll eat inside," he said to Viljo. Jason urged Kendal into the open hotel portico while Viljo set the plates in front of them and lit a citronella candle.

"You don't go running into the jungle at night. Vajaras has used women and children to trap people before."

"Why would Vajaras want to harm us?"

"Us? Not us, sweetheart. Me. I'm the American doctor who's heard too much, seen too much."

At Kendal's distraught look, he said, "Eat."

Jason dug into his food with gusto, but Kendal could hardly swallow a bite of hers, thinking about that frightened mother and her child.

CHAPTER NINE

AFTER DINNER they went upstairs and checked on that day's post-ops again, then Kendal typed her drug notes into her laptop.

Jason sat cross-legged on the cot opposite her and smiled. The way she jammed her pen into her thick hair was endearing. He was starting to think everything she did was cute. "You're very conscientious, but all the patients are doing really well," he said. "You work too hard, you know."

Kendal did not look up from her screen. "Would that be the pot calling the kettle a workaholic?"

"Do you like to dance?"

That got her to look up. "I love to."

"Then we need to have a little fun. Come on." He jumped up and took her hand.

As they cut through the lobby, Jason caught sight of Angelica, curled up in an ancient leather chair, reading. "Kendal and I are going to El Foco," he told her as they sailed by. "I'll be on my cell, if and when it chooses to work."

"I'll be right here." Angelica waved them off. "Try not to get your asses killed in that joint."

"What is El Foco, and why might we be killed

there?'' Kendal asked as they walked out into the humid night air.

''El Foco is just a charming little local joint. You'll see.''

''Ah. I'd be disappointed if you said anything else.''

Jason borrowed Viljo's Jeep and drove them over the short stretch of washboard jungle road rising into San Cristóbal de las Casas. He flew past the colorful facade of the cathedral in the central square, down a congested side street straight to a dark, hip-looking bar called El Foco. The Spotlight.

He parked the Jeep, hopped out, trotted around to Kendal's side and pulled her out. When she shivered in the colder mountain air, he hooked an arm around her waist, and holding her tight against his side, walked her down the narrow street. It struck him that he enjoyed just holding her. He had never been so happy just to hold someone, just touching her.

The sidewalk in front of the bar was littered with customers, mostly young men, who were busy smoking and leering at Kendal.

''They'll search us inside the door,'' Jason warned, ''so don't get all offended.''

But Kendal dug in her heels before they went inside. ''What did Angelica mean, 'try not to get killed in that joint'?''

''Angelica can be a bit of an hysteric.''

''Right,'' Kendal said. Her self-preservation instincts could not be squelched. He liked that. ''Why are they gonna search us?''

"Always happens. Especially to a pretty *chica*. Don't worry. I'll be right behind you so the guy'll restrain himself or pay the penalty. Come on. That's a great beat."

Kendal jerked on his hand. "Why?" she shouted over the music blaring out of place.

"Huh?" Jason seemed anxious to get in there and dance.

"Why the search?"

"They've had some trouble. Nearly everybody has in these parts. Just stick with me and you'll be okay." Jason reined in his impatience. "*Americanos* are perfectly safe in this bar. As long as we don't get too drunk or dance the naked Macarena or anything—unless, of course, you insist." His smile was purposely wicked.

At her disgusted grimace, he smirked. "Kendal, come on. Lighten up. This is Mexico." He pronounced it the way the locals did, *Meh-hee-coe*.

"Come on. I'll protect you." He raised the back of his loose denim shirt as if to give her a peek at something there.

Inside the waistband of his hiking shorts, Kendal could see the butt of his small gun secured under the belt. *Good Lord*, she thought. What kind of wild man had she come here with?

The search was nothing, if not stupid. They didn't even find Jason's gun. Jason cocked a warning eyebrow at the guy who then waved Kendal past. Inside, young locals and travelers, some Americans like themselves, were gyrating on a packed dance floor to a band playing a pulsing Latin beat.

Kendal saw immediately what gave the place its name. A single bare lightbulb dangled from a black cord in the middle of the dance floor, its weak halo surrounded by a cloud of flies, moths and mosquitoes. The general air of the place was very loud, very smoky, very…sexy.

"They usually get into some great salsa music around about midnight," Jason shouted. His face was gleeful as he pulled Kendal into the wildly dancing crowd.

"Won't somebody recognize *El Médico*?" Kendal shouted as he hooked an arm around her waist.

"Nah. This is a *turista* crowd. Not locals."

For a solid hour they danced. Jason seemed to have unending energy as he circled around Kendal. His moves were confident and hot, as if they were calculated to get Kendal that way. She decided it was certainly working.

When they slow-danced, it was as if he were hypnotizing her. He leaned low over her shoulder and hummed in her left ear. It sent an unfamiliar thrill through parts of her that had long been neglected. After a while they settled against each other and the rhythm of his breathing seemed to match hers.

Kendal hadn't danced in so long, she had forgotten how good it felt to melt into a man's body, to move with a beat. During the next fast set, Jason started giving her tiny, little pouty-mouthed frowns that said, *Ouch. Baby. You're hot!*

Finally, they stopped long enough to take in their surroundings while they sipped a beer. This was no elegant Mexican disco with patrons dressed to impress. The place was crammed to the gills with T-shirt-and-jeans-clad young drinkers and smokers in the mood to party.

But one man looked out of place to Kendal. He was too old, too hard-looking among the smiling young people. His graying hair was slicked back, Miami-style, his puffy face set in a grim mask. He sat, a mound of flesh off in a corner by himself, giving Kendal a slightly salacious perusal. When she gave him an offended frown, his cold eyes slid away.

"Don't do that." Jason set his beer aside and positioned his shoulder between her line of vision and the man's.

"What?"

"Don't make eye contact with that man. The locals think American women are brazen as it is. Don't reinforce the notion."

"I saw him outside on the sidewalk." Kendal leaned forward, nearly touching her lips to Jason's ear. "He followed us in here. And I'd swear he's been watching us."

Jason glanced over his shoulder, sizing up the man.

"Let's dance."

"Again?"

"Yeah. Now." He pulled her to her feet, then slung her against his body like a rag doll. Surging her backward with the Latin rhythm, he danced them on a crooked route through the crowd and finally out the door.

Outside on the sidewalk, Kendal was breathless from their hasty exit. "What was that all about?"

"If the guy was watching us, we can't stay. Come on." He grabbed her hand and hauled her along at a trot, heading toward their Jeep. His party mood had evaporated—he seemed completely sober now.

Kendal scrambled to regain her footing. She looked back over her shoulder and shivered, feeling the press of the cool mountain air even more keenly after the heat the two of them had generated inside the club. "But why would he be watching us?"

Jason slowed, wrapping her in his arms as he helped her the rest of the way to the Jeep. "Probably because you're so beautiful."

She made a wry face at him.

"Who knows? Ever since the Zapatista uprising, there's been a lot of fighting among opposing factions down here. And any foreigner who hangs around for long—that would be me, and by extension you—is suspect."

Kendal reverted to the same argument she always used when this subject came up. "But we haven't done anything except try to help these people."

"Sometimes we get caught up in it anyway. Last year some paramilitary types gunned down a bunch of women and children. I fixed some of the damage. I could be wrong about that guy. But he didn't belong in a place like El Foco, that's for sure. And it's also common knowledge that I bring a lot of drugs from the States with me. That's another reason I keep my operation hidden out in the boonies." He looked back. "There's some serious drug-running in this area."

"Vajaras?"

"Yep. That's why he wants to keep the villagers under his thumb."

Kendal looked back, scared now. "Do you think he saw us leave?"

"Hope not." He jerked open the Jeep door. "Hop in. We'd better get back."

He climbed in the Jeep, fired it up and lurched away from the curb. As he drove off he reached to his back, pulled out the gun and jammed it under his thigh.

On the winding road back, she noticed that Jason kept checking the rearview mirror. And he used his cell phone to make a warning call to Ben.

THE SECOND DAY of surgeries went exactly like the first. All day they worked. All day they stood on their feet. And all day Kendal could not shake the haunting images of the young woman who came out of the jungle holding the toddler and the hostile-looking man at the bar.

But Jason remained unrelentingly energetic and cheerful. Whistling. Joking. Giving orders. And when the long day was over, Kendal was surprised that he'd found another way to be alone with her.

Jason was full of energy because he had a plan. He really did enjoy seducing a woman, especially this one. He asked Viljo to pack a picnic and told the innkeeper he and Kendal could be found in a secluded spot in the jungle should he be needed.

"*El Médico,* what about that *loco* watching you in the bar?"

"What about him?"

"*Señor,* the jungle is full of Zapatistas and robbers," Viljo said as he handed over a basket of cheese, *bolillos* and fruit wrapped in a tablecloth and covered with a brightly striped woven blanket. "Not the place to take a *chica* alone. Let me go along. I got a gun."

"I've got my gun," Jason took the basket. "We're only going as far as Agua Luna." On Jason's first trip here Viljo had shown him the high waterfall that cascaded into a broad, deep pool. Long ago, when the hotel had first been built to attract wealthy vacationers from Mexico City, this was the romantic spot that had drawn them. Jason had been down to the falls alone many times. Now he wanted to take Kendal.

"We'll only stay out until the moon rises." Tonight the moon would be full, pouring light over the water. Perfect for what he had in mind.

He felt like he was in high school again, planning such ploys. He couldn't remember when he'd been this attracted to a woman.

They took Viljo's rattletrap Jeep again, descending a short road that was so narrow the tropical vegetation whacked into the open windows.

"Where are we going?" Kendal asked as she slapped at a mosquito.

"You'll see."

"Would you please stop saying that?"

He drove the rutted road farther down into the jungle, deep into the cloud forests that were cloaked in mosses, lichens, ferns.

Kendal heard the waterfall before he'd even stopped the Jeep.

He grabbed the basket and her hand, and led her along a narrow path through dense tropical vegetation.

Kendal came up short and gasped when they emerged into a clearing where a fifty-foot high waterfall thundered its frothy whiteness into a crystal clear turquoise pool.

"Oh, my!" she cried, staring at the beauty below.

"Agua Luna," Jason said quietly as he watched her face, her reaction.

"The water of the moon," Kendal translated.

Jason set the basket on a nearby mossy boulder and turned to her.

"Come here," he said and pulled her slowly toward him.

He studied her eyes in the twilight. "You have beautiful eyes." In a move that was very swift and very sure, he slid one arm tight around her waist and the other around her shoulders. He tipped her backward so that he had full access to her mouth, supporting her back with his strong arm while he swooped in to tenderly take, then ravage, her mouth.

Kendal felt the impact of the kiss all the way to her core. It wasn't the way he was holding her, though that was just right, very powerful, very masculine. It wasn't the way he used his lips, his tongue, with exactly the right mixture of softness and pressure. It wasn't the way he tasted, which was moist, but not sloppy, fresh and tangy but not too sweet. It was something else that made her breath come short and started her head spinning. The roar of the falls only intensified the roaring that had started within her own ears.

He broke away long enough to find a better fit—for their bodies, for their mouths—before he kissed her again, this time plunging his tongue deeper. Kendal could not stop herself from answering his passionate strokes with her own. Somewhere high in the trees, a bird called out, echoing the cry building inside Kendal's body. *More!*

Both of them simultaneously made an urgent sound from deep in their throats, and Jason's breathing grew husky and harsh as he descended on her mouth for a third time.

Kendal was astonished at how rapidly, how hotly, her passion built. It had never been like this with Phillip! But when Jason's hands started groping under her clothing, she found the strength to put a stop to it.

"I'm sorry," he removed his hands instantly when hers pushed against them. "I got carried away. I've wanted to do that from the minute I met you that morning in my office."

His honesty—like his kisses—was totally disarming.

"I…," Kendal was struggling to return her breathing to normal. She put up a palm, a signal for patience. "Wait."

"I understand." He enveloped her in his arms and

gently stroked her back. "I didn't plan on kissing you like that, but I'm glad we were here when I did."

"Why?" Kendal couldn't seem to manage anything beyond these one-word responses. She pressed her forehead against his chest.

"Because I want us to remember this moment." He laced his fingers up into her hair.

She was amazed at his candor, which seemed to inspire her own. "That was all just a little too fast for me."

He kissed her temple. "I'll slow down then." He took her hand and picked up the food basket. They left the steep path and crossed high above the pool on a crude hanging footbridge.

Kendal felt like she was crossing that bridge into another world. A wild and dangerous world that was under Jason's control. And she could do nothing to stop herself. She wanted to go to whatever mysterious places he chose to take her.

He found a mossy spot by the pool and spread the woven rug. Then they ate.

Kendal found she didn't have much of an appetite. Not for food, anyway. She'd lost her taste for food after they'd arrived in Chiapas.

Their conversation seemed charged, and when Jason noticed that she wasn't eating he stopped talking altogether. He leaned toward her on one palm and hand-fed her a bite of *bolillos*. She swallowed it as if she were swallowing a stone.

"You don't want any more?" He stopped the second piece of bread short of her mouth.

She looked at her hands nervously. "I don't know what I want."

"I think *I* know."

He slowly tilted her back to the blanket. Pressing his muscular body over hers, he bracketed his large hand around her jaw. This time his assault on her mouth was not tender.

While he kissed her, he whispered things against her lips. About what he wanted to do to her, about how he'd been going crazy with fantasies about her. His hands were everywhere on her skin, large and warm and confident and skilled at touching.

Kendal had not been touched like this in so long, maybe never, she thought with astonishment as his touches grew even more intimate. He was not shy about pleasuring a woman. "Your skin is amazing," he whispered against her lips while his expert fingers found the sweet spot at the inside of her thigh.

THE SUN HAD gone down and the moon had come up, but Jason was in no hurry. The falls made a rushing counterpoint to his soft, exploring touches, his lingering kisses.

He didn't care if they actually did The Act yet. It was enough for now to touch Kendal intimately. He wanted this to unfold on her terms, when she was ready. Anything she was willing to give, any boundary she set, was fine with him. But boy, she seemed more than ready. She was every bit a woman. Still, even if she was making him crazy with desire, and she was, he was willing to wait until the time was absolutely right. Though the condom in the pocket of his vest said otherwise. Angelica and the Mexicans called the things *angels custodios*—guardian angels.

He smiled faintly against Kendal's lips, thinking that though he intended to protect her, he was no angel.

His wry thought was interrupted by a sound that made his head snap up.

"What was that?" Kendal raised her head beside his. Her hair was a delicious mess—he had reveled in the feel of it.

He reached across Kendal to the basket and flipped the cloth up, producing the gun. He sat up, pointing at something moving in the foliage across the narrow pool.

Kendal bolted upright beside him, peering into the dark jungle. "What is it?"

"Shh."

In the same instant they both saw the figure move. It was a young woman, crouching in the undergrowth like a frightened animal.

"Tell her to step out into the moonlight," Jason said.

With a shaky voice, Kendal did. The woman obeyed and surprised them by striking a match and lighting a candle, holding the flame close to her face.

"It's the same girl who was outside the hotel," Kendal whispered at Jason's shoulder. "The one who had the little child with her."

She emerged into the moonlight and beckoned

them. "*Venga*," her voice carried above the sound of the falls. *Come.* "*Por favor.*" *Please.*

Kendal started to get up, but Jason grabbed her arm. "That little child!" she protested. "What if he needs us?"

"I told you—" he kept his voice low "—there are all kinds of desperate people out in this jungle who wouldn't be above using a kid as bait. Tell her not to pull any tricks. Tell her I've got a gun on her."

Kendal did as she was told.

"*Sí. Está bien*," the woman called back in Spanish. *That's okay.* "Just help us. Please." She beckoned with her hand, pointing into the jungle with the candle.

"Stay behind me." Jason shoved Kendal around to his back.

Kendal kept a hand on his shoulder and the gun trained on the woman's dark form as they made their way across the narrow bridge.

When they got to the other side, the *chica* maintained her distance and led them into the jungle over a dappled moonlit path to a small cave where trickles of water dripped over the opening. "*Aquí*," she said softly, putting a finger to her lips. *In here.*

Inside, there were a couple of stubby candles in the rock niches, illuminating the sleeping form of a tiny child, curled on a brightly woven blanket spread over a bed of fronds. He was pretty, like his mother, except his mouth and jaw didn't look right. As quiet as they were being, the toddler blinked awake, though he didn't make a sound. He had obviously been well-trained to keep silent. The young woman dropped to her knees as the toddler sought his mother's arms. He only stared at the strangers with huge black eyes that bulged oddly, sparkling in his elfish little face like two obsidian stones. To Kendal the boy looked plucked out of one of those cheap paintings of the waifs with enormous eyes and sad little mouths. He pressed his tiny, trembling, malformed lips together, biting back tears.

"Oh," Kendal breathed, feeling her heart melt. "He's so adorable. What happened to his little face?" she asked the mother in Spanish. "And his little hands?" She reached toward the child's tiny webbed fingers.

But Jason answered for the woman. "He was born that way, or rather, he's grown that way because of an inherited defect. Crouson's or perhaps Apert's syndrome is my guess." Jason dropped to one knee to examine the child. "You see variable penetrance with those sometimes. Whatever the syndrome, something has caused a cessation of midfacial growth."

Jason reached forward to gently trace a finger along the tiny, severely recessed jaw, and the baby withdrew with a frightened shriek.

The mother babbled urgently in Spanish. She seemed distracted, almost terrified of something, glancing at the opening of the cave while she talked. And then in the dim candlelight, Kendal noticed massive bruises on the girl's upper arms.

"You've been hurt," Kendal said in Spanish as she reached out to touch the woman's arm.

"*Sí, El Chancho,*" the woman said in a matter-of-fact tone. "Help my baby," she pleaded.

She asked the young woman a series of questions in Spanish, then turned to Jason to relay the woman's answers in English.

"Her name is Lucia. His name is Miguel," Kendal translated. "He's two years old—almost three—and she's begging us to take him, to fix him. She says he's very bright, likes to color and already tries to talk, but he can't very well because of his deformed mouth." Kendal finished her English explanation sadly. "She has no money."

"Kendal, get real." Jason turned on her with a look that bordered on the incredulous. "What I'm doing down here is cut-and-run stuff. This child needs extensive craniofacial work. That requires a team. And the kid needs far more than a plastic surgeon. He needs a neurosurgeon, an otolaryngologist, maybe an audiologist and an ophthalmologist. An orthodontist, a geneticist, a psychologist, a social worker even! Don't you get it? This is serious."

Again, Jason tried to examine the child, but again the toddler shrieked and recoiled.

"Stop it. You're scaring them with all those big words." Kendal stroked the mother's arm and murmured something soothing in Spanish.

"What did you just say to her?" Jason found himself getting annoyed. With the balky toddler. With the secretive mother. With Kendal's attitude toward him—switching from sensuous to censoring in two seconds flat.

"I told her we'd help him, of course."

Lucia kissed her child's head, bit her lip, then thrust the toddler into Kendal's arms. Instinctively, Kendal hugged the baby to her breast.

"I can't help this kid!" Jason protested. "I see kids like this all the time down here, sometimes more than one in a family. I've seen twelve kids growing up in a two-room shack with no running water and no electricity, half of them with the same genetic problem." Jason again tried to examine the child, but Miguel recoiled. "But you can't do surgery like this in a hut in the jungle, for crying out loud!"

"Shh!" Kendal hissed as she patted Miguel.

"Lower your voice. You're scaring him."

With tears in her eyes, Lucia was removing a medal on a long gold chain from around her neck.

"Santa Lucia," the girl intoned meaningfully, then she spoke in a long, unbroken string of Spanish as she pressed the medal into Kendal's palm.

Staring at the medal, Kendal spoke rapidly in reply. Jason's frustration mounted as the two women continued in an exchange that sounded like they were reaching some sort of accord. "*Sí, Sí*," Kendal repeated. He had no idea what kind of deal they had struck.

"*Gracias.*" Tears started running down the mother's cheeks as she backed out of the cave.

The toddler started to scream.

"Wait!" Kendal called in Spanish. "Where are you going?"

"She won't be back," Jason said cynically as the

woman disappeared into the dark. "Her problem is solved."

"No. You're wrong," Kendal said as she patted Miguel's thin back and held out the medal on her palm for him to see. "She gave me this medal and said she'd come back for it. It's pure gold, one of a kind, handcrafted for her mother, who is dead. She said it's a medal of Santa Lucia, who brings light to the blind. She said it would bring us blessings for helping her baby."

"Superstitious B.S.," Jason rolled his eyes and plucked up the medal, examining it in the candlelight. "It's gold all right, but I doubt she'll be back." Despite his cynical tone, he reached up and rubbed the crying toddler's little back most tenderly. "Looks like we've got us a little boy to take care of."

DAY THREE was a repeat of day two—long, hot and fraught with difficulties. When it was over, Jason sought out Kendal, who had taken Miguel back to her room at the hotel as soon she'd finished her records.

He tapped on the door, and she said, "Come in."

She was giving the toddler a bath in the small sink. A half-eaten banana, crackers and a cup of milk rested on a paper towel on the bedside table.

"What are you doing?"

"Taking care of him. He has no family."

"The *curanderas* can do that."

Kendal turned on him. "I have not shirked any of my other duties." But she had pushed herself mercilessly, shuttling all day between comforting the frightened toddler and monitoring the other patients. Continuing to teach, to encourage, but assuming the care of Miguel, as well. Jason was amazed at how determined, adaptable and just plain gutsy Kendal was. How could he refuse anything to a woman like this?

"I've decided to fix his palate," he said from the door.

She whirled around, her expression resolute. "When?"

Jason rubbed his eyes in exhaustion. "Early next week. The sooner the better. Even under the best of circumstances he'll have a complicated recovery."

"After surgery, he can stay in my room with me, since he has no family. I'll do all of his nursing care." She lifted Miguel out of the sink and wrapped him in one of her own towels. "Ruth is already helping me."

Jason smiled at the beautiful woman before him. Only three days in Mexico and Kendal Collins was ready to tackle anything. Was he getting emotionally attached to her? Not good. He made a mental note to keep his cool.

But later that night, after he finished his post-op rounds, Jason gravitated back to Kendal's room. She answered the door with a finger pressed to her lips.

"Miguel's finally asleep."

The child lay curled in a ball on Kendal's bed, covered with her fleece jacket. Ruth appeared in the hallway, walking up behind Jason and poking him in the ribs.

"'Scuse me." Ruth squeezed past him, carrying a cotton blanket.

"Found one," she said to Kendal.

The two women carefully removed the scratchy athletic jacket and covered the child with the softer, lighter cotton blanket. When they had succeeded in performing the task without waking the child, they smiled at each other. *Women and their baby dolls,* Jason thought.

"He keeps crying for his mother," Kendal whispered to Ruth. "It just breaks my heart."

"I know. Let's hope he sleeps all night."

"I was wondering if you'd like to go get something to eat," Jason said when he finally had Kendal's attention. "I'd like to talk to you."

"Go. I'll watch him," Ruth responded to Kendal's worried glance at Miguel.

"Thanks, babe." Jason winked at Ruth. "Remind me to give you a big fat Christmas bonus." He gave his nurse a grateful smile as he whisked Kendal out the door.

"I'm not very hungry," Kendal protested as they walked down the broad stairs.

"How are you going to take care of your little lost puppy if you don't eat?"

"Miguel is a human being."

"I know he is, Kendal. That's what I want to talk to you about. Come on. Let's eat. I'm starving, and I figure I won't get to see much of you now, especially once I do surgery on the kid."

"Okay, but I only want something light. And no dancing tonight, or anything like that."

"Fine." By "anything like that" he figured she

meant "hands off." But he knew for a fact that he couldn't keep his hands off this woman.

Jason asked Viljo to bring them some *sopa Azteca.* Aztec soup—he thought she'd like that. And a plate of margaritas with a knowing smile. Viljo threw in a couple of cheesy quesadillas for him. Viljo threw in a couple he and Kendal were becoming somewhat of an item, out here in the middle of nowhere. What would it be like when they got back to Integris? The thought made him smile. He was already thinking of places he wanted to take Kendal, people he wanted her to meet.

After they ate, Jason said, "You worked awfully hard today. You need a little fresh air," and took her by the hand. "Walk with me while we talk."

"You can't let yourself get too attached to these children," he said after they'd walked a bit. "You can't get too emotionally involved. Miguel will have to go back to his people."

"I can't harden my heart, Jason. I told you that. I won't."

He stopped on the path and studied her eyes in the moonlight. "I know. I think that's why I'm starting to get attached to *you.*"

Kendal's lips dropped open at his admission, and Jason couldn't resist leaning in to taste them. The nibbling instantly became a devouring kiss.

When it was over, she was breathless. She pushed at his chest and said, "Jason."

"I know," he murmured. "Don't go too fast. So I won't. We'll take it slow."

But before long he had his arm around her waist,

then his hands on her hips. And before long he was kissing her again.

And before long they had found their way back to his tent.

CHAPTER TEN

IN THE TENT, he guided her to the narrow cot and urged her to lie down. "You rest here," he said, "I'll sit on this sleeping bag on the ground beside you."

There was only the barest bit of light, fainter than candle glow, which came from a lantern down on the overgrown path that led to the hotel, reflecting off the tent walls. Still relaxed by the tequila, they talked on and on in the quiet darkness.

At a pause in conversation, Kendal said, "Thank you so much for doing Miguel's surgery."

"I want to." He shrugged. "It's what I do." But he felt strangely lifted by her gratitude.

"Still, I know it's a risk. Have I told you how much I admire the work you do?"

He kissed the palm of her hand with an intensity he himself did not understand. "That means a lot to me," he whispered.

While they talked, they had started to touch. First faces and arms, then hair. As she lay there, letting him stroke her thick hair back from her brow, he could feel her yearning for more.

Beneath Jason's hands she felt soft and delicate… and exciting.

He massaged her feet, then her calf muscles and when his hands gently glided higher, he was pleased that she didn't stop him.

With one hand moving intimately just below her waist, he slid her T-shirt up with the other, pressing a hot kiss where her bra dipped low between her breasts. "Stop me if anything makes you uncomfortable," he whispered.

Apparently nothing did.

He performed all of his ministrations kneeling beside the cot with her body, finally lying open and vulnerable, spread before him. Kendal felt no awkwardness about this, letting him touch and stroke and suckle her in a gradually escalating pattern that brought every nerve ending in her skin to excruciating life.

She felt herself peaking, reaching toward a place she'd never known before. Even in the darkness of the tent, when she looked in his eyes, she could read them. They glowed with passion, with triumph, watching her as he made her spiral higher.

Finally, her eyes slid closed in ecstasy. Blindly she reached, bracing one hand on his shoulder and gripping the cot with the other as he brought her to a shattering climax. "Oh, baby—" he encouraged at the zenith of it "—you are so beautiful."

When she was spent, he pulled her limp body down off the cot onto the sleeping bag beside him. *When had he removed his clothes?* Kendal wondered from a blissful haze. But she couldn't seem to form any words; instead her mouth begged silently for another kiss. He kissed her first, then stroked and massaged until she was again writhing in neediness. Finally, positioning her above him, he drove into her, and as they joined she heard herself uttering his name again and again.

Jason's jaw clenched as Kendal moved over him. She seemed totally surrendered to her passion now, totally unaware of anything but him. Unaware of the way she moved so sensuously, the way she tossed her head and said his name over and over, drove him wild. Wild. Yes. The woman was wild. In fact, he'd never seen anything so wild, yet so feminine.

His eyes had adapted to the faint light, or more likely his pupils were dilated with desire, and he marveled at every detail of her as she moved. Even the thin sheen of sweat on her skin fascinated him. Her skin was like a miracle. Milky. Flawless. As soft as whipped cream. Everywhere, so soft. He ran his palms over her hips, up her back. He'd never felt skin like this. He could have touched her forever.

Her movements became more intense, and as he rocked to match her rhythm, his universe threatened to erupt in an apex of dazzling pleasure. He focused his gaze on her beautiful pale breasts. There, between them, was the golden medal, swaying as her body swayed. Jason fixed his eyes on the rhythmic movement of it for one hypnotic second before Kendal shifted forward slightly and the thing started to tap gently against his chest. Again and again, the little medal buffeted his heart while Kendal thrashed against his body. Crying out, suddenly she came again. He watched in awe as she arched back for one stunning moment and then he exploded inside of her.

When it was over, Kendal collapsed onto his chest, with the medal lodged between the hardness of his muscles and the softness of her breast. She lay very still on him and he kissed her temple, feeling her heart beating wildly. Or was it his?

"I feel so close to you," he whispered. The words seemed so inadequate, compared to what he was really feeling.

"Hmmm," she moaned in sleepy satisfaction and snuggled her curvy body tighter against him.

After a while he toyed absently with the medal. "Why are you wearing this?" he asked.

"Lucia said to," she murmured from the edges of sleep. "She said it would bring us together."

"You and me?"

"Yes." Her voice was fading still. "You...and me."

And for one tiny, fleeting instant Jason felt an overwhelming sensation, something that brought tears to his eyes, something that felt like—rapture. Or was it redemption?

KENDAL WOKE from a deep sleep, disoriented and feeling slightly frazzled, emerging from the clutches of a disturbing dream. An incredibly erotic dream. Her skin felt as sticky as flypaper, her tongue as dry as a pumice stone.

Water. She needed water.

She pulled at the sheet that bound her as she lay on

her side, and some part of her brain was already registering that she was definitely not in her own bed. And she was...naked.

Oh, God. With a rush, her body jolted fully awake. She was in Mexico. In a tent. On a sleeping bag. With *him.*

The murky light of predawn was seeping through the grayish ochre sailcloth of the tent. As she allowed her eyes to adjust to the strange, humid interior, she heard a moan behind her. She was afraid to turn onto her back, afraid of what she might see, but cautiously she eased over. Her pulse shot up and her chest tightened at the sight of Jason's profile. He was even more handsome in sleep, though at the moment his expression was becoming pinched, anguished, as if he were having a bad dream.

He moaned again.

Well, she was having a bad dream, too. Except she was wide-awake. Memories of their night together came flooding back. Euphoria flashed through her, quickly extinguished by a wash of pure guilt. Why had she lost her head with him? This was not the way she wanted her next relationship to start. She wanted true love, dammit, and this guy wasn't going to give her that. Ever. He was The Wolf.

Again he moaned. She studied him as closely as she could in the dim light. He was definitely asleep, but seemed to be growing more restless, more fitful. He'd kicked free of the sheet, and in the waxy jungle light his body looked like sculpted marble. More beautiful than Michelangelo's David. His long, muscular legs were splayed wide, one hand draped near his genitals. A glance there made Kendal's dry throat tighten. His other hand was curled protectively over his heart, the fingers flexing with tension. He was definitely having a bad dream. Her theory was confirmed when his brow contorted into a pained grimace as he twisted a shoulder up slightly and groaned again.

Kendal felt like some sort of voyeur, but she couldn't look away. She pressed her palm over her mouth and stifled a squeak of chagrin as she studied his powerful body. What had she done, allowing herself to be seduced by this Adonis?

She'd succumbed to his charms. Despite her vow not to, that's what she'd done.

And eventually he'd leave her, like he'd left every other woman before her. In the night. On a motorcycle.

She had to get out of here while he was still asleep. *Where were her clothes?* She sat up, clutching the sheet to her breasts with one hand, while with the other she fumbled behind her and to the side, finally landing on the flashlight amidst the rumple of sleeping bags. Not that the thing would do her any good. Flicking it on would only serve to wake him, and she preferred him unconscious. Awake, looking at her with those eyes, Jason Bridges had proved to be a very dangerous animal, indeed.

A fresh ripple of desire coursed through her at the memory.

He tossed an arm her way and she dodged it.

Her clothes!

She searched again with blind hands. Her top and shorts were dark denim, indistinguishable in the murky light from Jason's forest green sheets and black sleeping bag.

Jason gave another low groan, mumbling, "No, Amy. No." Then his tone became urgent, pained. "No!" he repeated louder. "The fire! Go back!" He bolted upright, eyes wide open, obviously not comprehending the reality of the darkened tent. He was in the grip of some terror, flailing his arms as he fought a demon in a nightmare world. He battled the tangled sheets as if they were alive.

"Jason!" Kendal recoiled from his buffeting, trying to decide what she should do.

But before she could do anything he grabbed her, crushing her upper arms with his huge hands. He shook her, *hard*, then threw his head back and howled, "No-o-o!" so loudly that Kendal was afraid the other volunteers would come running from the hotel. Part of her wished someone *would* burst into the tent. She didn't recognize this maniacal Jason who had her in his grip. He was possessed—a madman.

He shook Kendal by the shoulders again. "No!"

"Jason, stop!" she cried, pushing against the muscles of his powerful chest as he gripped her. "You're hurting me. Let go! Wake up!"

But the harder she struggled against him, the tighter he gripped her. Twisting her flesh painfully in his strong hands, he flattened her against his chest, crushing her.

"Amy!" He struggled to his knees, trying to pick her up in his arms.

"Jason, let go," she pleaded.

"No! Amy!" He shook her. "I'll never...let you go," he choked out. He clutched her to him and buried his face in her neck as his voice broke with a sob, with very real, wrenching pain. His arms encircled her back, and from each side his fingers splayed up, grasping at her bare breasts, digging into her flesh, not with sexual passion, but with a strange clawing desperation.

"Jason, stop! You're hurting me!"

His head snapped up and he stared at her, his blue eyes looking eerie and confused for one last mad instant before he came to.

"It's me," she said softly as his grip relaxed and became more gentle. "It's me. Kendal. You were dreaming."

He released her as abruptly as he'd grabbed her. "Kendal?" His breathing grew ragged and rapid as comprehension dawned. "Oh, man." He raked his fingers back through his hair. "Gimme a minute here."

"It's okay." Kendal covered her front with one arm and placed the other palm on his shoulder. His skin felt incredibly hot and taut, and she felt the muscles twitch under her touch. "It's okay," she repeated. "You were having a bad dream. But it's over now."

"Oh, man," he groaned and sat, bringing his knees up, turning away from her in profile. "I can't believe this."

"It's over now." She touched his shoulder again.

"You don't understand. It'll never be over." There

was such defeat in his voice that it made her heart ache.

"What do you mean?" But even as she reached out to touch him again, she felt him closing off.

"It was only a dream," she repeated in an effort to keep him focused, to keep him engaged. It was also the only consoling thing she could think to say.

"Right." His voice sounded more normal now. "Only a dream. And I've had it before." He gave a dry chuckle and looked at her as if *she* had something to do with all of this. "It's been a long time, but it's still only a dream."

His cryptic tone puzzled her. "Do you want to talk about it?"

"No, I don't." And suddenly Jason's voice had gone from sad to cold. He scrubbed a hand down his face. "What time is it?" He fumbled in his shorts and produced his watch, checked it with the flashlight.

"Listen, babe. We gotta get some real sleep. I'm gonna be carving on people in a couple of hours." He jerked on his pants. "I'll walk you back to the hotel." And with that Kendal realized he'd dismissed her.

She bit her lip to hold back sudden tears. She couldn't decide if she was hurting for her loss…or for his.

CHAPTER ELEVEN

THE NEXT DAY Kendal had to ask.

When they finally managed a break and took their food out onto the steps during *la comida* she asked him straight out, "Who is Amy?"

It was pouring rain, and they were sitting on the top step under the thatched roof of the pavilion. They had heavy pottery plates piled with Viljo's spicy food balanced on their knees. The dried fronds of the roof kept the water out surprisingly well.

Jason and Kendal were alone. The rest of the staff was inside tending patients. Ben had gone to check in with the missionaries in San Cristóbal. Jason and Kendal were alone. The others would not stop to eat until Jason and Kendal were finished, so they were shoveling their food in fast, not talking. Her abrupt question seemed even more loaded, interrupting the silence. Kendal immediately felt she'd crossed a line, made a mistake.

When he said nothing, she sipped her bottled Coke, staring out at the sheet of shifting water pouring off the roof and blurring the jungle beyond.

Jason didn't even look at her. He chewed his steamed rice and pinto beans, his eyes fixed on some point in the distance well beyond the curtain of water. His jaw worked furiously as he chewed.

"Well?" Kendal prompted.

"Well what?" He cut her a glance, shoved in another forkful of beans. His voice was nasty, unpleasant—meant, she was certain, to punish her for asking, for trespassing.

But his coldness wouldn't work. Her instincts told her the nightmare was important. And somehow Kendal felt she had had a role in it. It was linked to her, to the things that happened between them during their lovemaking.

"Who is Amy?" she asked one more time.

"This is about that nightmare, I suppose."

"Yes. You kept crying out to someone named Amy. Who is she?"

"That's private."

Kendal stared at his profile. Private? When they'd been making hot, sweaty love right before it happened? How could anything be more private than that? She almost laughed out loud.

"In case you've forgotten, we were sleeping together when you had that dream."

"Oh, I certainly haven't forgotten what we were doing." He set his empty plate aside on the step. "And I imagine you haven't forgotten, either." He gave her a wicked smile as he wrapped a hot palm around the inside of her thigh and moved in to steal a kiss.

But his sexy smoke screen didn't deflect her.

"Didn't you tell me you hadn't had that nightmare in a very long time?"

"Did I?"

"I'm certain you did. And if that's true, don't you think its appearance has some connection to me somehow, to us getting involved like this?"

"I'd like to get *involved* with you again. As soon as possible." He moved in for the kiss a second time.

She avoided his lips by lowering her gaze to his hand, which was pressing into her thigh with blatant sexual urging. His touch probably would have felt great at any other time. "Here's what I remember." She swallowed, working up the courage to speak the truth. "I remember how your eyes looked when you were talking about your high school sweetheart. How'd you put it? Your one and only? And I remember what your eyes looked like while we were making love. And I remember how close you said you felt to me afterward. And then we went to sleep and you had that nightmare. I don't think it's all a big coincidence, do you?"

He extracted his hand from her thigh as if she'd slapped him. "Close? Did I actually use the word *close*?"

Kendal couldn't believe this. She wasn't going to argue semantics with him. She didn't ever have to tell her who this Amy woman was or what had happened if he didn't want to, but she wasn't going to let him deny what had happened between them, either.

"That doesn't sound like a word I'd use. Close," he persisted. "Must have been the tequila talking."

"Don't do that."

"Do what?"

"You're telling me you don't remember any of it? How you felt? What you said?"

"Well, of course, I remember the good parts." The grin he gave her was rakish. Infuriating. He was avoiding something very important with all this sex talk.

"The good parts? Don't you mean—" her voice rose with disbelief and indignation "—the intimate parts?"

"Whoa." He threw up his palms. "What're you getting so worked up about?"

"Listen. In my world you don't do the things we did last night and then act like you hardly know the person the next day. I'm concerned about you because you had a horrible nightmare only hours after we made love, and all you can say is 'it's private'? Making love is about as private as it gets, mister."

"Look." His expression hardened. "We had a great time together, but that doesn't give you the right to crawl inside my head."

She stared at him, openmouthed. She wanted to say something like, *I don't think I even know you.* But that would be ridiculous. Of course she didn't *know* him. That was precisely the point. She'd slept with him, but she didn't know him. Big mistake. She saw that now. It was like a flashing red sign at the edge of a cliff. *Big mistake! Big mistake!* Only she'd already gone over the edge of that cliff. It was a little too late to heed the warning signs. Somehow, she'd put herself on the begging end of a relationship again.

He was looking at her with narrowed eyes that she couldn't quite read.

"Apparently it doesn't give me any right to crawl inside your heart, either."

He took another pull on his Coke to cover the silence. Jason had closed himself off to her. It was as palpable as a dead bolt turning into place.

"Jason, you were hurting. I saw it. Why can't I help you?"

Now he smiled, but it wasn't a warm smile. "You need to learn the difference between sex and psychotherapy, baby."

Was he playing some kind of game? Or was he truly that wounded?

Maybe he really was simply The Wolf, after all. And maybe she'd walked right into his jaws. But the terror in his eyes when he'd been held in the grip of that nightmare had been very real. And his voice had sounded so tortured. Like a lost soul. Strangely young. Hurt. Inside The Wolf, Kendal decided, there was a terrified young man. Who was Amy? Now she wished she'd never asked.

His sardonic grin was replaced by a frown. "Eat your beans, sweetheart." He took another pull on his Coke. "And stop trying to fix stuff that can't be fixed. We've got a long afternoon ahead of us."

That afternoon was, indeed, the longest one yet. Endless rain. Cloying humidity building inside the O.R. pavilion. The damp air trapped under the thatched roof grew fetid with the smell of medications and blood and Jason Bridges's sweat.

Kendal tried not to think about what Jason had said, about the night she'd spent tangled in the sheets on top of that sleeping bag with him, but it seemed impossible when they were literally rubbing elbows all day.

At first she tried to remain professional and calm, tried to let it pass when he snapped at her in Spanish in front of a patient. But the second time he did it, she brought him up short in plain, loud English.

They were between surgeries. Ruth and Angelica were doing post-op recovery on the last one, and Jason and Kendal were supposed to be cleaning the instruments. Jason had stopped to reinforce a child's dressing and threw a roll of tape back at Kendal when she handed him the wrong kind. *"Ése no!"* he snapped. *Not that one!*

"Doctor, I need to speak to you, please," Kendal said when they finished the dressing. "Now."

They stepped over by the scrub basins.

"Do not speak to me with such nastiness in front of the patients," she warned him. "Or ever, for that matter." From across the pavilion, Angelica shot them a quizzical look. Kendal picked up a bottle of alcohol and a stack of four-by-four gauze.

Jason cut Angelica a dismissing glance, then his handsome mouth quirked into a smile. His voice was low. "Sorry. I'll confine my *nastiness* to the times we're alone."

Kendal wanted to slap him. Across the room, she

noticed Angelica wore a worried frown. But Kendal was beyond caring what anybody thought. Except for Jason. She most certainly wanted *him* to know what she thought. She tossed down the gauze she'd begun to saturate with alcohol. "I think I need a break," she said under her breath, "from you."

She turned on her heel and marched across the floorboards, toward freedom and the fresh, rain-soaked air.

"Where are you going?" he said from behind her.

"Angelica can interpret for you." She kept on marching.

"Angelica's English sucks, and she's got other stuff to do," he called after her.

But Kendal dashed out into the weather.

"Hey!" She heard his footsteps on the wooden steps behind her. "Come back here!"

But Kendal marched on toward the jungle, which was blurry through the sheeting rain and her building tears. She didn't know what she would do when she got out there, but she wasn't going to take any more of Jason Bridges's brand of crap.

She reached the edge of the clearing and batted aside the wet fronds of growth as she plunged into the dark shade. She tore down the soggy narrow path for several yards before she stopped, gasping back tears.

How dare he speak disrespectfully to her, especially after they'd slept together!

"Kendal." His voice, a sharp command slashing through the hiss of the rain, startled her.

"Leave me alone!" she called back and headed farther down the path.

"Wait!"

She heard his footsteps splashing in the puddles, heard thrashing as he knocked aside foliage, getting closer.

She took off running again, but the path quickly dwindled, and she was forced to slow her pace as she clawed at the undergrowth.

"You'll get lost, you stupid woman!" His voice sounded like it was receding behind her.

That made her come up short. What if she really did get lost? Without the sun, she had no sense of direction. He was right, but she'd spend the night out here with the snakes before she'd let him treat her like crap.

"Kendal!" he called again.

All right. They could just have it out, right here in this rainy jungle. She didn't give a big green bean what Jason Bridges thought anymore. She turned, squared her shoulders, blocked the path.

When he came around the bend, she saw his anger, heard his rapid breathing. His hair was plastered to his forehead as water ran in rivulets down his face. He raked it back as he stepped up to her. He was practically soaked to the skin.

"What do you think you're doing?" he rasped between breaths. "Even the natives get lost out here, especially when there's no sun to orient you."

"Just leave me alone." She swiped the rain—and the tears—from her eyes while trying to calm down.

"Believe me, I'd like nothing better, but unfortunately, I feel responsible for your little butt." He mopped the rain off his face angrily.

"How dare you speak to me that way?"

"How dare you run out of the O.R. that way?"

"And how dare you talk to me like that in front of Angelica and the patients." When she'd spat out "patients," rainwater sprayed from her lips.

"Look." He heaved a big sigh. "I don't treat you any differently than I treat anybody else."

"Exactly. And that would be like crap, *Doctor*. I'm beginning to think that's why you come down here every year."

"What in the hell are you talking about?"

"You get to be a little god down here. Passing out candy." She spat water droplets with each word. "You feel free to treat these people like the ants at the bottom of one of those Mayan pyramids." She pointed in the direction of the Palenque ruins. "Down here, you're the mighty Doctor Jason—" she went on while his eyes blazed at her through the pouring rain "—the savior, with his magic hands and his limited lottery. Down here, you don't have to worry about disguising the fact that you are basically just a rude asshole."

Jason's jaw tightened and he squinted at her. "Nice theory." He raked a hand through his rain-soaked hair again. "But it won't wash, excuse my pun." He ran a hand like a squeegee over his face. "I don't need to come all the way down to Mexico to get my ego stroked, because I happen to be the mighty Doctor Jason back home, too.''

Her eyes widened at his arrogance before she turned away in disgust.

But he grabbed her arm and spun her around.

''Take your hand off of me.'' She turned her face away, closed her eyes tight against him.

He released her arm.

All around them, rain pattered against jungle leaves in a steady, foreign-sounding *shushurush* that reminded Kendal just how far from Oklahoma she really was.

''Look,'' she heard him say. ''You can think whatever you want about me.''

''Oh, I will.'' She opened her eyes and looked up into his in challenge.

His eyes shone steely blue in the misty light, and she could read remorse in their depths. But not enough to satisfy her wounded pride.

''I don't have time for this, and neither do you,'' he continued. ''We have a job to do. Now let's get back there and do it.'' He grabbed her elbow again.

When she stiffened at his touch, he loosened his fingers and tried a gentler tack. ''Listen. We're both tired and saying things we don't really mean.''

''Oh, I meant what I said.'' Kendal kept her voice lethally quiet. ''I think you're an asshole.''

''Fine. Think it. But the patients still need us. Now come on.'' He pulled on her arm.

''Stop ordering me around.'' She took off down the path again.

"Kendal! You are acting like a child!"

But she only picked up her pace, jogging in splashy steps down the twisting trail. The path branched again and she lurched off into one fork. How deep could she go into this thicket before she actually got lost? She decided to note landmarks, but the foliage was all starting to look so...*same.*

A startled howler monkey came shrieking out of a sapodilla tree. Big as a chimpanzee, the animal flew down into Kendal's path like a furry streak. Kendal screamed and fell back.

"Kendal!" Jason yelled.

She lay in the mud with her hand on her heart, gasping. This humid air! Unbelievable. Like breathing underwater. The screaming monkey had disappeared into the thicket.

Jason knocked dense foliage out of his way and fell to one knee beside her. "Are you all right?" His worried expression totally disarmed her. "Did he hurt you?"

"I'm fine. Just a little muddy." She swiped her hair out of her eyes and succeeded in smearing mud on her face.

"You're sure?" He rasped out each breath, winded from the humidity and the chase. His hands seemed to be everywhere on her, touching her shoulders, arms, hips, ankles, brushing the mud from her forehead.

"Yes. He ran in the opposite direction."

"Can you stand up?"

She nodded and he helped her get up.

"Listen." He put out both hands in supplication. "You're right. I'm an asshole. And I'm sorry."

She stared down at those hands. Those hands that had given her so much pleasure the night before. Those incredible hands would surely be her downfall.

"I had absolutely no right to snap at you," he continued, "or at anybody, for that matter."

She knew she had to keep their bodies apart, or even in the pouring rain in the middle of a jungle they'd be doomed. "I was probably overreacting. It's just that I've had it with this god-awful place!" She was trying to wipe the rain and mud from her face with her shirttails, which were too dirty to do much good.

"I don't blame you. I get worn down, too. Then I don't know what gets into me. All I can think about is getting the next surgery done, and the next, and the next, and then I push too hard. Ask anybody on my staff. But that doesn't excuse my rudeness. I shouldn't talk to anybody that way. Ever. Particularly you. Please. Come back to the pavilion."

He reached for her, but when his warm fingers dug insistently into the chilled damp flesh of her upper arm, she had to pull away. She couldn't—could *not*— let this go.

This wasn't about his rude behavior. It was about the way he'd shut her out at lunch, and even before that, right after he'd had the dream.

"Jason, what do I mean to you?"

"I...you know I need you...."

For a minute she thought he meant physically, perhaps even emotionally, but when he went on she realized he was evading her real question by talking about their work.

"Ruth's Spanish is of the high school variety and Angelica's English sounds like something from another planet. You're the only one who can do both well. Your role here is crucial to our mission. Things will get bogged down without you here. Things will get too crazy."

"That's not what I mean and you know it. How do you feel about me?"

"How can you ask that? After last night?"

"Why wouldn't I ask, after the way you've been treating me?"

She'd almost said "today," but she wasn't just talking about the incident today. She meant in general. In general, Jason had not been treating her the way she wanted to be treated by a man who had just become her lover. But was she being fair? She accosted herself. His reason for coming here was to help these people, not to court a woman. And he worked harder than anyone else on the team. The fact that the two of them had become lovers was purely an accident. Or was it? She was so confused.

"Angelica's right. I can be an *asqueroso* sometimes. Like I said, it's not right, but sometimes the stress just gets the best of me."

"We've dealt with that." She turned away from him.

He stepped up behind her and tried to wrap his arms around her shoulders but she stiffened. "Then what's wrong?" He brought his face around close to hers. He looked like a vulnerable boy. "I can tell you're still mad at me. Please let me hold you," he begged. "Please. We're just tired. We didn't get much sleep last night."

She didn't know whether to be angry or to melt into his arms. When he tried to wrap them tighter around her, she sank against him. Somewhere along the way, it had stopped raining, but Kendal only just now noticed the profound silence that surrounded them as they embraced on the jungle path.

They were both steamy with rain and sweat, but it absolutely did not matter. Kendal felt a hum, a singing, start along her veins as he pressed his lips to her damp temple. "Thank you," he murmured.

Kendal closed her eyes. The smell of his damp shirt, his warm throat, was intoxicating to her.

They were standing in a wide, unshaded place in the path. The low afternoon sun had broken through the dense canopy overhead. Above them, exotic birds called out, flitting to and fro, high in the dripping trees.

Kendal opened her eyes and stared down at the soaked gray-green leaves packed on the muddy jungle floor, and thought she was in the most remote place on earth. She looked up into Jason's serious blue eyes, and it seemed that they were suddenly radiant, on fire. Maybe it was the strange jungle light. Whatever it was, he appeared to glow as he held her in the circle of new golden sunshine.

"Kendal." His voice grew hushed, husky, as he

pulled her to him and spoke against her temple, as he rubbed his rough chin against her cheek. "I can't keep my hands off you. I wish we hadn't started this down here, where I don't have the time for you that I'd like to have." He lowered his head and planted a hot kiss at the corner of her mouth. Softly, he slid his mouth fully over hers. Their lips clung gently for one beating second, then quickly fused as tongue met hungry tongue. Then they turned heads to taste again, more forcefully.

He had swallowed hard just before the second crush of contact, as if his throat had tightened with emotion. He had spoken, too. Her name. "Kendal." An entreaty. A plea. Now his mouth told her that those signals had meant what she knew they must—her name had new meaning to him. He was becoming emotionally involved with her, whether he liked it or not.

The kiss grew deeper, far more fierce. He cupped his hands tightly around her buttocks and slammed her body up to meet his. When his hot mouth moved down to devour her neck, she rasped out, "Jason!" and this time it was she who had formed his name into a plea.

"Yes, sweetheart." He pressed her body tighter and worked his mouth down to the vee of her halter top. "Tell me. Tell me exactly what you want. Anything."

"You," she breathed. "What I want is *you*."

"And I want you." His breathing was harsh as he kissed the snowy white skin he had exposed at the tops of her breasts. "Come with me…this evening," he breathed between kisses. "Be with me…again."

At this very moment, Kendal wanted to say yes, but she knew that within an hour, when her body had cooled down, when he wasn't touching her like this, or if he started acting distant and harsh again, that her yes would turn into a no. She remembered a saying her grandmother had taught her, *Let your yes be yes and your no be no.*

He must have sensed her hesitation and loosened his passionate hold, letting his arms relax into a gentle embrace with his palms supporting her back.

"Kendal, I've gotta be honest. I've never felt this way before and it scares me."

"Because of losing——" she took a chance "—Amy?"

He studied her eyes, then nodded.

"What happened?"

"I can't talk about it and then go back in there and do surgery. Just believe me when I say that I've tried to love before, and it didn't work. I'm not sure I can ever love again. Kendal, don't get attached to me. I'm no good for you."

She clung to him, with her arms around his neck, tilting her head back, shaking it *no*. No. He had to at least try, to at least give them a chance to fall in love. Was it love? She knew she had definitely never felt this way before. Or was it merely chemistry? Merely physical attraction—this amazing sexual heat between them? She had definitely never felt that before, either.

"I don't think I can be with a man who can't love me." She told herself she was being courageous, telling him the truth. But in her heart she knew she was being a coward. She couldn't be with him and she couldn't be without him. She wanted it both ways.

He dropped his arms and took her hand. "Okay. I can accept whatever you decide."

"It's not that I don't want you… I just…"

"It's okay, sweetheart. I've never coerced a woman. And I never will. It's entirely up to you now that you know the truth about me. We have to get back to the patients." He tilted his head back and studied the sparkling green foliage above them. "Good thing the sun came out. I wasn't exactly sure where we were before."

"You mean we really could have gotten lost out here?"

"Get real." He smiled his old wolfish smile as he led her back down the path, taking the forks in all the right places and with absolutely no hesitation. The man had an unerring sense of direction, Kendal mused, except when it came to relationships.

"Are you going to be grumpy when we get back in there?"

"I will be grumpy no more forever." He threw her a sheepish smile. They both knew it was likely a lie. But right now he was holding her hand, most warmly, most protectively, as he led her along the jungle path.

"Only two more surgeries left today," he said cheerfully now that the fragile peace between them was restored. "And then I've got a surprise for you."

THE SURPRISE came back from San Cristóbal with Ben Jason had given him the cash to buy crayons and paper and scissors and glue and storybooks and building blocks, and even a small CD player and children's CDs. Enough for all of the children, but Kendal knew Jason had been thinking of Miguel first.

The two of them were sitting on the bed in Kendal's room, playing with the toddler when Ruth came bursting in. "Chief, we've got a problem with Mr. Alvarez's wound."

"Mr. Alvarez?" Kendal said. "You mean you did surgery on him?"

"I'll be there in a sec, Ruth."

"Even though he didn't draw a number?" Kendal persisted.

Ruth left and Jason faced Kendal. "Yeah. I worked him in. And because he didn't draw a number, I'd like to keep it quiet."

"When?" She knew Jason had surgeries scheduled from dawn to dusk.

"This morning before sunup."

"You did his surgery by those crappy portable lights?"

"I squinted a lot."

Kendal couldn't believe he could make jokes like this after he'd made love to her all night, and then stayed awake to do surgery on that poor old man. No wonder he'd been grumpy. And if Jason did a surgery, that meant the rest of the team had lost sleep as well. "Why wasn't I told?" she said. "I could have helped."

Instead he had walked her back to the hotel and practically tucked her into bed.

"Which is exactly why I didn't want you to know. You don't need to be up all night, working yourself to death."

"Why not?" she countered. "I can handle it if the rest of you can."

"When you're burning the candle at both ends already, taking care of Miguel? You need your rest, Sleeping Beauty." He smiled. "Especially now that the Prince has kissed you awake."

CHAPTER TWELVE

ANGELICA SOUGHT Kendal out while Jason and Ruth were out tending to Mr. Alvarez.

"It was nice of Jason to bring the kids these things," Angelica said.

Kendal could tell that the tall Mayan woman had something else on her mind. "Jason's a nice guy," she said.

"He's a complicated guy."

Kendal didn't pretend not to know what Angelica was talking about. "You don't think I should be getting involved with him."

"I don't think you know what you are getting into here."

"How well do you know Jason?" Kendal asked. She sincerely wanted to know.

"We never got involved as lovers, if that's what you're wondering. But I've been his friend ever since his first trip to Mexico. And I've watched him go through a lot of women. And I know some things about him that you should know.."

Kendal waited in silence.

"Did he tell you about his girlfriend? The one who died?"

Kendal's heart sped up. "You mean Amy?"

"Yes. Amy. She didn't just die. She killed herself." Kendal sucked in a breath, shook her head in disbelief.

"His family owned a big house in Dallas. Jason was a star football player...and a bit of a wild boy, a party boy. I am told *Norteamericano* kids are quite spoiled."

"Some are," Kendal said. Coming to Mexico had made her see that she had been a little spoiled herself.

"The big house caught fire one night when Jason and Amy had sneaked out to a party. Jason's *madre* and *padre* were home, though. When Jason and Amy drove up, the house was already in flames. He thought his parents were still inside. He tried to go in after them. Somehow—I never got the full story, he was telling it from the bottom of a bottle of tequila, after all—Jason went in and Amy followed him." Angelica sighed heavily.

"He escaped unharmed, but Amy was badly burned, badly disfigured. She couldn't live with her face like that. Two years later, at about the same time Jason's parents were in the process of getting a divorce, Amy took an overdose of her mother's sleeping pills."

"Oh, Angelica." Kendal shook her head again. The story was far worse than she had imagined. This was the source of Jason's driven behavior...and his cold detachment.

"I don't know why I'm telling you this. Jason will be mad as hell if he finds out. I think he only told me because I'm safe, way down here in Mexico where I can't tell nobody. Except in all the time I know him, I never seen Jason acting the way he has about you. I never seen him look at anybody the way he looks at you. I just thought you should know.''

''I'm glad you told me,'' Kendal said. ''It helps me understand him.'' But at the same time she was thinking that understanding Jason was one thing. Loving him, and *being loved* by him, was quite another.

''HAS THE LITTLE BOY'S MOTHER come back at all?'' Jason asked Kendal after they had completed two more days of surgery.

Miguel was busy coloring, clutching a crayon with his webbed fingers. Kendal thought his drawings were amazing for a child his age. She could see crude figures in the pictures. But Kendal worried sometimes as she watched the boy slash violently at the paper with a red crayon, yelling.

Kendal shook her head sadly. ''I'm afraid you were right about her.''

''I don't even wanna touch this kid without an operative permit of some kind, and I want a parent in the vicinity after the surgery.''

''What if she doesn't come back?''

Jason made a sour face. ''Then I guess you'll have to adopt him.''

''I just might.'' Kendal wasn't kidding. She was getting more attached to Miguel with each passing hour.

"I told you, Kendal. Don't get attached. These children need to stay with their people."

For two days Kendal had watched for some sign of Lucia, hoping she'd at least show herself at the edge of the jungle. When she asked a couple of the older women from the village about the young mother, Miguel reached up and grabbed for the medal.

"This was hers." Kendal held the medal up for them to see.

The women reacted to the sight of the unique medal with horror.

"The daughter of Vajaras," one of them said and covered her mouth.

"Who?" Kendal asked, though she was sure she heard the name correctly.

But the *curanderas* wouldn't answer. They had started to back away from Miguel as if he were possessed, and they refused to say another word.

Kendal asked Ben to find out everything he could about this Vajaras. She had to know more about him.

"A terrible man. A criminal," Ben told her the next day. "He hides up there. In the mountains. He terrorizes the people out in the villages. Miguel is his grandchild. That's why the locals shun him, I suspect. Lucia wasn't supposed to bring him here. Vajaras wouldn't want this surgery to be done. He doesn't even want the child seen in the village."

"Why?"

"The rumor is, he looks like his grandson, has some of the same defects. The indigenous people think the child is cursed."

When Kendal went to Jason and told him this, his jaw tightened. He turned to Ruth. "We're doing his surgery first thing in the morning. You'll have to help," he told Kendal.

"I'll do anything you say," she responded.

They started Miguel's surgery as soon as the sun was fully up. Jason repaired the tiny hands quickly enough.

"He's holding up well?" he asked Angelica.

"Great."

Jason went on to repair the maxilla and tiny nose. Though she'd gotten used to the sight of blood in the past week, Kendal still found aspects of the surgery upsetting. But she steeled herself and did whatever she could to help Jason and Ruth under these crude conditions. Despite the impediments, Jason did his job with elegant precision.

"How's he doing?" He checked in with Angelica, who was monitoring Miguel's pulse and blood pressure every few minutes.

"He's a little tiger."

"Then we'll go ahead and finish his little palate and lips," he said to Kendal.

The final repairs went beautifully.

"To do the work on his eye sockets, I'm afraid I'd have to have him back at Integris," he told Kendal when the surgery was done.

"I wish we could take him home with us."

Jason eyed her compassionately. "I don't think his mother is coming back."

Kendal shook her head, wishing it weren't so.

In the days ahead the team became like Miguel's family. Every detail of their most challenging patient's care was endlessly weighed, discussed at every meal, during every free moment. Gauging the dosage of Paroveen particularly was difficult. On a child as young as Miguel it was very fine-tuned. By the third day he was showing some discoloration.

"We still need to increase it," Jason said.

"But it's untested at such high doses," Kendal argued.

"I can't let the edema get too severe."

Kendal nursed the toddler night and day, and though he was cranky and combative, he seemed to be healing well. But on the third post-op day, Miguel spiked a raging fever.

Kendal was deep into the first sound sleep she'd had in days when someone shook her awake. "*Chica! El bebé!* They take him."

"What?"

"The child. They take him away. Because of the blood mark," she whispered.

Kendal swung out of the bed, slipped on her sandals and jogged down the hall.

In the dim room, two of the local nurses were standing over Miguel, who lay red-faced and limp. One was rubbing Miguel's thin little legs with an old bone while the other balled up the edges of his sheet, preparing to lift his tiny body off the cot and carry him away. "We have to get him away from the others," the first one said.

"The baby is burning," the other one said, and crossed herself, "for the sins of the grandfather."

"Stop!" Kendal pushed their hands away and reached to feel Miguel's purplish forehead.

"The blood mark!" one of the women cried and snatched Kendal's arm back.

Anger sluiced through Kendal when she realized the superstitious women had done nothing to help Miguel because of their irrational fear of his discoloration. "The purple marking is from the drug we've given him! *Llame al médico*," she ordered and got to work sponging Miguel. *Go get the doctor.*

But the women only shook their heads and backed up. "The mother, now the child," one of them said.

"What are you talking about?" Kendal demanded.

"His mother. Found dead in the jungle."

Kendal wanted to burst into tears at this awful news, but instead she stared at the woman and forced herself to be strong. "Go get the damned doctor. Now."

The women disappeared.

Soon Jason ran into the room and Kendal said, "Could the fever be another reaction to the increased Paroveen?"

"More likely a post-op infection." Immediately he set to work restarting Miguel's IV.

While Kendal held Miguel on her lap and sponged him, Jason changed the dressings, checking the incisions for infection. Finally, after an hour of such efforts, the child's fever started to come down.

"You have surgeries in the morning," Kendal said.

"I'll stay with him now."

"I'll sleep in here." Jason brought a sleeping bag and slept on the tile floor.

Kendal tended Miguel all through that night. In the wee hours her humming woke Jason up. Through slitted eyes he watched Kendal, sitting on the edge of the cot with Miguel in her arms. She rocked the child, soothing him with her humming and a cool cloth that she dipped in a basin beside her. Her hair was a mess, she had dark circles under her eyes and her thin T-shirt was dirty and soaked. Through it, Jason could clearly see her breasts, her nipples. And as she held the baby with such tenderness and devotion he felt his heart melting.

She looked up at him and saw that he was awake.

"He finally drank a little Coke." She smiled.

Jason thought he had never seen anything so beautiful in his entire life.

THE NEXT DAY Kendal came down with the fever herself.

Angelica dashed to fetch Jason. "It's an autochthonous virus, probably. I see it all the time," she said.

"I agree." He hurried to the alcohol basins, disinfecting his hands.

"The little boy is already bouncing back, but Kendal, she got no resistance the way the child did."

Jason turned to Angelica. "I'll take care of her myself. Put the rest of today's surgeries on hold."

He found Kendal lost in the same fevered sleep that had gripped Miguel the night before.

He closed the shutters in the room and ordered Angelica to leave.

"I got resistance," she countered in a whisper. "What about you?"

"It's my fault she's here. I feel responsible for her." He didn't take his eyes off Kendal as he spoke. "I should never have talked her into coming to Mexico where her health would be endangered."

"You could not know this would happen."

"Bring me some IV supplies. I should never have brought this woman down here." *And, I should never have let myself get attached to her.*

But during the long, hot vigil at Kendal's bedside, Jason found himself at her mercy.

All of his hands-on ministrations—starting the IV in her delicate arm, sponging her beautiful body, threading his hands in her hair while he lifted her head to make her sip water, counting the rise and fall of her chest while he checked her shallow respirations—all of these things only bound him tighter to the woman.

With each passing hour he watched her sleeping face, and her features were etched more deeply into his mind.

But it was her feverish words about Miguel that tore at him most, that finally stole his heart completely.

"Where is Miguel?" She repeated again and again as she tossed and turned. "Did his mother come?"

On the second day Kendal grew so agitated that Jason agreed to let Ruth bring Miguel to her bedside. They lay the toddler down next to her. Miguel, now fairly recovered and taking nourishment, patted Kendal's face with his bandaged hands, his little eyes smiling around his bulky dressings. Though weak, Kendal looked immediately relieved, revived somehow to see that Miguel was doing better. As she laid her head back with tears leaking from the corners of her eyes, Jason realized that, at last, he had found his treasure.

"WHAT DO YOU MEAN, the child is ill?" Benicio Vajaras paced beside his enormous dining table.

"An old *curandera* from Chamula told me she saw him nearly dead with the fever." Flaco was sick of watching all this spying and telling. He was sick of watching the gringo doctor playing games with his gringa whore.

"This old woman knew who the child was?"

"Many have seen him. Many knew. But this one saw Lucia's medal on the neck of the woman taking care of the child."

Vajaras cursed. "My willful daughter. So stupid. I should never have let her set foot off the hacienda."

"The gringo doctor, he worked on Miguel—"

"I told you never to say his name again. I don't want to hear about the bastard son of the stinking Zapatista snake who got my daughter pregnant."

"*Disculpe,*" Flaco apologized. "But what I must

tell you is very important. *El Médico norte-americano*, he fixed the child's face."

Vajaras's eyebrows shot up with interest.

"I do not see the child's face yet." Flaco swiped a hand in the vicinity of his own face. "The bandages, you understand. But the workers at the old hotel, they say this man, he is a miracle worker.

"One other thing, *El Capitán*, there are many drugs in this jungle hospital."

"I don't want to touch the things. We get the *Amer-icano Federales* on our necks that way, stealing American pharmaceuticals. You Chiapas hillbillies are blind in your greed. If we rob one of their clinics, the Doctors Without Borders people might sic the internationals on us."

"No, *Capitán*. This doctor is not with them. He is alone. We could take the place."

"I see." Vajaras tapped his recessed chin while his deformed lips curled into a deformed smile. "In that case, perhaps the drugs would be useful after all. We could get to this grandchild of mine that way. I don't want a hair on his little head harmed. The child could come in very handy, very soon."

"I don't understand, *Capitán*."

"You told me this gringa is fond of the baby and the gringo doctor and this woman are lovers?"

"*Sí*."

"Then I want my grandchild back. We may need him."

THE VIRULENT INFECTION that had ravaged Kendal's body had caused her to lose weight. Her waist, waspish to begin with, had almost disappeared in profile. Jason resorted to tricks to get her to eat. He sent Ben into San Cristóbal to find anything American. Today it was to be fried chicken, her favorite.

"You sure you can spare me?" Ben questioned. The team was already busy to distraction that day, trying to catch up on the surgeries Jason had delayed while he took care of Kendal.

"Go. She has to eat. Take Viljo's Jeep. It handles the roads at higher speeds."

No sooner had Ben disappeared over the top of the jungle road than the robbers appeared, seemingly out of nowhere. Three men wearing dirty ski masks and soiled kerchiefs in the sweltering jungle heat. They pointed assault rifles from the doorway of the pavilion, and in Spanish a grossly obese man told everyone to freeze and raise their hands.

"Shit," Jason cursed. He was up to his elbows in a complicated resection of a burn contracture and it pissed him off to no end that these pigs would come busting in here like this.

Ruth threw a sterile towel on the patient's wounds and angled her upper body to shield the unconscious man on the table.

"Give us all of your drugs," the fat one ordered.

"You gotta be kiddin' me, man," Jason muttered in English.

The other two bandits were already patrolling the room, quickly checking each patient in each bed. The ones who weren't drugged had raised their hands.

"Get away from my patients," Jason ordered in Spanish as he lifted his bloodied gloves and angled himself between Ruth and the line of fire. He was grateful that Kendal and Miguel were over at the hotel. "What do you want?" he asked in his most careful Spanish. "I have a very critical patient here."

"The drugs," the fat one repeated.

Angelica pointed to the key ring at her waist. "I need to open the lockbox."

"Do it," the fat man said.

While Angelica unlocked the narcotics, the masked man jerked the gun at the Merrill Jackson boxes beneath one table. "What's that stuff?"

"Vaccines. Antibiotics. No use to you," Angelica answered. She handed him the narcotics.

"*Flaco!*" the tall one called to his comrade after he'd seen every patient. "He is not here."

"Miguel Vajaras—" the fat bandit swung his gun on Jason "—where is he?"

"You have no business with any of these patients," Jason took a step, but the bandit waved the gun.

"That one *is* our business. He is one of us. A Zapatista child. We will take him."

Above her surgical mask, Jason saw Ruth's eyes flash toward the hotel before she bit her lip and looked down at the patient on the table again.

"Go." The tall one pointed his gun barrel to the hotel. "There."

The three men clamored down the wooden steps. When Jason ran after them and yelled, "Stop!" the hind gunman turned and fired a round at Jason's feet.

They disappeared into the hotel as Jason darted back into the pavilion, stripping off his bloody gloves. Frantically he dug out his gun from his supply bag. He dashed outside, staying low as he approached the hotel.

The sound of Kendal's hysterical cries and Miguel's wailing propelled him inside. In the lobby, a few steps up the stairs, she was being held back by one of the masked robbers while another attempted to wrench Miguel from her arms. The third aimed his gun at the group.

"Let the kid go," Jason said in Spanish as he aimed the gun. The one not holding Kendal whirled around at the sound of Jason's voice and fired at him again. Jason dodged and fired back, sending the man sprawling backward on the stairs and grabbing at his shoulder.

In the same instant, the other robbers succeeded in ripping the screaming Miguel from Kendal's arms. She fought back like a tigress, but the man grabbed her by the waist and hauled her along with him.

Jason lurched forward, ready to shoot again, but the man was using Miguel and Kendal as shields. One bandit held a gun to the back of Kendal's head while the other pulled his wounded comrade to his feet.

"Give us the child—" Jason bargained while he kept his gun trained on the men "—and I'll supply you with all the drugs you need. I'll give you everything we have in reserve, plus I can ship even more from the States."

"No," the fat one spoke rapid-fire in Spanish, "we

don't leave without this child. He belongs with his people. Put the gun down, Doctor, or we bring back more men and kill every one in this compound. All the volunteers. All the patients."

Miguel, who had only recently started to speak, gave a terrified cry that sounded like, "Chancho," while he stared at the masked face of the fat man.

Jason began to feel a snake of tension in his gut about this whole business, a suspicion that went beyond his immediate terror. These were not Zapatistas. Why did these men have such an interest in one skinny toddler who was going to require complex medical care for many years to come? The eyes of the short fat one seemed familiar, but Jason could not think where he'd seen the man. "What did he say?," he asked Kendal, to make sure he understood the bandit's terms, that he was doing as they asked.

Kendal's face was contorted, her eyes wide as she, too, studied the fat man. "He called him a pig."

"No, before that," Jason urged.

"If we don't let them take Miguel—" her voice broke ", —they'll attack the clinic and kill us all. They want you to put your gun down."

Jason knew they meant their threat. There had been massacres, uprisings, violence and tension in this region for years. He could not endanger all of these innocent people for the sake of one child, even if he was the child Kendal loved. Slowly, he lowered his gun to the tile floor.

"No!" Kendal clutched at Miguel, who tried to

hook his tiny arms around her neck. "*Mi Mamá!*" the toddler cried.

The men shoved Kendal back as they tugged Miguel from her grasping arms yet again.

"Kendal, let him go," Jason said in a level voice. He came up behind her and clamped one arm across her shoulders, strong-arming her around the waist with the other and pulling her back. "The struggle might tear his suture lines."

Kendal and Miguel continued to reach for each other with outstretched arms, but Jason held her back.

"Miguel!" she sobbed, dissolving into tears as the men ran off.

Jason held her tightly and stroked her hair, turning her to his chest, trying to console her. "There was nothing else we could do."

"But he's Lucia's child," she wailed. "And I told her I would take care of him."

"He also has a father somewhere. Maybe these men know him."

"What if he's the one who killed Lucia?" Her eyes blazed with accusation. "Those men are obviously monsters. Criminals. Threatening to kill helpless patients. They probably won't even take care of Miguel. They won't see that his wounds heal properly."

"You don't know that, Kendal. Just because they have stolen, that doesn't mean they will mistreat Miguel. There are some traditional Maya medicine men in the highlands."

Angelica and Ruth came running in. Viljo emerged from his hiding place.

"You have got to leave pronto, *El Médico*," Viljo urged as he rushed forward. "And take your nurses with you. The presence of the americanos is dangerous."

"I'm afraid he's right," Angelica agreed. "You got to leave immediately. And we'll have to move these patients back to town or send them home with their families. Those weren't Zapatistas. They were thugs pretending to be Zapatistas, wanting to intimidate the people. They do it all the time. And now that you've shot one of them they'll be back to get even and use that to stir up more trouble among the factions."

"What about Ben?" Ruth argued. There was no answer on Ben's cell phone. He was apparently not where he could get a signal.

"What about Miguel?" Kendal's face was tear-streaked and her expression was wild, nearly hysterical. "I won't just *leave* him."

"Angelica's right. We have to go," Jason agreed.

"But I must finish closing that burn resection."

"I'll close the surgery," Angelica said. "It won't be the first time I play doctor. We'll get word to Ben to stay with the missionaries in San Cristóbal."

Except for quickly grabbing and wiping Jason's instruments, they had no time to load the medical supplies. Viljo wouldn't even allow them to gather personal belongings out of the hotel. Jason was yelling last-minute instructions about the patients to Angelica even as he boarded the van.

The young driver Alejandro looked wild with fright

as he steered the careening vehicle back to the main highway.

It wasn't until they were airborne from Tuxtla Gutiérrez that Jason began to sense Kendal's very real withdrawal from him. Ever since takeoff she had clutched the St. Lucia medal, running it back and forth on its long chain, staring out the window at the breathtaking scenery below, saying nothing.

"Kendal," he started, "I'm sorry about Miguel—"

"*Chancho*," she whispered. "That's the word Lucia used that night in the cave. Why would they want the child?"

Jason was afraid to answer that one. Despite what he'd said about the boy's father and the "good" medicine men in the jungle, he feared the worst for Miguel. In the surgery pavilion, the fat man had said Miguel's last name was Vajaras. Was the child being taken to Benicio Vajaras? The man was notorious for using children to further his evil plans but Jason wasn't about to put such worries into Kendal's mind.

"I don't know," he answered truthfully.

"I don't blame you for what happened." She seemed to be far away as she spoke. "I blame Mexico. I wish I'd never come to this godforsaken place." She stared at the mountains.

"But if you hadn't come here—" Jason tried to console her "—we might not have found each other."

He hoped it wasn't too late to admit how much that meant to him.

But Kendal shocked him when she said, "That's

the worst part. What was the point? For us, there'll never be a future." She glanced at him, emitting a sudden burst of air as if seeing something for the first time. "You warned me not to get attached, didn't you? To you or Miguel." She looked out the window again, away from him. "I should have listened to you, Jason. And I should never have come to Mexico."

CHAPTER THIRTEEN

BACK IN OKLAHOMA, the story of their narrow escape from Chiapan insurgents was told and retold in the local media over the next several days. Jason's picture was even on the front page of the *Daily Oklahoman*. He was touted as the renegade doctor who had been a hero in more ways than one.

Jason made his usual jokes to the reporters, to his staff, to his admiring but faintly envious colleagues. The hospital's media coordinator had fielded some interviews and TV live shots, grouping them to conserve Jason's time and energy.

The media coordinator also asked Kendal and Ruth to appear at each one. Kendal dreaded seeing Jason again. But she used the opportunity to make some heartfelt statements for the cameras about the urgent plight of the children in Chiapas. All the while she had to make an effort of will not to make eye contact with Jason, standing next to her.

But even if she managed not to look at Jason, Kendal could feel the heat, the physical longing, radiating off of him.

"I can't do this anymore," she said when the camera lights went off after another session.

"The media storm will die down soon," Jason said.

"I don't mean press conferences. I mean I can't see you. It's tearing me apart."

He claimed that he didn't understand, wondered why being together wasn't enough.

"I told you, because for us there is no future. For us, there's no happily ever after."

They only saw each other a few more times after that, and only from a distance in the hospital corridors. They spoke once, after Kendal started getting regular e-mails from Ben. She let Jason know that Ben was okay and had decided to stay in Mexico to work as a missionary.

Jason tried to call her, leaving messages on her machine. She was screening her calls, of course, and didn't allow his to make the cut. Still, he left message after message, hoping to wear her down. But for some reason he couldn't tell her what she needed to hear. None of the messages said, "I love you. You are my one and only."

Kendal would see his number on Caller ID or "Dr. Jason Bridges" in the Sender column of an e-mail and her heart would fall. The subject line always read, "Talk to me."

At first she opened them, but the setup he seemed to be proposing—can't we still be friends…and lovers?—was not what she wanted. Kendal knew that she was transformed. Her experience with Miguel had taught her that she was the type of person who gave her whole heart. She couldn't go back to living a safe half-life now. No compromises. She wished for the same for Jason eventually, but in the meantime she was certain she couldn't have a relationship on his limited terms.

Still, it was painful to think about him. It got to the point where even thinking of the name Jason was painful. She erased all the messages, dumped all the e-mails and tried to be strong. He was the right man in every way but one.

WHAT WAS LOVE? Jason argued with himself. So many women had tried to trap him into marriage in the name of "love." But Kendal wasn't "so many women."

Kendal was Kendal. Over and over, he tried to figure out what had happened to his heart when it came to Kendal Collins. Had he lost it…or had he found it?

He tried to forget what happened in Mexico. All of it. Mexico was Mexico, he told himself. A weird place where weird stuff happened. He couldn't know how he truly felt about Kendal Collins until he had tested their relationship in a more normal environment.

And for that, they'd need to be at least friends, and he had to admit to himself, if he had his way he'd like to be lovers, too. He'd never wanted a woman so bad. But commitment? That was scary. Somewhere deep in Jason's heart, commitment equaled pain. More pain than he cared to think about.

The kind of pain amplified many times that Kendal Collins was causing him already.

He gave up trying to contact her. A man could only stand so much outright rejection.

But once, he was caught off guard when he saw her

wrestling her little luggage cart onto an elevator in the doctor's tower. He rushed to help, lab coat flapping, and came face-to-face with her just as the doors started to close. Their eyes met for one full second before the cold metal doors slid shut between them. To him it seemed that more pain and longing and meaning were exchanged in that split second than in a thousand years of ordinary human discourse.

"Kendal, wait," he had said at the last millisecond, but she had lowered her eyes, refusing to press the "doors open" button. When the doors touched he wanted to pound them to bits.

As the weeks passed, he sank to a new low—pumping their mutual acquaintances and friends, especially Ruth, for updates about Kendal.

"I wouldn't say she's actually happy," Ruth allowed one day as they stood side by side at the deep sinks outside of surgery, performing their routine scrub with Betadine-saturated brushes.

"Why's that?" He focused on his scrub strokes, trying to act casual, although when it came to Kendal Collins, his feelings were anything but.

"Oh, it's hard to put my finger on it." Ruth's brush strokes became slower, more rhythmic as she thought about his question. "There's a sadness about her. Maybe she still hasn't gotten over having to leave Miguel behind like that. She really had made up her mind to rescue him, you know, after she found out that Lucia was dead."

"She told you that?" Jason tossed his scrubber into the trash and started rinsing.

"I was helping her check into an adoption. We found out the process was going to be ridiculously expensive. But you know Kendal. She hasn't given up. She's saving money, scaling back her lifestyle, selling her town house, stuff like that. She says she's going to go back to Mexico to find him someday."

"That's crazy." Jason held his dripping hands aloft.

Ruth shrugged and did the same. "Maybe. Or maybe what's eating her isn't about Miguel at all. Maybe it's because she's working too hard. Something's making her unhappy. Not that she doesn't have her act together. She does. She looks good lately. She *really* does. All that weight she lost in Mexico? She's determined to keep it off. I see her at the gym all the time."

His head snapped around. The Integris gym! Of course. He'd forgotten that all the drug reps bought memberships there. He could pretend to run into her at the gym. "When?"

"Jason." Ruth gave him a reproachful glance as she pitched her voice lower. At work Ruth always called him *Doctor*, so Jason figured something pretty serious was coming. "Listen. Kendal doesn't want to see you anymore. Time to move along to your next conquest." Jason could imagine Ruth's condescending smile behind her surgical mask. *Women.*

"Just tell me *when*, Ruth."

And even though her face was covered, Jason could tell that the grin had vanished, and Ruth's lips had snapped shut tighter than an old lady's purse.

"When does she go to the gym?" he insisted.

"You are determined to break her heart, aren't you?" Ruth turned away and marched off toward the O.R.

"Okay," he called as he followed her. "You're fired."

"Oh, *right*." Ruth pushed the O.R. door open with her backside and held it for him. "She doesn't want to see you," she repeated, this time loud enough for the whole surgical team to hear. But as Jason shouldered by, her mean jab must have made her feel guilty because she relented, mumbling, "Usually around eight."

So for the next week, every evening around seven forty-five, Jason made sure he was at the Integris gym.

He badgered his buddy Dr. Mike Lewis to increase their usual number of raquetball games that week. He lifted weights in the weight room. Many. Slow. Reps. He loitered in the gym like some kind of pervert outside the ladies' locker room, pretending to tie his running shoes over and over while a constant parade of women went in and out through the swinging door. All manner of women, some of them very toned beauties, winking or smiling as they passed him. Some of them winked *and* smiled. But none of them were Kendal.

"Have you seen Kendal Collins lately?" he finally asked Mike at the end of the week. The two men were in the cardio theatre. Side by side on identical treadmills, wearing headphones as they watched an ESPN rerun of a boring golf tournament while they worked off their stress. Except for Jason, the exercise wasn't working. His stress seemed to increase every time he thought about Kendal, whether his feet were pounding the treadmill or not.

"*Who?*" Mike huffed. Teddy-bear soft, Mike didn't stay in shape like Jason. The workout was actually making the poor guy's breathing ragged.

"You should come here more often, you know. Kendal Collins."

Something in the way Jason said the name made Mike stare at him curiously. He slowed his pace and pulled down his headphones. "Who's that?"

Jason looped his own headphones around his neck and glanced around. Everybody else in the room was minding their own business, treadmilling away. The noise of the machines would cover their conversation.

"Kendal Collins. You know? The woman I took to Mexico in February. The Merrill Jackson rep."

"Oh, her." Mike picked up his pace again and his heavy breathing resumed. "Yeah…she hits the office about…once a week. Very thorough. She's been giving me some…some great patient education materials. Handy little models of the naso-pharynx… stuff like that."

Funny, she didn't *hit* Jason's office once a week, even though he *was* prescribing Paroveen like crazy now. She didn't give *him* any great *stuff.* As far as he could tell, Kendal only dropped off boxes of samples and split. She never asked to see the doctor.

"How does she seem to you?" Jason glanced down at the green number on his machine. It indicated his pulse rate had shot up at the question. Crazy. Under his skin, that's what the woman was. Digging around under there like some stupid liposuction wand.

"How does she *seem*?" Mike gave him that curious look again.

"Yeah." Jason knew he was being an idiot. He just couldn't stop himself. "When you see her, does she seem...okay to you?"

"Yeah, she's okay. Very professional, like always. Are you hung up on this woman or something?"

"No! I just... I was just wondering how she was doing since we got back from Mexico. That whole deal down there was really hard on her. I should never have taken her with me."

"Oh. Well, she seems just fine." Mike shrugged like he failed to see the relevance. To a ridiculously happily married man like Mike, Kendal Collins was just another attractive little drug rep. He probably didn't give her much notice. "The woman works night and day as far as I can tell. But she's always pleasant. Very classy chick." His friend eyed Jason again before he continued. "Hey. Why *don't* you ask *her* to the Miracle Makers Ball?"

The Miracle Makers Ball was the annual spring fund-raiser benefiting the Integris burn center. The tables went for a thousand a pop, and anybody who was anybody showed up—politicians, bankers, musicians, artists. And of course, the event was a command performance for all the Integris docs. Jason and Mike and a couple of their other friends had gone in on a table. All of the other guys were married, razzing Jason about cleaning up his act so he could get a date. De-cent women didn't cotton to picking out a formal dress at the last minute, they warned.

"She's single, isn't she?" Mike pressed.

"Yeah. So I hear," Jason grumbled. He'd eat dirt before he'd ask Kendal to Miracle Makers. Why should he float a big old balloon like that just so Miss Priss could shoot it right out of the sky? Not on your life. She'd have to at least push the "doors open" button for him first.

He asked Mindy McCane.

And on the night of the ball, Mindy McCane turned out looking great, just like he knew she would. Tall. Blond. Exceptionally hot. Wearing a glittery backless black dress that looked like it had been poured over her curves like black lava. He backed Mindy up against the wall of the elevator as they rose to Oklahoma City's posh Petroleum Club on the top floor. He leaned in to give her a sound, mind-numbing kiss. Might as well get her all warmed up for the dancing.

Her eyes sparkled with a most satisfying fire when he was finished with her. "It's been way too long since we've seen each other," she murmured.

Absolutely. He'd pined over Ms. Kendal Collins just about long enough. He was going to have himself a great time tonight.

Then, out of the corner of his eye, he caught sight of the "doors open" button on the panel. He shot a determined look at Mindy and saw her eyes widen with surprise just before he plastered another kiss on her, a fiercer one this time.

But the effort was no good. Images of Kendal had already intruded. It was as if she were right there in the elevator, refusing to push that damned button for him.

"We're gonna have a blast tonight, baby," he growled in Mindy's ear, giving her trim little bottom a quick pinch as the elevator doors glided open.

And there she stood.

In profile to him, near the cash bar, chatting and laughing with some balding old porker in a tux.

He stopped in his tracks, wanting to curse. Kendal looked even more beautiful than the last time he'd seen her. She turned to say something to the man next to her and Jason got the full view of her face. That face. It was emblazoned in his mind, his heart, in a thousand ways, in a thousand poses. Most of them in a moonlit tent in Mexico.

He sized up the man she'd spoken to and hoped to goodness that wasn't her date—the guy looked old enough to be her father. Wait a sec. Maybe, he hoped to goodness The Porker *was* her date.

Her dark hair tumbled in a lush, curling cascade over one shoulder. Her dress was black, like Mindy's, and backless. Far more so. In fact, it had no back whatsoever. From a high neck in the front only two tiny sparkling straps crossed behind and bisected her shoulder blades. The rest was pure…skin. He willed her not to turn any farther so he could keep on enjoying the sight of all that perfect milky beauty.

"Jason? What's wrong?" It was Mindy, leaning

into him. She followed his line of vision. "Who is that?"

"Nobody. Listen." He took Mindy's elbow gently and pointed toward some tables near the high windows. "Mike and his wife are right over there. You remember Dr. Lewis and CeCe, don't you?"

"Sure." Mindy waggled her fingers at the couple as Mike and his wife took notice of Jason and his date. He had escorted Mindy to social functions before. She came in handy any time he needed a classy, accommodating chick on his arm. "Why don't you go ahead and join them? The crowd at the bar looks pretty deep. I'd better go ahead and fetch our drinks while there's still a drop or two of hooch left."

Mindy smiled at his lame joke and glided away.

Jason gave his tux lapels a brisk tug as he strode across the room. Another prominent physician tried to waylay him en route, but Jason only nodded politely and plowed past. The attendance at the ball was always a record-breaker, and tonight was no exception. He feared if he didn't make contact with Kendal now he might lose her in this crowd.

"Kendal," he came up behind her and felt his gut tighten. He had to exert an effort to keep himself from gliding his palm over the warm skin of her bare back.

She turned, and there were her eyes, looking into his. Green and soulful and beautiful as ever. Her social smile slowly faded. "Jason."

"Hi." He smiled bright enough for both of them.

"How are you?"

"Fine."

"I didn't expect to see you at this shindig."

"I come every year. It's the least I can do for the Burn Center." Her tone was flat but she had pasted the social smile back in place. "Roger, this is Jason. Jason, this is my date, Roger." She canted a languid hand toward The Porker, who gave Jason a tight smile with slightly dingy teeth.

This kind of competition, Jason figured he could handle.

The guy put a hand on Kendal's back, right on the *skin* of her back, and Jason felt his own palms go sweaty. His fingers flexed with tension, and he had to force them to relax when Roger stuck out the other hand in greeting.

"Roger Newls."

"Nice to meet ya." Jason shook the guy's hand, maybe a tad too hard. "Jason Bridges."

"Jason is the premier plastic and reconstructive surgeon at Integris," Kendal explained. "He works on a lot of the burn patients. Roger is an investment banker."

And a porker.

"A plastic surgeon, eh? You know, you look familiar." The Porker's eyes narrowed behind his Ralph Lauren glasses. "Do you run one of those photo ads in the Sunday paper? So many of the plastic types do these days. You look at those ads and wonder why they don't do a little work on their own faces." Roger chuckled.

Funny guy.

The Porker had directed that last quip to Kendal.

The man was definitely acting threatened. If he weren't coming across as such a prig, Jason would have felt sorry for him, but as it was, he'd had about enough. He wanted to say, *I'm running a two-for-one special on faces, Roger. If you have any friends, feel free to bring one along.* But he didn't want to act like an ass in front of Kendal. And he wasn't ready to leave her side.

He settled for a watered-down comeback. "I've never run an ad. The space is always taken by the investment bankers." He smiled cordially.

Kendal laughed lightly. The familiar sound only made Jason's gut tighten all the more.

"Actually, I expect you did see Jason's picture in the paper." Kendal was looking at Roger, but Jason felt her energy rising toward *him.* "Jason is the physician who had the run-in involving the Zapatistas in Mexico. The man I narrowly escaped from Chiapas with?"

"Oh!" The Porker's round face lit up. "*That's* where I've seen your face before. Well, let me extend my heartfelt thanks to you, my man, for getting this darling girl out of that hellhole alive." The Porker ran his fat hand up and down Kendal's back in a possessive gesture. "Kendal's the best thing to come into my life in a very long time."

Jason wondered if Kendal could possibly be serious about this guy. She'd only been back from Mexico for five weeks. But when he replied, "She's pretty special all right," and looked into Kendal's eyes again, he was relieved to read her feelings plainly. She had feelings for *him*. Still. But just as plainly, he saw her immediately cloak those feelings. *Guarding her heart.*

No happily ever after.

Jason's gut tightened again with the queerest sensation. He looked down at his shoes, then up at the couple. Roger was smiling at Kendal with unmasked adoration. When The Porker drew her against his side, Kendal looked the way she had right before she puked on Jason's plane. Would she really let herself be trapped into a relationship with a fat geezer like this? After the passion the two of them had shared? Was a commitment, security, really *that* big a deal with her?

"Well, it was a pleasure to meet you, Roger." Jason backed away. Kendal would not look at him, so he said, "Nice to see you again, Kendal," very pointedly.

"Yes. It was." She barely flicked him a glance.

"Well, I'd better get my date a drink before every last drop of hooch is gone." *Great.* It was going to be that type of evening—sweaty palms, recycled jokes.

Jason made up his mind to act like a gentleman, to stop gawking at Kendal and pay attention to Mindy. But before the evening was out, he crossed the room straight to Kendal again. Like a quivering divining rod in the pull of some deep magnetic field.

He stood over her, looking down at the top of her beautiful hair until she slowly turned her face up to him. He smiled and extended his hand. "Care to dance?"

She didn't look too sure. Her cheeks pinkened while

she hesitated. But then she turned to Roger with a bright smile. "Would you mind?"

The Porker smiled at Kendal and shrugged. He got up from his chair and held Kendal's while she stood. Above her, he narrowed his eyes imperceptibly at Jason. "Take good care of my girl," he said with ineffectual suaveness.

"I'll give it my best," Jason took possession of Kendal's hand, then her waist. He swept her onto the dance floor, feeling a great rush of relief when he finally had her body close and his palm pressed to the luscious skin at the small of her back. He couldn't resist pulling her body tighter against him. "What's with that guy?" he murmured near her ear.

She leaned back from him. "What do you mean?"

"Is he your boyfriend or something?"

"Don't be ridiculous." She stiffened away from him, as if the question offended her. "We barely know each other. Sarah fixed us up."

"Sarah? Your best friend?"

"Yes. She works at his bank. We're just keeping company."

"Keeping company? It didn't sound that way when he was thanking me for saving your life."

"I have no idea why men talk possessively like that sometimes. They just do."

"I know why." *Because you're hot,* he added in his mind, but decided against saying it. Plenty of men had probably wanted to possess Kendal Collins. Himself included. He pulled her body back flush with his. "So did *you* ask *him* here?"

"Yes. I had the tickets. It's good PR to be seen at these events."

"Why didn't you ask me?"

She frowned at him. "You know why. Besides, you seem to have brought a very nice date with you." Her eyes darted to the fabulous silhouette of Mindy, who was busy flirting with a group of doctors over by the cash bar. He could see Kendal practically biting her tongue to keep from asking about their relationship. He smiled.

"Mindy? Mindy's just...she's just somebody I keep company with."

She winced at his teasing. Not in the mood, he guessed.

"Look. What about us?"

"What about us?"

"You won't answer my calls."

"I already said everything I have to say. If neither of us has changed our minds about commitment, I can't see any point in fanning the flames." Her own cheeks flamed a bit at her choice of words.

"So, we can't even keep company?"

She gave him an irked little look for mocking her choice of words again. "I don't think that's really wise."

"Why not?" He slid his hand low on her back. Very low.

"Why not? Why *not?*" She arched back, tilting her head and looking him directly in the eye. "*This* is why not, and you know it." She reached behind herself and replanted his hand higher up.

"All right. So I can't keep my hands off of you. So sue me. You feel the same way about me, and don't you deny it." She tried to pull her body away from his, but he jerked her flush against him again.

"You are a piece of work, you know that, Doctor Bridges?" She stopped resisting and let their bodies meld together. The feel of her was driving him wild. But at the same time her next words challenged him like a slap. "What are you planning to do next? Throw me down on the floor right here in the Petroleum Club?"

"If I thought it would slam some sense into you, I would."

"Stop it," she hissed. "Physical attraction isn't everything. That's where a relationship begins, not where it ends. You don't seem to get that."

"And you don't seem to get this, Kendal." He pressed his palm lower on her back, subtly mashing her hips into his, canting his face over hers as he spoke. "What we have doesn't happen every day. Don't be a fool. You can't start up some guy like that—"

"Roger is a very nice man."

"I'll bet. You can't go back to a guy like that after what we had together. You'll go crazy."

Her cheeks were flaming higher, with anger now, he suspected. "What I do, or do not do, with another man is absolutely none of your business."

"Roger's *safe*, isn't he, Kendal? You're back to that now, aren't you? Choosing safety over passion. Looking for some tame little pet, some guy you can put on

a short leash, who'll fit in with all your other acces-
sories, the way Phillip did.''

Kendal's chin jutted forward. ''I ought to slap your
face right now.''

''Except that's not what you really want to do, is
it? *This* is what you really want.'' He swooped in on
her mouth like a tiger on a kill. He would have her
again. By God, he would have her again. He forced
her head back, bending her to his will as he ravaged
her mouth.

He didn't close his eyes. Instead he watched her
through slits that burned with passion as he gloried in
her face. The deepening furrows between her brows
told him she was spiraling into something between
pain and ecstasy.

Somewhere in the back of his mind, he realized
people were staring while he kissed the stars out of
Kendal. For him, what people thought didn't matter.
His reputation in the love department was pretty well
shot. But Kendal was another matter. Maybe she was
right. Maybe she should have slapped him. But it was
a little late for that. He was kissing her. And she was
kissing him back. *Hard.* Then he felt her stopping herself, withdrawing.

He released her. She stood staring at him, wide-
eyed and angry. Breathing fire. It was clear she hated
him. So why did a part of him feel like he had to save
her from herself? ''Choose passion, Kendal,'' he said
softly while he did nothing to protect himself from the
impact of her blazing eyes. ''It's all we really have in

this life. And we can have it again. Again and again. For as long as we both want it."

For an instant he thought he saw tears spring to her eyes, but then she blinked them back. Her body went rigid. "For as long as we both want it?" She pushed at his chest, and he allowed her to put more distance between them.

The music continued but they had long ago stopped moving to it. Kendal glanced around at the dancers gliding past them. She kept her voice low, under the cover of the orchestra. "I'm choosing a lot more than passion, Jason. What I'm choosing is decency and commitment over your head games. I'm sorry you can't make a commitment. I understand why. I know what happened to you, but that doesn't change anything. I hope you get help for your problem."

"I don't have a problem." Why did she insist on talking to him like some kind of radio show psychologist? "I know what I want and I go after it."

"Oh, yes you do have a problem. You're choosing to run from woman to woman instead of finding genuine happiness. But if you can't see that, you are certainly not the man for me." She looked at the other dancers again, clearly embarrassed, but Jason was way, way beyond caring what anybody else thought.

"Goodbye again, Jason." She turned and as she walked away, her head tilted slightly sideways. Her long hair shone softly in the dim ballroom light as it fanned in a heavy veil across her bare shoulders. He saw her hand go up to her face, her fingers splayed out near one eye, trembling slightly. It looked like she was swiping at a tear.

Jason stood rooted to his spot for endless minutes, unaware of the other dancers flowing around him. Watching her go. Blinking and watching her go. Watching that dark hair, watching that luminous back depart from him yet again. And as he watched her, the strangest feeling hollowed out his gut. It was like an organ had just been ripped out there, or something. He stood there and wondered where he and Kendal Collins had gone wrong. And then he thought, *Mexico, that's where.*

CHAPTER FOURTEEN

KENDALL TOLD ROGER that she was sorry, but she had suddenly developed a vile headache. She said that she wanted to go home and would have the security guard downstairs summon a cab for her. Roger offered to take her home himself, of course. Even though she protested that she couldn't ask him to leave the ball so early, he obliged anyway, departing with her immediately.

Roger was a nice guy. On the drive through the quiet downtown Oklahoma City streets, he said nothing about her embarrassing scene with Jason on the dance floor. Nothing. A real gentleman.

But where was the honesty? Kendal wondered as Roger took both of her hands in his at the door of her town house. Jason Bridges would have come out onto the dance floor to cut in and end that nonsense, or he would have at least teased her about it. Or at least he would have said, "Who the hell was that?" later. And he definitely would have kissed the fire out of her once he had her alone. But not Roger.

"I'll just say good-night here," her date said quietly. "You seem very tired."

Tired? She wasn't *tired*. She was humiliated and

pissed off. Jason Bridges had ruined her evening, possibly her life, and now this Milquetoast of a man was not helping by worrying a hole in the tops of her hands with both of his thumbs.

"Roger, I—"

But he interrupted her before she could apologize for cutting his evening short. "Kendal, it's okay. I know you have a past with Dr. Bridges."

"You do?" How would a downtown banker know what was going on across the city at the Integris Medical Center? But she thought of the answer before he said it.

"Sarah told me."

"Ah." She didn't care. She didn't try to deny or explain any of it. Jason, blast his hide, had nailed the problem back there at the Petroleum Club. As long as she was willing to kiss Jason Bridges like that, what was she doing with a nice guy like Roger? Getting ready to break his heart the same way hers had been broken by Jason?

"Good night, Roger. I'm sorry the evening turned out so badly. I just couldn't stay there after...after...."

"I understand. May I call you sometime?"

"Sure. It would be nice to talk to you."

"Just to talk?" He leaned closer, finally seeking a kiss. But it was too late. He brought himself up short the instant she tilted her face aside.

"For now." Kendal kept her voice light, though she was feeling a little more than awkward. "I think we'd better stick to friendship."

"If that's the way you want it. Friendship it is,

then.'' Roger's tone was also light, but his eyes betrayed his deep disappointment. ''Good night, Kendal.''

''Good night.''

She went inside and tossed her purse and keys on the entry table, and pressed her fingers to her temples. She really did have a vile headache now.

Why couldn't she make herself feel anything for a nice guy like Roger? She thought of all the nice men who had asked her out in the year after Phillip had dumped her. Guys who could probably make a commitment. At the time she'd told herself she was grieving over her lost relationship.

But the truth was, she hadn't met anyone like Jason Bridges in that year. The truth was, she hadn't met anyone like Jason Bridges ever, and probably never would again.

She climbed the narrow stairs to the top floor of the town house, the master suite. She didn't need a bath, but yet she *needed* one. She turned on the tap and let her black thoughts run amok while the tub ran full.

She was never going to get married, never going to have a family, never going to be happy. She was back to thinking the way she had after Phillip left.

She went into the walk-in closet and kicked off her four-inch heels. She removed her black formal dress, hung it on the padded hanger, carefully arranging the support straps to keep it from sagging. A few weeks of wild living in Mexico hadn't eradicated the neatnik in her. She went into the bedroom to her highboy and slid open the narrow velvet-lined drawer at the center where she stored her jewelry. She removed her glittery earrings, and when she laid them in their assigned place, her eye was snagged by something as surely as if it were a living thing, lying there. The St. Lucia medal. She touched the cool gold and closed her eyes, seeing it flash around her own neck, against her own skin, on the night when Jason had first made love to her.

She picked it up and wrapped her palm around it and squeezed. She would keep the medal always because she'd promised Lucia, that night in the cave, to safeguard it and Miguel. But she'd never be able to wear it again. Too many memories. Memories of Jason. Memories of falling in love. Had she actually sent up some kind of quasi-superstitious prayer to this saint, a plea to let *this one* be her true love? And now look what had happened. She'd gotten emotionally involved again and ended up lonelier than ever.

She'd gotten involved with the wrong man. She tried to tell herself that, but the memory of his kiss tonight invaded her mind, making him feel so right.

One kiss. One kiss and Jason had brought it all rushing back. All the raw energy, the passion, the heat. Tears filled her eyes. Angry tears. Confused tears. Lonely tears. Oh, God. Was she going to spend another night letting her tears pour into this bathtub? She swiped at her cheeks. She would not let Jason Bridges do this to her. If only she hadn't been so foolish in Mexico. *Mexico*.

Thoughts of Mexico brought thoughts of Miguel, reminding her that she had more urgent things to worry about than her foolish affair with Jason. Where had those men taken Miguel? Was he being properly fed? Was he cold when the chill of night fell upon those high mountains? Was there anyone with him who would rock him to sleep or sing to him or read him a story? Somehow she had to find her way back to Mexico and rescue the little boy who had stolen her heart. The idea of finding Miguel gave her purpose, put steel in her spine.

For Miguel, she could be strong. She heard the water, still running, and went into her luxuriously appointed master bath. Already, she had put this town house up for sale. If Ben ever found out where Miguel was, she wanted to have ready cash so she could go and get the child without delay. A simple apartment was good enough for her. The thought of a spare, simple life actually made her heart light. Miguel would think any place was a palace after the conditions he and Lucia had been forced to endure in Mexico.

Ben had e-mailed that local peasants told the missionaries that Vajaras had a compound somewhere in the jungle near Palenque. And the jungles near Palenque were vast and dense. If Vajaras had taken Miguel there, how would she ever find him? Somehow she would find a way. And she would bring her beloved child into the bosom of her new life and she would be happy, even without a man.

She felt the medal still pressing into her palm, and slowly opened her hand to look at it. "I have a new request for you," she whispered to the feminine profile carved into the gold. "Help me find Miguel. There must be some way. Help me find him. I don't care how.''

Tenderly, she placed the medal on the marble countertop, slowly looping the chain in a small circle around it.

She turned and ran a hand through the swirling water, testing. As she prepared to take one last bath in the luxurious tub, she thought about how much she'd changed. She wasn't going to cry her eyes out in the bathtub over some guy ever again. And she thought how sad it was that Jason Bridges would most likely never change. But she could force herself to accept that. She was a new woman now, one who looked the truth in the eye. And the truth was, whatever ghosts were keeping Jason Bridges a prisoner in his private shell, she did not have it in her power to put those ghosts to rest.

IN THE LONG DAYS that followed the Miracle Makers Ball, Jason mulled the whole scene with Kendal over in his mind. Endlessly.

Though he kept up his surgery schedule, it was as if his mind and body had split apart, totally separated. No, it was his mind and his heart that were separated, divided. His body was functioning like the same precision machine it had always been. Albeit now it had become a very, very frustrated machine.

He'd thought about finding himself another woman, a stand-in, as it were. Easy enough to do. Mount the bike. Roar up to some local C&W dive. Billy Bob's was a favorite one. Buy some little hottie a few too many beers, dance with her real slow until she melted beneath his hands, strap her onto the back of the bike, and off they'd fly for a night of the wild thing.

But he didn't want the kind of women who wanted that sort of one-night stand anymore. He wanted Kendal, and only Kendal. He couldn't get the feel of her, the taste of her, out of his blood. Why settle for a trinket when somehow, some way, he was certain he could have the real treasure?

But the "treasure" seemed to want nothing to do with him. She'd made that clear—*again*—at the Miracle Makers Ball. A fact that was making him just a tad crazier as each day ticked by.

He never imagined he'd love someone as much as he loved Amy. But here it was. Love.

Maybe, just maybe, she had really meant what she said about commitment. Every time he had one spare second, took one blank, unaccounted-for breath, Kendal's last words in Mexico came back to plague him.

No happily ever after for them.

What the hell did she mean, *for them* there would be no happily ever after? He couldn't believe she had said that. Did she mean that the two of them were not the kind of people who could ever be happy? Or did she mean they just couldn't be happy together? And how could she be so damned certain of that? Did she have a crystal ball tucked away in that damned little rolling cart of hers? No one could predict the future. Certainly not when it came to relationships. He'd learned that lesson early and well.

They were too different, she had said. Well, duh.

Wasn't that rather the point of him being a man and her being a woman?

Did she expect some kind of homogeneous existence where they both agreed on every dot and chittle?

He felt some irritation, even some anger, rising up when he started mulling the whole deal over like this. Let her find someone like old what's-his-face, that sterile-as-bleach buttoned-down drug rep who had done her bidding for five straight years. What was his name? Phillip? He'd seen the guy. He'd made it his business to get a good look at the guy. Handsome in a gay catalogue-model sort of way. Not a hair out of place.

Or maybe she'd be happier with The Porker paying her bills and doing her bidding. Go get 'em, sister, and live happily ever after, with every hair in place.

No happily ever after? Suddenly his anger dissolved into a wave of genuine sorrow. No, not sorrow. This was deeper than sorrow. This was real grief. The kind of grief that harkened back, all too sharply, all too distinctly, to the loss of Amy.

Jason closed his eyes, bit his lip. Maybe Kendal was right. Maybe he ought to have his head examined.

"Are you okay?" Kathy Martinez thrust the stack of morning charts at his chest.

He opened his eyes. His nosy nurse was giving him the fish eye. "I'm *fine.*" He yanked the charts from her grip.

But Kathy ignored his grumpy attitude and continued to eye his appearance skeptically, just like she always did.

Jason worried that she might see through the veneer this time, straight to his broken heart. "Stop your hovering, Mother Martinez."

"Did you pull another all-nighter or what?"

"No." He gave Kathy an irritated scowl.

But he *had* pulled an all-nighter. He'd pulled a bad one, though he'd stayed right in his own bed the whole time. Right in his own bed, alone. Twitching around, gyrating like one possessed, until he was wrapped in a wicked tangle of sheets. He'd used all of his old medical school tricks and finally willed himself into a choleric sleep, but he only ended up in the grip of a dream about Kendal. He woke up in a sweat, cursing in the darkness.

No happily ever after? The words had come back to him, over and over, in the predawn hours as he lay there and wondered what the hell was happening to him.

What did she mean by happily ever after anyway? Wasn't it being *known*, the way he had let Kendal know him in Mexico? The memories brought a physical wave of longing to his loins. But it was the accompanying feeling of longing in the vicinity of his heart that disturbed him more.

Being *known.*

He imagined, again, a future with Kendal. A future they would likely never have. Still, he thought of what life would be like with her. He imagined kissing her every day, in all kinds of places. In the kitchen. In the car, rushing off to work. In the park. God, he did love to kiss Kendal. And not just her mouth. Her face. Her hands. Her hair. Her body. With Kendal, kisses meant what they were supposed to mean. They conveyed the message he so deeply felt: *I adore you.*

When had he decided he adored her? It didn't matter. What mattered was, he did.

He'd covered his eyes with a restless arm, trying to shut out the images, but it was like an endless slide show that would not stop.

A child. For some weird reason, images of a child came into his vision next. In his mind's eye, he and Kendal were each holding on to a toddler's little hands, swinging him high off his feet between them, the way he'd seen couples doing in the park or at the mall. The child's face became Miguel's little face. As clearly as if he were still down in Mexico, Jason imagined Miguel's first healthy smile, quickly replaced by the wrenching image of the crying child being ripped from Kendal's arms. That's when Jason had hurled himself from the bed and gone in to the bathroom. He'd gulped down a glass of water while his heart twisted with guilt.

Wishing he could roll back time, he'd looked in the mirror and thought, *Why? Why hadn't he helped her get Miguel? Why hadn't he given the woman he loved the very thing she'd wanted? Why?*

"We're going to be busy today," Martinez said, pulling him out of his reverie.

"Yeah?" he said as if emerging from a torpor.

"Yeah." She frowned at him. "I'm gonna ask you again, Dr. Bridges. Are you sure you're okay?"

"I'm fine."

"Umm-hmm. The way you keep saying that word makes me think you are *not* fine. You want to tell Mother Martinez what gives?"

Martinez was well aware that Jason had no family he could count on. They'd talked about it. Or rather, she'd brought it up once, back in his office when he'd been having a bad day. He'd told her then that all of that business about his family was a long time ago and it didn't matter.

"I expect it does matter," the unflappable black woman had folded her arms across her bosom and used the same skeptical tone she was using now. "I expect it matters a whole lot." She'd given him the same look then that she was giving him now.

Women. Why did they feel compelled to heal everybody of all their afflictions? Especially nurses. They wouldn't quit until they had you lying down on the couch with a cold cloth on your forehead, spilling your guts. Especially this one, who looked like she wasn't about to give up.

"Does this...mood of yours have something to do with Kendal Collins?"

"What are you talking about?"

"The whole hospital heard about that little scene at Miracle Makers Ball."

"I put a lip lock on a chick in a hot dress." He flipped open the first of the charts. "I know that's terribly shocking, but eventually people will get over it." He headed toward his office, hoping to leave Martinez and her stupid questions behind.

But Martinez dogged at his heels. "Don't be a

smart-ass. Ruth said you stood there for about five minutes, looking like you'd been gut punched.''

Ruth. She'd been there with Doug Lippert. ''This is not cool.'' Jason made his tone as exasperated as he'd ever made it to Martinez, but she was not deflected.

''And now you're functioning like some kind of robot that's wound too tight. Running around this hospital all day, running around on that motorcycle all night—''

''For your information, I've been working out at the gym. Now, I don't want to talk about it.''

''Well, the gym's not helping. I'd say you'd better talk to *somebody* about it, or you're gonna blow a fuse. If you won't talk to me, then confide in a friend. Or better yet, get professional help for your problem.''

Professional help? Almost the exact words Kendal had used. Did absolutely everybody think he needed a shrink? When he didn't comment right away, Martinez headed for the door.

''Martinez. Wait.''

''Yes?'' She turned with her hand on the knob.

''Do you think I have a problem?''

She seemed to weigh her answer for a bit before she shut the door with a soft click and faced him.

''Yes, I do, Doc. I think maybe you have a problem.''

''With women?''

Martinez came around and lowered her bulk into one of the chairs facing the desk. ''How old are you, Doc?''

''Thirty-one.''

"Did you ever think it might be time to settle down?"

"You mean get married?"

"Well, that would be nice, but that's not the goal, necessarily. I just meant find a steady woman in your life, a long-term relationship, instead of always running from one woman to the next."

Almost Kendal's exact words again. "You think I can't commit?"

"The signs are all there."

"You think I'm sick? That I need therapy? Is that what you women think about guys like me?"

"It doesn't matter what *we women* think, but if you're not happy, I'd say maybe at the very least you need to do a little soul-searching."

HE WAS RUMINATING over these thoughts again, torturing himself for the hundredth time, when the call came.

He was back in his office late in the afternoon, trying to concentrate on the lab reports from his post-ops when Mary buzzed from up front. "Dr. Bridges, this is long distance. He says it's urgent. Can you take it?"

"Sure," he said into the intercom, then snatched up the receiver. "Hello."

"Is this Dr. Bridges?" The caller spoke in English, but even in those four words, Jason could hear the hint of a Spanish accent. "The plastic surgeon who recently visited Mexico?" It was a man's voice. An older man's voice. Cultured. Sibilant. As if he had a speech defect. Something about the sound of it made the hairs on the back of Jason's neck stand on end.

Jason kept his tone cool and professional. "Yes. May I help you?"

"I believe so, Dr. Bridges. My name is Benicio Vajaras and I believe you truly can help me. In fact, I believe you are perhaps the only man who can truly help me."

Vajaras. Jason wondered if the man was toying with him, introducing himself this way. Surely this thug, who had done everything in his power to terrorize the people around San Cristóbal, realized that Jason had heard the stories, had treated some of his victims.

"How is Miguel?" If this guy was into some kind of game, Jason wasn't playing along. He didn't know for sure that this thug had Miguel, but he was trying for any advantage.

A nasty chuckle answered Jason's question. "The little *steenker* is very well, *El Médico.* Better than I've ever seen him, in fact. That is why I'm calling you. I want to express my gratitude for the miraculous work you did on my grandson."

Somehow, he doubted that was what this man really wanted. Men like Vajaras didn't feel gratitude, much less express it. "What do you want?"

"Ah. A man who prefers to cut to the chase is a man after my own heart." Jason could hear the sneering smile in Vajaras's voice. There was a stony silence before Vajaras continued in a soft voice. "I want you to come back to Chiapas."

"I always do. Every single year."

"Not next year. Now."

"Now?"

"Perhaps some of the villagers told you that I am afflicted with the same defect that my grandson bore before you performed your remarkable handiwork."

"No, as a matter of fact, the villagers didn't." Jason didn't want to make things any worse for the peasants.

"It's true. I bear the same devastating scars on my face and in my heart that my little Miguel would have borne for the rest of his life were it not for your miraculous work."

There was that word again. Miraculous. Jason was surprised by the man's command of English. This guy was no Chiapas peasant. "There's nothing miraculous about it. I practice medicine."

"*Sí*. You practice, and because of all that practice, you have become a most impressive expert."

"I have patients waiting, Mr. Vajaras, so you'd better tell me what you're getting at."

Vajaras continued in his obsequious tone. "Until I saw what you did for Miguel, I never dreamed there was hope for me as well."

"Mr. Vajaras." Jason did not bother to conceal his impatience with this arrogant man. "Surely you can afford any number of fine surgeons who operate in Mexico City." The wealthy in Mexico had access to good medical care. Jason was only concerned with the poor.

"Ah. *El Médico*. Few doctors are as skilled as you, despite their reputations. A very expensive butcher in

Brazil tried to fix this sadly deformed old face once. That fool only made it worse. I had given up hope until I saw Miguel. Will you help an old man, Doctor? I heard how you helped *Señor* Alvarez, so I know that old age is not an impediment to you—that you are willing to help elderly people like me. You, Doctor, have the power to relieve an old man's torment, to make an old man's final years peaceful and content.''

Vajaras didn't sound that decrepit. His self-pitying attitude irked Jason. If he was contacting a plastic surgeon in the United States, the man had far more resources than the average Mayan in Chiapas. As far as Jason was concerned, if this ''elderly'' man wanted his services, he could get in line like everybody else.

''I suggest you enter yourself in the lottery when I come next year, along with all the other villagers—''

''No!'' Suddenly Vajaras's soft voice became sharp, like a blade waved in Jason's face. ''You will come. Now.''

''Look, I come whenever I choose to. And I'm not interested in your money, so don't even mention it.''

''*Señor*—'' Vajaras started, but Jason charged on.

''And I don't care about your political connections. I will be in Chiapas again next February. You may try to get your surgery then.'' *After I've taken care of the people that you and your kind have oppressed for decades*, Jason added in his thoughts.

Another chilling silence persisted on the line. ''Have it your way, *señor*,'' the soft reply finally came. Jason didn't even want to honor such nonsense with a response. He just hung up.

CHAPTER FIFTEEN

THREE DAYS LATER the second call came.

"There are some things you *do* care about, I assume." It was the soft lispy voice of Benicio Vajaras again.

"What the hell are you talking about?" Jason was running out of patience with this arrogant bastard.

"As you know, these have been dangerous times in Chiapas. I am forced to place men in the villages, Doctor Bridges. Men who watch. Men who know everything that goes on down there. Who is born. Who dies. Who falls in love. With *whom*."

The hair that had stood up on Jason's neck when he first heard this man's voice did so again, and along with it, a warning coiled in his gut. A sudden image of Kendal's tear-streaked face as her arms reached out to hold on to Miguel flashed into his mind.

"If you come to Chiapas," Vajaras continued without encouragement, "I will release her to you—unharmed—after the surgery."

Jason's heart thudded with a sickening rhythm. "Release who?" he said, but he feared he already knew. "Who are you talking about?"

"The woman you were screwing in that tent on your recent visit. She is here. With me."

The top of Jason's head felt like it might come off. Some overlord's spies had been watching them in the tent? And now Kendal was back in Chiapas?

"I believe you know *Señorita* Collins rather well."

"You have Kendal there?"

"*Sí*."

"If you've done anything to her, I will personally hunt you d—",

"She is here of her own free will. She came immediately when I called."

"Let me talk to her."

"*Señor*, first you must—"

"*Now!*"

The next sound on the line was Kendal's voice. "Jason?" she breathed. She sounded scared.

"Kendal? What in the hell are you doing in Mexico with Vajaras?"

"He..." Her voice choked off. She sounded so very scared, as if she were about to cry.

"Sweetheart. Angel. Don't cry. Just talk to me."

"He...he called me the day before yesterday and he said...he said I could come and fetch Miguel. So like a fool, I jumped on a plane without thinking. Oh, Jason, it's terrible here. You've got to come and get us. Miguel is okay, physically, but I can tell he's frighten—"

There were scruffling noises, and then Vajaras's voice returned on the line, low and evil-sounding now. "So you see how it is, *El Médico?* No surgery, no girlfriend."

"I understand."

"I'm sorry, *señor*. You forced me to take drastic action. Right after I talked to you, I called *Señorita* Collins. She is overly fond of my grandchild." Again the nasty chuckle. "I could have discovered that part, of course, even without my spies. The whole village could see it. The peasants chatter so. I told *Señorita* Collins that the boy was hers if she wanted to come to Mexico and get him."

"You lured her there using your own grandchild as bait?" Jason was starting to see the whole ugly picture. When Vajaras didn't get what he wanted on his first try, he moved along to stronger tactics—blackmailing Jason to do the surgery on Vajaras's terms. Miguel was the bait for Kendal. Kendal was the bait for Jason.

"I have no interest in the boy." Vajaras's voice indeed conveyed his lack of feeling. "Why would I want to keep at my side a constant reminder of my daughter's willful disobedience? A reminder of the Zapatista fool she chose to make this baby with. A Zapatista fool who is now dead, I should point out."

Jason had no idea what in the hell this madman was talking about, and he really didn't care. So the man's daughter had been involved with a Zapatista. All that mattered to Jason was Kendal's safety.

He heard a squeak, a female yelp, in the background.

"Don't you touch her!"

"She is unharmed," Vajaras said smoothly. "But she does not like to hear me talk of Miguel this way, I suspect. The fact is, I cannot keep the boy. I am leaving Chiapas soon in any case and cannot have a child burdening me.''

''I demand to speak to Kendal again.''

''Of course,'' Vajaras said. ''She is right here. *Uno momento.*''

Jason stood up behind his desk. He planted his feet wide and thrust one hand into his hair, already forming a plan while he waited.

When Jason heard Kendal say ''Jason?'' again, his heart actually hurt.

''Hold on, sweetheart. I'll be there as fast as my plane will fly.''

''No, Jason. That's what he wants. Don't come.''

''Have you got a cell phone?''

''No. They took it.''

''You just take care of Miguel, sweetheart, and leave the rest to me.''

''Jason. Don't come. I...we're okay. He won't hurt us as long as he thinks he can get what he wants and—''

Again, there was the sound of the phone being wrestled away.

''I think you will come, *señor.*''

''You bastard,'' Jason spat out, imagining driving a fist into that *sadly deformed face.*

''Indeed I am,'' Vajaras crooned. ''But that is hardly the point. When will you arrive?''

''Where am I going?''

''You do not need to worry about the where. I know you have a plane. Fly into Tuxtla—alone—and we will bring you to my hacienda.''

So Vajaras was holding Kendal hostage at some remote compound. Jason's mind whirled but he could see no way out. He had no idea where that compound was hidden. The eastern highlands and Lancandon jungles were vast and treacherous. "I'll leave to-night," he said, clenching his jaw.

"I will pay all of your expenses, of course, coming and going."

"That's extremely generous of you," Jason spat, fully intending the insult.

Vajaras ignored it. "I will also guarantee your safety, and the woman's, on your return trip to the United States. I will see that you have all the medical supplies and equipment you need when you arrive. We can do the surgery right here, in my home. It is a comfortable place, I assure you. When you are satisfied with my recovery, you can return to the United States with the woman. Unharmed."

This guy was nuts. "I can't do surgery on you *sin-gle-handedly*. This kind of procedure requires a team."

"I will supply all the auxiliary personnel you need."

Jason's thoughts flew into overdrive. If Ruth would agree to it, he wanted her to make the trip with him. First of all, no one could scrub and assist with Ruth's level of expertise. Second, she was strong and smart, and one more ally—one more witness, one more American with ties at home—in this mess couldn't hurt. And most importantly, Kendal and Ruth had a bond. Kendal and Miguel might need the care and support of a good nurse when he couldn't be with them. He hated to ask such a thing of his good friend and longtime nurse, but hopefully the ordeal wouldn't last for long. And as soon as he got off the line, he was going to call in the cavalry, though he'd have to tell them to hold back until he'd gotten Kendal and Miguel out. "I insist on bringing my own scrub nurse along. No one else is capable of the kind of anticipatory planning necessary to assist me in such a complicated surgery."

There was a long, tense silence, and Jason felt a frisson of panic as he wondered if they'd lost the connection. "Bring the nurse," Vajaras finally grumbled. "But no one else. And do not be so foolish as to contact the authorities, either in your country or here in Mexico. You will fly into Tuxtla Gutiérrez. Let us know the time. My men will be waiting to escort you."

Right. They'd escort him with a gun jabbed at his back. Rage pumped through Jason's veins, anger at himself as much as at this evil man. He should have listened to Kendal. He should never have made her hand Miguel over to those men. He should have fought the bastards that day at the old hotel. "I'll have to clear my surgery schedule and get back to you." He was amazed that he could keep his voice so calm when his whole being was roaring with outrage.

"I understand."

"Kendal Collins—and Miguel—had better be in good shape when I get there."

"*Señor*, I have nothing personal against the

señorita. As long as you do as I ask, they will remain safe.''

"Put her on the phone again," Jason demanded.

"Of course."

He heard shuffling again, then Kendal's frightened voice. "Jason?"

"Have they hurt you in any way, sweetheart?"

"No. I'm fine."

"And Miguel's okay?" To a man like Vajaras, the toddler was no more than a pawn, an inconvenience. The baby had probably only been given minimal care.

"We have to get him out of here."

"Try not to worry, honey. We'll get him out of there somehow and take very good care of him from now on. I promise."

"Oh, Jason." Her voice dropped, became hushed, as if she were determined to speak intimately despite the fact that she probably had a gun aimed at her head at this very moment. But the words she spoke apparently couldn't wait. "I love you."

A thick silence pulsed, excruciating in its length because Jason feared they would take the phone away from her again. Not now. Not now, when he needed to say the three most important words he'd ever said, ever would say. The words he should have said a long time ago on a moonlit night in Mexico. "I love you, too, sweetheart," he whispered.

"Jason." He heard her small mew, as if she were stifling a sob.

"I always have." He spoke more forcefully now, his heart bursting with the need to tell her everything, in case something happened. *No.* He wasn't going to allow anything to happen. "I love you. Do you understand me?"

"Yes."

"I've loved you ever since the first time I saw you, and I've been falling more and more in love with you ever since."

She was crying now; he could hear her gulping back the sobs.

"Sweetheart, I need you to be strong. For Miguel. I'm coming and I promise I'll get you out of there as fast as I can."

"Okay." Her voice echoed over the long distance line, very small, very far away. "Please hurry. And do just as he says. Please don't get anyone else involved."

"I promise I won't, sweetheart." He knew he'd have to find a way around that promise, but he was certain Vajaras and his goons were listening in on another phone. "No one will know where I'm going, except Ruth." But he knew that before he called Ruth he would place one other call. This had the makings of an international incident. He would have to contact the U.S. authorities to let them know what he was doing. But with Ben's help, maybe he could keep them waiting in the wings until the right moment.

"You just hang on. I'll fly down there just as fast as I can."

KENDAL HAD TAKEN a terrible chance. And within seconds of her arrival in Chiapas, she had sized up the situation and decided it was not good. They had picked her up at the airport in Tuxtla Gutiérrez in a state-of-the-art Land Rover—her first clue that something was amiss. Why would someone who could afford such an expensive vehicle give a grandchild up for adoption? Why had she assumed Miguel's family consisted of poor peasants? Glad that she had feigned ignorance by saying, *"No hablo español,"* when the driver gave her an order in Spanish, she quickly learned snatches of the truth by listening to the three men's conversation.

They worked for Vajaras, Miguel's grandfather. They were taking her to a hacienda far away, in the jungle. They had recently committed some sort of robbery. Kendal was apparently some kind of hostage, to be handled *con los guantes*—with the gloves.

And worst of all, they were the men who had killed Lucia. Hearing the man that the others called Flaco describe the way he beat Lucia to death, because she defied her father and sought medical care for Miguel, made Kendal physically ill. It took every ounce of her willpower to maintain an unaffected expression.

Lucia had called him *Chancho.* The man was a pig, all right. And Miguel had recognized him. With a fresh wave of nausea, Kendal wondered if Miguel had witnessed the violence against his mother.

They didn't start treating her like a captive until they had crossed the mountains and were descending the narrow road into the jungle. That's when the man in the back seat—*Chancho*—pulled out a gun. He used the barrel to push apart the lapels of her blouse as he ran the cold metal over her skin, ending with a jab at her heart. Kendal stifled a gasp.

The man in the front passenger seat turned to watch the performance with a gold-toothed smile.

"*Señorita*," Flaco said in the local dialect, "you dance a pretty hot Macarena."

With a jolt, Kendal realized he was the man who had watched her at El Foco. The way he was looking her up and down now made Kendal's skin crawl the same way it had that night in San Cristóbal.

"Maybe you make the dance for me real soon, eh?" He lowered the gun. "Maybe we find us a little tent out in the jungle."

Her heart hammered with the sudden knowledge that this man or one of his cohorts must have been spying on her and Jason when she spent the night with him in the tent. What else did he know? That she spoke Spanish obviously.

She showed him just how thorough her command of the language was. "*Tendrá que esperar, cabrón*."

The sentence meant *you'll have to wait*, but the last word was open to interpretation. Whether Flaco took the word to mean billy goat or bastard or faggot, it was still a huge insult. She kept her face neutral and her eyes cold, training them in steady defiance on his beady ones. This lowlife wasn't about to do anything to the hostage that needed to be handled "with the gloves."

But Flaco raised the gun as if to strike her.

"Flaco," the man in the front seat stopped him.

"The *Capitán* said she's not to be harmed and she got to stay with the boy."

Flaco, *the Pig*, gave Kendal an evil stare that turned her stomach inside out. "When the *Capitán* gets what he wants, he will no longer care what happens to this *chica*."

CHAPTER SIXTEEN

SET FAR BACK in the jungle, the Vajaras compound was well-defended with high-tech monitoring equipment, guard dogs and men dressed in paramilitary clothes—all armed with automatic assault rifles.

Kendal was not sure how many acres surrounded this walled estate, but she assumed it was huge. The hacienda was very old, a nineteenth-century fortress perched on a high plateau with a breathtaking view of the valley and the mountains below. The house itself was swallowed by tangled vines and probably crawling with poisonous vipers.

Beneath the impenetrable foliage Kendal could make out a warren of balconies and long arched walkways built of the area's light pinkish cantera stone, interspersed with wrought-iron gates.

Kendal was escorted up wide stone steps through an immense wooden door, then up more steps and down a long vaulted stone passageway.

At the end a door opened, and there was Miguel. He was playing on the floor in a room with a single high, arched window. He looked well, obviously being tended by a stout woman the guards identified as Miguel's *"niñera,"* which loosely translated meant baby-sitter. Kendal rushed into the room and fell to her knees beside the child. Once she showed him the medal she was wearing around her neck he warmed up to her, but she was not allowed to stay with Miguel for long. She was soon taken into a huge dining room where at a table that was at least fifteen feet long, under an elaborate rusting scrolled candelabra, sat a middle-aged man.

"I am Benicio Vajaras," he said. As her eyes adjusted to the dim light, Kendal realized he was the most grotesque-looking individual she had ever seen. He shared some of Miguel's deformities—the bugged eyes and severely recessed chin—but it was his expression, so angry, so cold and cruel-looking, that made Kendal avert her eyes.

"We spoke on the phone," he said in a hissing voice that caused her stomach to tense. "And I spoke to your doctor-lover as well. He was not cooperative. Perhaps now that you have joined us, he will be more so."

Kendal had barely hung on to her courage then, telling herself that at least she had seen that Miguel was okay. But two hours later, hearing Jason's voice on the phone had been her salvation. Then waiting half the night for him to arrive had been sheer torture.

When the sound of the Land Rover grinding up the jungle road woke her, Kendal jolted to full consciousness with a pounding heart. She dashed to the arched window and saw the top of the vehicle pull into the moonlit jungle clearing. The floodlights of the compound blazed on. The doors opened and two armed men crawled out.

The next figure to emerge was Jason. Kendal got

tears in her eyes at the sight of him. He looked up at the window, right at her, as if he sensed her presence in the darkened arch. She bit her knuckles to keep from sobbing with relief.

He was scruffy and unshaven, of course. His hair was sticking out in every direction. His clothes looked like an elephant had been sitting on them in the dirt. She had never seen a creature so beautiful.

Her heart sank when, behind him, she recognized Ruth's blond head as it emerged from the Land Rover. *Oh, no.* But of course, Jason could not do the complicated surgery Vajaras wanted without Ruth's skills. Jason turned and took Ruth's hand.

They walked forward hand in hand like martyrs facing the Romans while the guard kept an assault rifle trained on their backs. High on the hacienda steps, Vajaras had emerged.

Kendal checked the sleeping Miguel and woke the *niñera.* "If anything happens, keep him out of harm's way," she said, then rushed to the door.

She was confronted there by the guard Flaco. "Take me down there," she demanded in Spanish terms that left no doubt about her determination.

He grabbed her upper arm and hauled her along the terraced hallway, kicking the succession of huge planked doors open as they went down.

In the clearing she broke free from her captor's grip and rushed into Jason's arms.

From his lordly position on the hacienda steps, Vajaras put a hand up to stop Flaco from pursuing her. "Let them embrace," he said. "I want him to remember what she means to him."

Jason held her so tight she thought her ribs might crack, yet she wanted him to hold her even tighter.

"Are you all right?" he said in a throaty voice against her hair.

She nodded. She could not talk. Nothing had ever felt so safe as the warm, solid body of this man who had been her lover—once.

"Let me see you." He tipped her chin up and examined her eyes, her nose, her mouth. "Where is Miguel?"

"In there." She found her voice, but it was hoarse.

"Upstairs. He's okay." She glanced furtively at the depraved men flanking them. "Some of them speak English."

"I figured that out." His gaze traveled over hers.

Kendal put an arm out, beckoning Ruth, who had been standing to the side, alone and frightened. "Thank you," she mouthed as Ruth stepped forward and clutched her friend in a tight embrace.

"We'll be okay," Jason said as he wrapped a reassuring arm around each woman. "I'll get the surgery done quickly and get us all out of here." He led them up the steps to face their adversary.

VAJARAS INSISTED that the medical professionals check the room that had been set up for the surgery first, so it was another hour before Kendal saw Jason and Ruth again.

When the guard closed the door to their chamber, Kendal rushed into Jason's arms.

"Everything will be all right," he whispered.

"What does he want you to do?" Kendal asked in a whisper because Miguel was sleeping.

"Rebuild his face."

"Can you do that? Way out in the boonies like this?"

"We'll do our best."

"Jason's hands are our trump card," Ruth whispered from behind him.

"Oh, Ruth!" Kendal practically fell upon the woman, clutching her shoulders. "I can't believe you came with him."

"It was my own choice. Jason left it entirely up to me."

"Except," Jason whispered, "for threatening to fire her."

"I quit," Ruth shot back.

Having borne captivity for nearly twenty-four hours, Kendal was in no mood for these defiant jokes. "I can't believe I got us into this." She rubbed her eyes. "And I can't believe you two would risk your lives for me and Miguel. Especially you, Ruth."

"I came because I care about you both. And I wasn't about to let Jason face this creep alone."

"Remind me to give you a really big Christmas bonus." Jason's teasing grin was not as wolfish as usual tonight.

"Are we being monitored?" He sobered as he asked Kendal this.

"Possibly."

"I'm just glad there's someone to help us take care of you and Miguel," Ruth looked meaningfully at the plump woman who was keeping a vigil at the sleeping toddler's bedside, subtly indicating that the *niñera* could be a spy.

Kendal did not believe Flora could speak English, and she refused to believe that the quiet peasant was reporting back to Vajaras, but she conceded that Ruth had a point.

"Flora, this is Ruth and Dr. Jason," Kendal explained to the older woman. "Flora is Miguel's *niñera*, his baby-sitter, and she has taken excellent care of him."

Ruth went over to exchange a gentle handshake with Flora and to exclaim over how well Miguel had healed, how much he had grown.

Jason took Kendal to the dark side of the room by the arched window, where they stood in a shaft of moonlight. There he braced his palms on either side of her face and kissed her. Gently, slowly. A kiss so light at first it was barely there. A reverent kiss that grew imperceptibly stronger, then totally open and passionate. He was right, they certainly didn't need words.

But there were some words Kendal wanted, needed, to say out loud, even if they had already been communicated in other ways.

"Jason, I meant what I said on the phone," she whispered. "I love you." She continued rapidly, giving him no opportunity to interrupt before she'd finished what she had to say. "And I'm not saying those words because you came to Mexico to rescue me and Miguel. I love you. I thought you should know, in case something—"

"Shh." He kissed her lightly again then studied her

eyes in the moonlight. "Nothing's going to happen. We're going to get out of here. Alive. You understand me?"

She nodded.

"You've got to keep believing that, Kendal. And you've got to trust me." He moved his mouth very close to her left ear and whispered, "I have a plan." When she tried to look at his face, he held her head still and continued speaking near her ear. They were standing close, so close that she could feel his heartbeat. "And I meant what *I* said. I love you, too," he finished in an earnest whisper.

Kendal stood so still that her own pulse seemed to stop, and for a few seconds, his seemed to beat in its place. Hearing those words in person, while he was holding her, was far more powerful than hearing them on the phone.

This time when she tilted her head back, he let Kendal angle her face up to read his eyes. Deep-set, shimmering in the moonlight, Kendal thought Jason's eyes were the most beautiful she had ever seen, or ever would see. He brought his mouth down to hers and kissed her again.

"Oh, Jason," she breathed, "when did you realize you had fallen in love with me?"

"Right from the start, I think. I was just too scared to admit it."

"Scared of what?"

"Scared of losing you. I haven't felt this way since I lost Amy, and I think I see this now…I was afraid of ever having that kind of pain again."

"Oh, Jason." She pressed her forehead to his chest.

He smelled of the manly stress he'd borne for her. "Because of the way Amy died?"

She felt him become very still. Then he relaxed, and she knew there would be no more secrets between them. "Yes."

The pain in that one word pierced her heart. "Oh, Jason," she breathed again. "You were so young when those tragedies happened to you. You couldn't help but be scarred."

"Ironic, isn't it? I spend my days fixing other people's scars, but no one can fix mine."

"That's not true. We can find someone to help you." She offered him hope, praying he would accept it.

"I'll do anything for you. How did you find out what happened to Amy?"

"Angelica told me, right after Miguel's surgery."

"She told you everything?"

Kendal nodded, then pressed her cheek against his chest.

"So you've known all this time?"

She nodded again. "Like I said, I understood why you were the way you were, but that didn't change anything. It didn't change the fact that you had to realize you loved me, that you had to commit for me to feel safe. I can't help the way I am, either. That's what I need, that safety."

"We've wasted so much time." Like the pragmatic physician he was, he added, "But I guess we can't pretend our wounds are healed until they're healed. And some wounds take a lot longer than others."

In the soft illumination from the moon, Kendal

could see tears rimming his eyes as he went on. "I thought I'd gotten past it somehow by going to medical school and being a success and helping people. I always told myself it was a long time ago and it didn't matter. Now I see that I was just running away from the pain. But I'd be a fool to let my old pain keep me away from you. The first time I made love to you—"

Kendal placed a silencing finger to his lips. She tossed a cautionary glance at Ruth and Flora. Their private quest for each other, their history, suddenly too sacred to share, could not even be whispered about in the presence of others. But Flora and Ruth were both asleep—Flora slumped in the chair, Ruth curled in a graceful C at the foot of Miguel's bed.

"The first time I made love to you," Jason started again, keeping his voice very low, near her ear, "I felt like I was going to die. I wasn't sure I'd be able to function the next day, to do surgery."

Kendal gave him a teasing little frown. "And I tried so hard to be gentle."

He grinned and kissed her forehead.

She laid her head on his shoulder. "It was your heart, Jason, opening up at last."

He nodded and she heard him swallow. "Couldn't you tell I was dying inside?"

"No," she told him sincerely, "I honestly couldn't. Except for that nightmare, I saw no change in you. I thought you were physically attracted to me and that was all. I had no idea your emotions were involved."

Jason shook his head. "I hadn't felt that way since I was seventeen years old. I had given up on love. I told you that. At first I thought you were going to be just another great lay, but then…'' He stared up at the moon as a very emotional, faraway look came over his face.

''Then?'' Kendal encouraged.

''Then we made love and it was so different from anything I'd ever felt before. I tried to tell myself it was only the Mexico effect.''

''The Mexico effect! Me, too!'' she admitted with a palm spread on her chest, on her heart.

''Weird, wasn't it? I couldn't stop thinking about you.''

''Same here.''

''You want to know something else weird?''

She nodded. She was consumed with a desire to share everything they could possibly share.

''When we got back to Oklahoma City, I found another woman. I think I was trying to get you out of my system after you'd rejected me.''

''I'm so sorry I hurt you like that.'' Fervently, she pressed her forehead into his chest again. ''I didn't know what else to do.''

He tilted her face up and kissed it. ''It's okay. I know you thought I was being a shallow, coldhearted bastard about Miguel and us and everything else. It's just that I've had to leave so many of these children down here. You have no idea. Even though I knew Miguel was different, because of you, I just kept telling myself it couldn't be done, that it didn't matter. I even tried to tell myself that *you* didn't matter. But it was no good. To me, you matter. More than anyone else in the whole world.''

"Oh, Jason."

He kissed her again. Another light, tender kiss. A kiss fraught with meaning and feeling.

"What about this other woman?"

"I did the deed with her."

"Really? How trashy."

"Having sex?"

"No. Telling me about it. And while we're on the subject, let's get something straight. You're going to have to give up being The Wolf, Jason. Because I—"

This time he touched her lips to silence her. "Easily done. Here's why. When I was with that other woman...afterward..."

Kendal nodded.

"I kept wishing you were there."

"Kinky."

He gathered her tighter in his arms and squeezed her joyously. "You know what I mean. Here I was thinking of you, even though I had another woman right there beside me. That's when I knew I was a goner. That's when I knew you were my one and only, and always would be."

"Your one and only? What are you saying, Jason?"

"I guess I need to say some things, don't I?" He swallowed again. "The next few days are probably going to be hard. We're going to have to be strong. I don't want to wait to say this because I want us to have this moment to sustain us." He paused and drew a deep, solemn breath. "Kendal Collins, I can't imagine living my life without you. I want us—" he closed his eyes " —I want us to go for the happily ever after. Will you marry me?"

In the brief flash of a second, Kendal thought of how long it had taken her and Phillip to reach the point of talking about marriage. She thought of all the work she put into making that relationship happen. All the negotiations. All the compromises. And in her heart, she sent up a small prayer of thanks, like a dove set to wing, that the relationship with Phillip hadn't worked out, and that by some miracle she had been given this man instead.

And in the next second she felt as if her whole body were floating, rising to meet Jason's. This felt so easy. This was the way it was supposed to be. For them, a proposal made in whispers in the dark air of this steamy jungle, by the surreal light of this foreign moon, seemed perfectly right.

"Oh, Jason. Of course I will."

Let your yes be yes and your no be no, Kendal thought while he kissed her. And while they kissed, her yes was sealed between them, under that crumbling arched window, under that foreign moon.

"This is so amazing!" Kendal marveled, barely controlling her excited whispers.

"So I've been told," Jason kidded, whispering against her lips, nibbling in for another kiss.

After he kissed her, she backed up with a sly grin. "Your kisses are amazing, but I meant it's amazing that I've never been so sure of anything in my life, and we've only known each other for a couple of months!"

"Sometimes, granted it's very rarely, even a few

minutes can be enough." Jason smiled and she could see the peace in his eyes. The same peace she could hear in his voice. "Sometimes *you just know*, don't you? The rest is just playing it out. Making sure the timetable makes sense. Getting used to each other in the flesh. Working out the little details, like how you will get a little boy away from his destructive grandfather and get him legally adopted."

Kendal pulled back from Jason's chest and turned her head to look at Miguel. "How will we?"

"I'm going to bargain for Miguel in the deal. If Vajaras knows we'll adopt him, if we can arrange to destroy all the records, maybe he'll go for it."

"I've overheard that he wants to get out of Mexico, to go to South America. But to do that, you'll have to change his face. Authorities all over the world have images of him the way he looks now. So unless you change his face, he's kind of trapped out in this remote compound."

"Oh, I'll change his face, all right. I'll change it but good."

VAJARAS AGREED to let Miguel go almost too easily. "The boy's poor mother is dead—" the old man affected a sorrowful expression "—and I am his only living relative. I suppose I can oil the legal machinery now, since I am the child's legal guardian ever since my sweet Lucia passed on. There should be no problem in turning him over to you."

"Then you will let Kendal take him? Adopt him?"

"I will sign all the necessary papers."

"When?"

"I can have a lawyer come out from Tuxtla with them."

"Even if we don't have the papers, I want to leave and take the child as soon as the surgery is done."

"No, no, no, my friend," Vajaras shook a finger in Jason's face. "You do not leave this compound until the bandages are off and I am satisfied with the results. If you butcher me like that idiot in Brazil did, you die." Vajaras smiled mildly. *Comprende?*"

"I understand," Jason said, keeping his voice low, deferential. In his bag, he had stashed extra vials of Paroveen. The guards had taken his gun, of course, but they hadn't suspected this other weapon.

The anesthesiologist that Vajaras had imported from Mexico City was good at his job, no doubt, but that young doctor would not be familiar with a drug that had only recently been introduced into the American market. Jason could administer as much of it as he needed to. That would have to be the way.

MIGUEL WAS RESTLESS and cranky, scribbling the gruesome pictures again, and Kendal worried that she was communicating her anxiety to the child. She clutched her St. Lucia medal, begging for Jason and Ruth's safety as they operated on Vajaras, praying for an easy escape once this ordeal was done.

"The child needs to play outside," Flora had a knack for pointing out the obvious. They had been confined to this room for almost three days now.

"I know," Kendal went to the arched window and looked down. "But not now. Not while there are guards patrolling the clearing with submachine guns."

The hours ticked by, and finally Jason and Ruth returned to the captives' quarters.

"It's done," Jason groaned as he and Kendal hugged.

Over at her small hot plate, Flora was preparing some *té de manzanilla*, chamomile tea, for the fatigued *medicos*. The women had survived like this, only having contact with the guard when they went down the hall to use the bathroom.

Jason would check Vajaras every few hours, but the patient's personal care was in the hands of two excellent Mexican nurses from Queretaro who had trained at the Herman Hospital in Houston.

All they could do now was endure the confinement and wait for the bandages to come off. During this tense time Jason and Kendal managed to steal precious moments to seal their commitment. Every night before they settled into a restless sleep on the floor next to Miguel's little cot, they vowed to survive and build a future with each other and Miguel.

On the fourth morning, Miguel, whose mouth had almost completely healed by now, said, "Bad man hurt mi mamá," in plain Spanish.

Kendal looked at Jason. "He said a bad man hurt his mother."

"Bright child. Do you think that's what his drawings have been showing?"

"Yes. If Miguel witnessed someone abusing Lucia, what else has he seen in the Vajaras compound?"

"And what else will he be able to verbalize now?" They looked at each other, sharing in that instant their growing parental feelings for the child, and their fear.

"How do we keep a three-year-old from talking? We have to get him out of here, Jason."

"We will. I promise."

But even as he said it, Jason secretly feared that his plan to take out Vajaras would somehow backfire.

ALTHOUGH HE'D DONE an excellent job on the reconstruction, Jason thought he had never seen a face so ugly, so cold, as the one that vainly admired itself in the mirror.

Vajaras lifted his chin. "Uhh," he grunted, pointing at his neck.

"I think he wants to know when this bruising will go away." One of the Mexican nurses was doing his talking for him. The fat bandit Flaco was hovering in the background—a bodyguard, Jason supposed.

"In a few weeks," Jason lied. He hoped that within twenty-four hours of being exposed to sunlight, Vajaras would begin to exhibit the "blood mark" in a solid purple mask from his neck up. Jason had given him three times the normal dose of Paroveen. He had notified the authorities about the dark purple stain and told them they should have no trouble finding this killer as soon as he showed his new face in the civilized world.

"Satisfied with the results?" Jason wanted to move along and get Kendal, Ruth and Miguel to safety.

"Sí. Magni—"

"Magnifico," the nurse finished for him.

Though the patient was restricted to monosyllables

and grunts, Jason thought something in Vajaras's voice sounded even more hostile than before, but he couldn't worry about duplicity—his or Vajaras's—when Miguel was being dangled before him like a piece of meat.

"There is nothing more that I can do for you." Jason bent to look in the cold eyes in the reflection, trying to keep the contempt out of his own. "You need to rest now."

"Sí," Vajaras mumbled and fell back on the bed. Jason wondered if the Paroveen wasn't having some kind of weakening effect, leaching off too much potassium from his system. But he had no intention of reversing any ancillary damage.

"I want to leave immediately."

"We'll need time to fuel your plane, señor," Flaco said from the shadows.

"Then do it."

Flaco snapped his fingers and didn't bother to glance at the obsequious minion who immediately materialized. He kept his flinty eyes on Jason while he fired off some terse instructions in Spanish.

But the shifty look in the minion's eyes gave Jason a queer tightening in his gut. He suddenly wished he had Kendal at his side after all so that she could interpret the rapid-fire Spanish.

KENDAL, Miguel and Ruth were huddled in a corner of the room on one of the beds when Jason came bursting in. "Let's get out of here."

The women blinked to full comprehension as they stared at each other.

"He's letting us go?" Kendal said to Jason's back. He was already gathering up Miguel's meager clothes, drawings, art supplies, toys.

"Yes. Get Miguel ready."

"He's ready." Kendal stood and hoisted the toddler onto her hip. Ruth rushed over and started strapping on his little sandals.

"We're leaving right now?" Kendal shoved back her hair. She couldn't believe their captivity was coming to an end.

"Yes. The jeep's waiting outside."

Suddenly Flaco appeared in the doorway.

"Chanchol!" Miguel said plainly, pointing at the obese man.

Flaco's eyes narrowed at the child. "He talks now?"

"Very poorly," Kendal said as she pressed Miguel's head to her shoulder. "We can't understand anything he says."

"Your plane will be ready at the Tuxtla Gutiérrez airstrip within the hour, Doctor." Flaco continued to watch Miguel. "Shall we get you and your party loaded into the jeeps?" The heavy man swept a palm out, like a gentleman escorting his guests.

BY THE TIME they descended the steep road down into the hot, humid valley surrounding Tuxtla Gutiérrez, the sun was inching up over the mountains at their back.

Jason's plane had already been fired up and rolled

out onto the private airstrip, where the four captives were hurried aboard.

"Get in front in case I need you to navigate!" Jason hollered over the engine noise as Kendal started to crawl into the back seats with Miguel. Reluctantly, she let Ruth climb in beside the toddler instead. Jason helped her into the copilot's seat.

Jason wasted no time taking off, aiming the plane north/northwest in a straight line for Texas.

Kendal breathed a cautious prayer as they gained altitude. As long as the fuel held out, they would not have to stop until they crossed the Texas border. They would not stop until, at last, they were safe.

But she had barely finished that thought when they discovered the hemorrhaging fuel.

CHAPTER SEVENTEEN

"JASON! Can we make it?" Every cell in Kendal's body screamed alarm as she stared at the fuel gauges.

"Get the vests on!" he repeated. "Be ready to unbuckle yourselves as soon as we hit the water."

Kendal finished helping Miguel and Ruth with the life vests, then took one last hard, horrified stare at the dials. Scant quantities of precious fuel remained now. The flow rate, completely unstaunched, registered as high as it would go. Frantically, she pulled on the red knob one last time in a futile attempt to stop the fuel flow. Nothing happened.

Jason called in his Mayday message, then battled the sputtering plane as it tilted and careened toward the river.

Kendal tried to think how she could help. But when her hand went to the lever that engaged the landing gear, Jason yelled, "No! They'll catch on the water."

She studied his grim face and then turned to see the rocky red walls of the Canon del Sumidero hurtling past the window. Twisting as far away as she could from the horrifying sight, Kendal pressed one hand on Jason's shoulder and the other around the howling Miguel's tiny leg.

Jason turned his face and kissed her knuckles, so fiercely it felt like his lips might bruise her. "Stay with me, baby," he said through clenched teeth. "We're gonna make it and that bastard's going to the slammer." He pulled on the yoke with all his might to keep the nose up out of the water. "As soon as we hit the water, unbuckle your harness and open the door."

With the plane losing power and the brownish-green water of the Rio Grijalva zipping ever closer below its belly, Kendal could only clutch her St. Lucia medal and pray.

Jason pulled back on the yoke and bit back a curse.

The touchdown, when it came, felt miraculously gentle. There was an initial jolt when the plane splashed into the water, with the rear hitting first. The fuselage tilted, almost softly, for one instant, suspended on the surface. There was a sudden catch and drag as if they'd become weightless in molasses, and then they started to sink!

Kendal clawed at the door handle. "I can't get the door open!" she screamed as she pushed against the mounting pressure of the water.

Jason reared back and, with three mighty slams of his boot, kicked out the windshield. "Gimme the boy!" he yelled at Ruth.

Ruth passed the still-howling Miguel forward, and after Jason crawled out while clutching the child under his arm, the two women quickly followed.

With Jason pulling Miguel with him and yelling encouragement, they swam as fast as they could, away from the downed plane. Breathless, they stopped and grasped at each other's life vests. Miguel flailed his arms, screaming and crying for Kendal. Jason handed him over. Then they turned to watch the nose of the plane disappear below the surface of the water.

"The emergency...location transmitter...will continue to broadcast for rescue," Jason said between harsh breaths.

"Will there be anyone way out here?" Ruth asked above Miguel's crying.

"There should be some river cruises coming along soon."

Kendal saw a kingfisher diving for food near the bank. "Are there crocodiles in this river?"

"Probably a few—" Jason was speaking honestly "—but they only feed at night."

The surface of the river was surprisingly calm but the slow-moving current was already carrying them downstream. The banks of the river, far away and in most places nothing but sheer rock walls, did not offer hope.

"Don't fight it," Jason advised. "Lie back and ride your life vests."

Kendal got Miguel calmed down and the small party floated in the water for a while, with Jason swimming the perimeter and keeping them together.

Then they heard the drone of a plane's engine. The three adults all craned their necks and looked up at the sky at once.

Kendal couldn't be sure from this distance, but it

had to be the plane that the gunners had taken from Tuxtla. "Do you think they can see us?" she said.

"Even from that high altitude," Jason answered, "it's likely."

They were wearing orange life vests in the middle of a glistening field of water on a bright sunny morning. Had the plane above them contained their rescuers instead, these conditions would have been a godsend. But the plane circling above them contained their assassins.

"Don't splash," Jason warned. "Any disturbance in the water will create reflections, making us that much easier to spot."

They held their breath as the plane droned on by and disappeared beyond the walls of the canyon.

"What now?" Kendal asked.

"We've got to get out of this river."

Which would be no small task. The steep-walled canyon wound on forever, with little to give purchase on the banks except an occasional outcropping of rocks and vegetation.

Kicking against the water mightily, Jason herded them toward the bank. In time, they reached a rocky shelf barely large enough for the four of them to crawl up onto it, where they collapsed like exhausted travelers on a giant hotel bed.

Miguel was fussy, tugging at his life jacket, wanting out of it, asking for a drink, and Kendal had to sing to distract him so that the insectile buzz of a motorboat engine had grown to a roar before Jason realized what it was. He was on his feet as it came around the bend, waving his arms and yelling furiously.

The Mexican man driving the boat seemed astonished and disturbed to find four wet people in life vests stranded in the middle of his route along the canyon. And so were his passengers, three middle-aged couples, Americans who immediately began to help. They offered bottled water, their jackets, and one of the ladies even produced an umbrella from her big bag to shield Miguel from the sun.

Jason told their story. The tourists nodded and frowned as he talked, not seeming all that surprised to hear about the evil activities of Vajaras.

"We've heard tales of this man down in our mission," one of the men confirmed. He was a distinguished white-haired gentleman, whose bearing exuded leadership. "Turn the boat around." He signaled the driver. "We'll take you back to Chiapa de Corzo where the boat landing is," he explained to Jason.

That's when Kendal noticed a cross winking at one of the women's throats. "You're missionaries?"

The pretty lady nodded.

"You wouldn't happen to know a guy named Ben Schulman?"

"Gentle Ben?" one of the other missionaries asked.

Despite their trials, hearing that comment made Kendal smile. Apparently Ben's nickname had followed him to Mexico the way Jason's had followed him to Oklahoma. "Yes. A big blond guy from Oklahoma?"

"Of course we know him. He's in another boat

right behind us, in fact, with some friends of his—visiting missionaries from the States."

"Ben!" Ruth and Kendal said simultaneously. They swiveled their heads to look back as if they could catch a glimpse of their former protector and friend.

"Ben was attached to a medical party. They had to leave him during some kind of incident out in the jungle near Tonina."

"We're that medical party!" Ruth cried, getting as excited as the rest of them.

"But that was weeks ago," the white-haired gentleman looked puzzled. "We were told you were all back in the States."

"We came back to save this little boy," Kendal explained. "I'm Kendal Collins, this is Ruth Nichols—"

"And I'm Dr. Bridges." Jason shook the missionaries' hands. "I can't thank you enough for coming to our rescue.

"The men who want to kill this child, and us with him," Jason explained, "punctured the fuel lines of our plane and we went down in the river."

The missionaries looked horrified. "It's a miracle you survived," one said. "I thought we heard the plane screaming through the canyon."

"Wait!" the white-haired man said. "Oh, Lord," he muttered as he crawled to the back of the boat where the guide was steering at the motor. "Is there an alternate route out of this canyon?" he yelled in Spanish above the roar of the engine.

The driver shook his head emphatically. *No.* He yelled something back in Spanish, something about there being no way out of the canyon for the next twelve miles.

"Then turn around!" the white-haired missionary yelled, making a giant circle with his hand. "Turn this boat around!"

The driver started to argue in vehement Spanish and Jason yelled, "What is it?" to the missionary in the back.

With her husband busy arguing with the driver, one of the wives took up the task of explaining the situation to Jason, Kendal and Ruth. "Back at the jetty, when Ben and his people were waiting to board, some men commandeered their boat. They said they were looking for some kidnappers. We knew from experience in this region that the men were probably not what they said they were. Ben didn't argue with them."

"And Ben got in the next boat?" Jason asked.

"Yes. Our driver was already pulling out. We hollered at them to wait for the next boat and catch up with us later. We never worry about Ben. He and his friends are big guys and can take care of themselves. I believe my husband is trying to find a way to get you out of this canyon without going back and risking passing that other boat."

Jason and Kendal exchanged worried glances before he crawled to the back of the boat.

"Turn around," Jason commanded the driver. But it was too late. They heard another motor, and then the reason for the missionary's distress came around the rocky bend into view. Another fiberglass boat sped toward them, the figures of the male passengers holding clearly delineated silhouettes of submachine guns.

Jason grabbed the umbrella, tilted it for cover, then pushed at Kendal and Miguel, flattening them on the bottom of the boat. "Stay down." He pulled Ruth down alongside him as he pressed himself over their bodies.

"Lie," he yelled at the white-haired missionary, who nodded his understanding. "Ben has agents with him who will help us."

"The missionaries?" one of the women asked, clearly confused.

"Undercover agents," Jason explained. "Waiting for my call when my plane cleared the canyon. Now cover us."

The couples quickly arranged their legs to cover their passengers in the bottom of the boat.

LYING UNDERNEATH Jason's weight on the gritty bottom of the sweltering fiberglass boat was a claustrophobic experience, and Miguel started to squirm and cry. Kendal winced as she was forced to press a palm over the child's recently-healed mouth. She tried to sing a little song in his ear to calm him, but the boat's motor provided less of a cover as it started losing power. Above them she heard the familiar guttural voice of Flaco, ordering the driver to stop. Both boats' motors sputtered to an idle and then a standstill. Things grew so quiet that Kendal could hear the waves sloshing against the sides of the boat.

Miguel whimpered again, and Kendal covered his mouth, hushing him softly.

The missionary women picked up the song Kendal had begun to sing, a Mexican children's ditty, but again the voice of Flaco exclaimed, *"Cállese!"* Shut up!

This was followed by a warning staccato of machine gun fire ripping across the water.

In the silence that followed, Kendal could hear Flaco questioning the lead missionary, who did indeed lie very convincingly, even in Spanish.

"We are looking for kidnappers who have abducted the only grandchild of *Señor* Javier Benicio Alvarez Vajaras," Flaco said with false authority. "These criminals have escaped to this area in a small plane. We think they landed on this river."

The missionary answered the bandit as respectfully as if Flaco were actually a local authority looking for criminals. The older gentleman spoke intently, lying with just the proper mix of agitation and horror. "We saw a plane hurtling through this canyon an hour ago. We heard a crash, an explosion, and spotted debris floating on the river. I fear there are no survivors."

Miguel cried out and Kendal froze, terrified that the missionary's composed tones did nothing to conceal the toddler's outburst. Above her, she felt Jason's muscular body tightening for attack.

The missionary women began to chatter excitedly about the plane crash, interrupting each other, arguing with each other about the details, but their attempts at camouflage were too late.

Flaco waved his gun. "*Cállese!*" he shouted again. "Move aside!" He stepped up and spanned the space between the two boats on widespread legs.

Jason leaped at the outlaw, grabbing for his gun. The boats rocked precariously as the two men twisted and fought until they were both knocked overboard into the river.

While they struggled in the water, Jason saw one of the other desperadoes leaning into the missionaries' boat and grabbing Miguel's life vest, yanking him from Kendal's arms and pulling him up over the side of the other boat. Kendal tried to go after him, but the two boats quickly drifted apart. Kendal and Miguel screamed for each other just as Jason and Flaco surfaced again, locked in combat for the gun. One of the men on the other boat held the writing toddler while the other fanned his automatic rifle from the fighting duo to Kendal and back.

The next time they surfaced, Jason pounced on Flaco like a ferocious young lion savaging a grunting pig. In seconds it was over, and Flaco was left floating faceup, an unconscious blimp in the water.

The two men remaining in the other boat aimed their guns at Jason as he swam toward them with rapid powerful strokes. But when they fired they got nothing but empty clicks. Realizing they'd discharged all their ammo, they started the engine and turned the boat to make a getaway.

Jason wasn't going to make the same mistake twice. If they wanted Miguel, they'd have to kill him first. He swam like a demon and hurled himself through the water, throwing his arms up and clamping his hands over the side of the boat, being dragged in its wake as it sped away.

One of the outlaws swung his empty weapon at Jason's head, but Jason ducked below the side of the boat. The man then slammed the butt of his gun down on Jason's hands. Again and again, those gifted hands were bashed, but Jason held fast as he hauled himself up, hooking a leg over the side of the boat.

The driver left the engine to help his comrade subdue Jason, but Jason held on, tipping the boat with his weight, sending the two men rocking back and forth.

The sound of another boat motor approaching sent the pilot scrambling back to his post. But they couldn't pick up speed fast enough. The boat bearing Ben and the undercover agents nearly rammed the escaping vessel as it came up alongside, while Ben threw himself aboard.

Ben pummeled the two men as Miguel cowered in the bow, screaming and watching it all with terror in his eyes. Jason's hands were useless now, but he used his elbows, his shoulders, his head, to join in the fight. When Jason and Ben finally threw them overboard, the banditos swam for the canyon wall while the agents chased them down in their boat.

Jason rushed to Miguel and scooped the child into his arms, grimacing in pain. His hands, he knew, were probably broken in several places, but his heart had never felt so whole, had never beat with so much gladness.

The driver of the missionaries' boat brought it to a

bumping halt beside the other one and Kendal leaped from it. She threw herself at Jason and Miguel.

Kendal locked her arms around them as she looked over the child's head at Jason, and with tears in her eyes, said, "I love you so much."

The driver took them back to the jetty at Chiapa de Corzo. From there they made their way in the missionaries' Jeeps down the long road into the hot, humid valley surrounding Chiapas's capital.

Ignoring the injuries to his hands, Jason insisted on going straight to the authorities in Tuxtla Gutiérrez. Based on Jason's earlier call from Oklahoma, other undercover agents had been preparing to go into the jungle from this location to apprehend Vajaras as soon as the captives were set free.

"If we leave tonight," Ben volunteered, "I can lead the agents directly to the man with the blood mark."

"The blood mark?" a Mexican detective said.

"An unfortunate side effect of a drug I gave him," Jason explained, wincing as he held his hands aloft.

"You need a doctor now," Ruth said as she brought fresh ice packs for Jason's hands.

"All I need is Kendal." Jason winced as he lifted his broken hands to embrace the woman he loved. "And this little boy. They're all I really need for the rest of my life."

EPILOGUE

MRS. JASON BRIDGES, hugely pregnant, was feeling a teensy bit cranky. Maybe she was just jealous because she was too far along to make the trip to Mexico this year. Jason had offered to cancel his humanitarian expedition. "Mexico will be there next year. My family is my number one priority," he'd vowed.

But Kendal wouldn't hear of it. Those trips to Mexico were as healing for her husband as they were for his patients. "You'll be back way before the baby's due date," she assured her hardworking husband.

"It's important for Daddy to go to Mexico," she said to the three-year-old strapped into the rear seat of her minivan, but she was talking more to herself.

"Meh-hee-coe," the preschooler said.

Kendal smiled. Jason had taught Miguel to say it like that. Miguel seemed to be able to imitate any sound and loved to sing along with his little CDs in the van. The speech therapist had reassured them that Miguel was so bright that his speech would be up to a normal level within another year, maybe less.

"Yes. Mexico, sweetie. Where Daddy and I got you."

She parked her minivan and hauled the balky Miguel up on her hip as she made her way into his new daddy's medical tower. She was exhausted because Miguel had been restless last night—the final stages of his eye surgery had gone beautifully, but there were still discomforts to be borne—and she was due to deliver in eight weeks. She imagined she looked awful—baggy maternity sweats, no makeup, hair in a messy treetop—but Jason wouldn't care. How many times had he told her he loved her, no matter how she dressed or what she did to her hair.

Her goal today was simply to pick up the paperwork Jason needed for the vaccines and get it dispatched to her old employer in time for this year's trip. Then she was going to get the Hades out of here before anyone spotted her looking like this.

Inside the doctors' tower she pressed the elevator button, and while she waited, she remembered the time she'd refused to open the doors and let The Wolf in. Into her life. Into her heart. She smiled, remembering how dejected his face had looked as the doors slid closed. How wrong she'd been about him. There wasn't a more devoted husband on the face of the earth.

At her shoulder she saw Miguel pull a pouty frown at someone coming up behind her. Out of the corner of her eye, she recognized a vaguely familiar profile. She turned to get a full view of her old boyfriend.

"Phillip." By an act of will, she smiled and kept her hands off her disheveled hair. "How are you?"

Phillip smiled uncomfortably and said, "Hi, Kendal! I *thought* that was you."

No, he didn't, Kendal decided. He'd thought it was some fat cow with a wiggly toddler on her hip. She weighed a good thirty pounds more than she had the last time Phillip had seen her on the night of the Miracle Makers Ball...and in all the wrong places.

Phillip's appearance, on the other hand, was impeccable. Was that an Armani suit?

Phillip cast an abashed glance at her bulging abdomen. "I heard you got married, but I didn't realize you were having a baby. Congratulations!"

"Thanks." She adjusted Miguel, who was threatening to turn whiney now, trying to bury his face in her neck. "This is our little boy, Miguel."

"Oh, yes. Seems I heard something about you adopting a kid from Guatemala, too."

"Mexico."

"Right. Mexico."

"Meh-hee-coe," Miguel corrected and gave Phillip another disagreeable scowl.

"He's sure a tiny little thing." Phillip ran a hesitant finger over Miguel's underdeveloped arm. Kendal winced, remembering how he used to touch her that way.

"He's got some catching up to do, but he's growing just fine now," she said.

Miguel pointed at Phillip. "You go 'way," he said.

"Miguel. Talk nice." Kendal grabbed the tiny finger. She smiled defensively at Phillip. "He's usually very sweet-natured. But he just had surgery a few days ago," she explained. "You'll have to excuse him if he's a little grumpy."

"Kids have their bad days. Mine, too."

"Oh, yes! You have a little girl," Kendal said brightly, unable to believe that a year ago that very news had caused her to gnash her teeth in despair.

"She's a cutie," Phillip beamed. "But they *are* work, huh? Are you taking yours to the doctor?"

"No. His daddy's office is upstairs."

With conviction, Miguel informed Phillip, "I going to *color* at Daddy's."

"Yes, you'll get to color while we're at Daddy's," Kendal confirmed. "He's very artistic." She found she just had to show Phillip that Miguel was blessed with certain gifts.

"And what floor is Daddy on?" Phillip's eyes traveled over the brass directory plate on the wall.

Same old Phillip. Couldn't ever ask a direct question. If he wanted to make a point of the fact that she'd married the hospital's most sought-after bachelor, why not just say, Who did you marry?

"Tenth floor. Dr. Jason Bridges." Kendal pointed at Jason's name, etched at the top. "I married Jason Bridges." Months of living with Jason's forthright masculine honesty had left her with little patience for a furtive little pansy like Phillip.

"Oh, yeah? Isn't he that renegade plastic surgeon that's always running off to the jungle? I can't imagine what you two have in common." Having made that speech, Phillip sniffed, looking slightly snobbish. Then he dared to frown disapprovingly when Miguel started to whimper.

Kendal had to bite her lip to keep from blurting out,

Sex, Phillip. What we have in common is sex. Lots of it. The real kind. And we have something else in common you wouldn't understand. True love. Ours isn't a relationship based on one of your precious lists. But of course, she just smiled and said, "Jason's a really great guy. We're actually very compatible."

Suddenly she felt Miguel's weight being scooped out of her arms. "Come here, big boy." It was Jason's voice.

She turned to see her husband smiling down at her. "Jason! Where'd you come from?"

"Staff meeting." He inclined his head toward the walkway that led off to the main hospital. He kissed Kendal's forehead and hugged his little boy to his shoulder.

The child favored Phillip with a proud smile and said, "This ith my *daddy.*"

"Dr. Jason Bridges." Jason offered his free hand to Phillip.

"I know." Phillip shook it, but seemed suddenly disgruntled. "I used to try to make sales calls in your office. Phillip Dudley." When he squeezed Jason's hand too hard, Jason grimaced uncomfortably.

"Oh, sorry," Phillip said. "I heard stories about your injuries."

Aha, Kendal thought. So the little prick does know all about us, and Mexico, and Miguel.

"Pretty amazing tale, landing a plane on a river," Phillip added and his tone implied that most of the story was surely made up.

"It all seems like a long time ago," Jason replied

evenly. "Except on heavy surgery days like today when my hands still get a little achy."

Jason adjusted Miguel on his hip and focused his attention on Kendal. "Honey, you look beautiful as always, but kinda tired." He spread a protective palm on her side, supporting Kendal's rounded front.

"How's our little baby doing?"

"Little baby," Miguel echoed, leaning forward to pat the top of Kendal's abdomen.

Kendal smiled. At Jason. At Miguel. Even at Phillip. Suddenly it didn't matter that her hair was a mess or that she looked like a cow. And it certainly didn't matter what her snippy ex-boyfriend thought.

Kendal's world was right, complete. The man she adored was holding their beloved child in his arms and asking her how their soon-to-be-born baby was faring.

"The baby?" she said, pressing her hand over Jason's large warm one. "Baby Lucia is just fine."

If you enjoyed what you just read,
then we've got an offer you can't resist!

Take 2 bestselling
love stories FREE!
Plus get a FREE surprise gift!

Clip this page and mail it to Harlequin Reader Service®

IN U.S.A.	IN CANADA
3010 Walden Ave.	P.O. Box 609
P.O. Box 1867	Fort Erie, Ontario
Buffalo, N.Y. 14240-1867	L2A 5X3

YES! Please send me 2 free Harlequin Superromance® novels and my free surprise gift. After receiving them, if I don't wish to receive anymore, I can return the shipping statement marked cancel. If I don't cancel, I will receive 6 brand-new novels every month, before they're available in stores. In the U.S.A., bill me at the bargain price of $4.47 plus 25¢ shipping and handling per book and applicable sales tax, if any*. In Canada, bill me at the bargain price of $4.99 plus 25¢ shipping and handling per book and applicable taxes**. That's the complete price, and a savings of at least 10% off the cover prices—what a great deal! I understand that accepting the 2 free books and gift places me under no obligation ever to buy any books. I can always return a shipment and cancel at any time. Even if I never buy another book from Harlequin, the 2 free books and gift are mine to keep forever.

135 HDN DNT3
336 HDN DNT4

Name		
	(PLEASE PRINT)	
Address		Apt.#
City	State/Prov.	Zip/Postal Code